if we PRETEND

CHRISSY HOPEWELL

First US Edition: October 2023

ISBN: 9798988745808 (ebook), 9798988745815 (paperback)

Edited by Brenda Chin www.BrendaChin.com

Cover design by Stephanie Anderson, Alt 19 Creative

Proofread by Lindsey Hinkel www.LindseyHinkelEdits.com

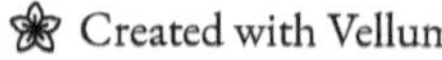 Created with Vellum

To my mom, who would have been delighted to know that the spicy romance novels I snuck from her shelves as a middle schooler planted the seeds for my debut romance novel, decades later.
Miss you, Mom.

1

REESE

Thursday, July 21
32 Days Before Departure
Peebles, Scotland

This idyllic Scottish village has to be the best place in the world for a reset of my life.

I tug the hood of my Rutgers sweatshirt over my hair as a light mist dampens my face. Rain won't bother me. Not today, not while I'm in Scotland. I'm delighted with my decision to stay for the month while Chelsea's at her camp, instead of dropping my sixteen-year-old daughter off as originally planned.

Maybe I'll never leave.

I practically dance down the main street of Peebles, out of the shop-lined town center toward the soccer fields where Chelsea's month-long, invitation-only program kicked off this morning. I still can't believe she's here—*we're* here—thanks to her exceptional talent for the sport she's been playing since kindergarten.

On my left is an adorable, well-kept stone home with yellow shutters and a lovely front porch, complete with a wooden swing. That one might be a bit out of my price range, but I could sell our house in New Jersey and buy the one over there—slightly less well-kept but still nice if you squint your eyes and ignore the overgrown weeds out front. And get myself a Highland cow as a pet and drink steaming tea in a cutesy mug with, like, a Scottish flag on it. Perfect.

Staying for the month instead of just leaving Chelsea wasn't a spontaneous decision, unlike what my ex-husband (of eighteen months) and my former best friend (also of eighteen months) will think when they eventually find out I'm *not* departing on the flight I originally booked back to Newark Airport this afternoon. After taking Chelsea to visit her Aunt Stella in London, I was supposed to bring Chelsea to Peebles and head back to New Jersey. Adrian and Britt—a giant diamond an anchor on her left ring finger—will be flying in and picking her up at the end of the month.

But two weeks ago, after the happy couple dropped my daughter off in my driveway—they were clearly dressed up to go out on a fancy date—an uncontrollable banshee scream welled up in my throat. My hands clenched so tightly at my sides that my knuckles had turned as white as Britt's wedding dress was sure to be. So I slunk back inside, drank a jumbo glass of red wine, and changed my return flight to four weeks later.

I need to sort through what's going on in my head. I should be able to handle them being together. After all, Britt didn't cause our divorce. Not really. She simply removed herself from our lives. Which shouldn't have mattered . . . except *our lives* had been so intertwined. Sharing a beach house down the Jersey Shore. Christmas Eves together. Our kids being best friends. It was a big deal when she said she needed space from us . . . and it started the whole chain of events.

There'd been no outright betrayal, even though Adrian and Britt were together within weeks of the divorce. I *might* have completely lost my shit when he eventually told me they'd fallen in love, and Chelsea *might* have walked in on me screaming at him.

But since then, I've pulled it together. I'll be the best example for my daughter if it kills me.

And honestly, my heart warms when I see Chelsea and Britt's son, Jackson, giggling together. It's sweet to see an almost high school junior being besties with her future stepbrother, an incoming freshman boy. So who am I to be causing problems? And Britt's been through some bad stuff recently, too—things I can relate to—so I gave them my blessing and have opened the door to her gentle requests to be friendly again.

Still, when I see them together these days, instead of feeling neutral-to-positive as I intend to, my insides end up a swirling, confusing mess, angry red and fiery orange mixed in with a bland tapioca to create a muddy brown.

So, here I am. Clearing my head. Figuring out my shit.

The soccer fields are a half mile outside of town, away from the small one-bedroom flat I'll be calling home for the next month. Last night I confirmed that yes, it does smell like the fish and chips shop below, just like the leasing agent had warned, and no, the smell never dissipates. But it's a perfect place for me to work remotely over the summer, despite the scent of fried haddock.

I turn into the fields just as my phone buzzes in my pocket. I pull it out and head toward the bleachers, where a few scattered parents are watching the girls run a passing drill.

The new text is in the group chat with my sisters.

STELLA

How's Scotland?? Miss you already! Wish you and Chelsea could've stayed in London longer.

I miss her already, too. Chelsea and I had a great time in London over the past week with Stella, my fiercely independent sister. The middle one. She moved to London to get her MBA six years ago, and she's the one I worry about most. She's determined not to get married or have kids, always pushing people away, usually sabotaging her relationships in some subtle way. While we were visiting, I didn't get the chance to question her about the not-quite-right vibe I was sensing with her current boyfriend.

I hate having an ocean between me and either of my sisters. But I'm thankful we talk and text daily, especially these days, with a best-friend-sized hole in my life.

MADDIE

You better come back to New Jersey, Reese. I don't like having both of you over there.

At least at home, I'm around to keep an eye on Maddie. After our father died when I was fifteen, our mom fell apart a bit and I had to step in to help, giving up field hockey and other school activities to make sure my eleven- and nine-year-old sisters were taken care of. Maddie's always been the one who needs my help the most. Or accepts it, at least. I guess this is what it's like being the oldest of three sisters.

Smiling at the other parents, I settle down at the end of the bleachers, my butt instantly wet. I point my phone at the girls on the field and click a photo for the text chain, then turn and take another of the low, rolling green mountains in the background, spotted with white sheep and tinted with purple heather.

ME

Not sure I'm coming back. Miss you both!

STELLA

Gorgeous. And, oh! That coach!

I crinkle my forehead and look up. The girls switch to a complicated shooting drill, relentless on the poor teenaged goalkeeper. There's a man in his early sixties with wispy gray hair and glasses in a full tracksuit on the sideline with a clipboard, watching the girls and taking notes. I don't think Stella was referring to him. The other coach is younger, also with a clipboard, but he's on the field, pointing, gesturing, and shouting soccer-y things like *find the open space* and *two touches before you pass*.

Oh, he must be the one Chelsea was freaking out over when the camp added him to the coaching roster. She's been obsessed with UK soccer for years. Having him for a coach was even more exciting for her than finding out she'd be working with the head coach, who works for a women's soccer team in Scotland.

The younger coach is definitely cute. I start from the bottom, shamelessly objectifying him. Black athletic shorts show off glorious calf muscles adorned with at least one tattoo and lead up to thick, muscular thighs. His t-shirt allows a peek into more ink on one arm and a shit ton more muscles on both. He's probably in his thirties, but for sure younger than my thirty-seven years.

I hope Chelsea isn't going to be distracted. She was giving off intense crush vibes on this ex-professional soccer player before we left. If I were a teenage girl, I'd certainly be. But I'm not a teenager nor am I remotely interested in any kind of relationship. With anyone. I'll stick with my cat, Peanut Butter, and objectify cute men from a distance.

I make an effort to wipe my face of any inappropriate expression and steal a glance at the other parents, who are acting quite normal and not drooling or staring.

ME

No, thanks. I think I'll avoid hooking up with the soccer coach my daughter is crushing on.

STELLA

Ohhh, that's who she was going on about last week.

ME

Yup, pretty sure it is.

MADDIE

Aw. No fun. But you should definitely find a hot dude with an accent.

STELLA

Just for a fling. Don't get sucked in.

MADDIE

She deserves a little adventure, Stella.

STELLA

She doesn't need a dude for an adventure.

I bite my lip and grin. And what, exactly, would I do with said hot dude? On my to-do list: go on long walks, appreciate the gorgeous countryside, maybe pet a sheep, and figure out how to show Chelsea I am a strong, independent woman—not someone whose life is a hot mess. I only have two more years before Chelsea goes to college, probably somewhere far away, wherever could help her get to the next level of soccer. I want to give her the best example of someone who has their shit together in the time we have left. Someone who can be mature and act friendly with her ex-husband and his fiancée.

Not do things like destroy thoughtful gifts from said fiancée.

A few months ago, Britt bought me a birthday present—an adorable mug with cat ears, personalized with Peanut Butter's name on one side and *Don't Stress Meowt* on the other. Chelsea watched as I flung the mug into the trash so hard that the poor cat's tail—which was the handle—broke right off. I immediately regretted the reaction and glued the mug together before shoving it in the back of a cabinet. My daughter rolled her eyes and went back to staring at her phone, not buying the explanation that it slipped from my hand.

We've had one heart-to-heart about the divorce. One time where I broke down and admitted how hard it was to rebuild my life and see her father and Britt together. I assured her everything would be fine, that I could handle it. She was angry, grinding her teeth together, and I'm sure she thinks I'm weak.

That's why I always remind myself that the most important

thing is Chelsea: setting a good example and co-parenting in a way that won't stress her out.

But yeah, I *don't* exactly have my shit together, as much as I try to pretend it's all okay.

Adrian and Britt do, though. They are mature about their relationship, and kind to me. Hell, they even offered to take care of Peanut Butter while I was away. I politely declined and called Marisa, my soccer mom bestie (and basically only friend post-Britt) and asked her to cat sit.

ME

Hard pass. A vacation fling isn't my style.

STELLA

I'm not saying you should have a fling. I'm saying just do what you want and what you want only.

MADDIE

Stella, you're impossible.

ME

Ladies. I'm fine. I don't need you worrying about me. It's my job to worry about you.

STELLA

That's not your job!

I laugh and slip my phone back in my pocket before I get sucked into the debate. I breathe deep and close my eyes for a second. I need this month, so I can figure out how to not be a hollow shell of a mother. So I can figure out what the next version of myself will be.

I'll head back to the flat soon for my next call. My current client is based in Europe, so it's ideal that I only have an hour time difference, which is another reason my boss immediately said yes when I brought up working in Scotland this summer. My project management and digital graphic design work is always virtual anyway.

The older coach blows his whistle. "One hour and fifteen minutes for lunch, lassies!"

I stand and step off the bleachers. Guess I should introduce myself to the coaches before heading back. Even the hot one. Honestly? I'm zero percent intimidated. Zero percent is roughly the same likelihood that I would ever be on his radar, with my soccer mom uniform of leggings and a hoodie. The only reason I put makeup on this morning was because of an early video call.

Given that, I'm not sure why there are butterflies flitting around in my stomach as I make my way across the field.

I intend to head for the older coach, but he steps aside with a pair of parents who were quicker than me, so I approach the younger one, trying to keep my gaze on his face, not let them wander over his muscled, inked biceps.

I pause in front of him. He's all broody, clinging to his clipboard, eyes focusing beyond me at the lush green mountains. He looks lost somewhere in the gray clouds lingering above.

"Um, hi?" It feels rude to interrupt, but it's weirder to just, like, stand here.

He startles and focuses on me, seeming surprised to find someone in front of him.

"Hallo," he says in a thick Scottish accent, his icy-blue eyes locking on mine.

I can totally talk to a hot man. This is no problem. A squeak escapes my throat, contradicting me.

"Have a second? You look deep in thought." I run my hand through my long brown hair, pulling it over my shoulder, suddenly self-conscious.

"Aye, sorry, must've been daydreaming."

Sweet baby Jesus, that accent. A lilting, melodic cloud of floating words. I could listen to it forever. Maybe I can ask him to read me a bedtime story, like I used to do with Chelsea when she was little.

"Daydreaming about soccer drills?" My cheeks grow warm as he looks me up and down with a quick scan. Did the hot soccer coach just check me out? It's an uncomfortably pleasant feeling.

He chuckles. "Where ya fae? America?"

"What gave it away?" My face contorts in a goofy grin. I'm *so* not cool. "I'm Reese. Chelsea's mom. We're from New Jersey." I extend my hand and it lingers in the air for a second.

"Of course. Chelsea's our only American footballer." He stares at my outstretched appendage with wide eyes, as if it's some foreign object, before grabbing it. He visibly swallows, which draws my attention to the bear claw tattoo that reaches out of his shirt and up his neck.

"I'm Oliver Vass. From Stirling originally, just about an hour north of here. And in Scotland, we call it football, not soccer."

I wonder if he's got the whole bear under there? Does it cover his entire chest, or is it just the vicious claws reaching up out of his shirt? With a repressed giggle, I pull my hand away.

"Well, that doesn't make any sense." I tilt my head. "We already have football in the United States, and it doesn't look like this." Heaven help me, I'm attempting to flirt with him.

"American football." He grunts. "We have something like that, too. It's called rugby and we dinna bother with helmets or padding." He lifts his eyebrows.

I stick my hands in my hoodie pocket and shrug. "Don't blame me. I'm not a big fan of football."

"*American* football. This is *real* football." He gestures to the field.

"Whatever." I roll my eyes, Chelsea-style. "If it makes you happy, keep telling yourself that."

Oh lord, someone stop me. I'm making a total fool of myself. But I'm grinning, he's grinning, and my cheeks are burning.

"Did you want to talk about Chelsea?"

Right. Soccer. Chelsea. That's why I'm here.

"I just wanted to introduce myself. I'm staying in town the whole month, so I'll be around, but I'll do my best to keep out of the way."

"Sounds braw. An extended holiday? Traveling with your significant other? Chelsea's father?"

I blink about a hundred times.

"Nope. No husband. No significant other." I want to do a dance that my ex-husband is three thousand miles away. "I'm working remotely. Here. It's, uh, a reset month. Trying to get my life together. Clear my head."

And now my cheeks are even hotter. I must look like an over-ripe tomato. Why am I oversharing with Chelsea's soccer coach? He doesn't give a shit about why I'm staying the whole month.

Oliver makes a nondescript sound.

"Sorry. That was too many details, I think."

"Dinna fash. Tis a bonnie place to have any kind of reset." His face tightens, and I'd like to know what he's thinking about. He pushes a strand of wavy hair back from his face.

There's a surprised yelp from the sideline that distracts me from the coach.

It's Chelsea, and it takes me a few seconds to register who she is approaching. A tall, handsome man with a gorgeous woman standing next to him, her white-blond braid laying on her shoulder, a smile as bright as the absent sun. They are two faces I know so well, people I used to love with all my heart.

A couple who isn't supposed to be here for another four weeks.

The woman's gaze moves across the field to lock with mine, her jaw dropping open. She reaches out to grab the man's arm, then points in my direction.

For fuck's sake. It can't be them.

But it is. It's Adrian and Britt.

2

———

OLIVER

A reset month? That feels like what I attempted for the past year in Ireland, hiding away from the world with Patrick, my old football club's ex-goalkeeper, hanging out in his mate Ian's tattoo parlor, drawing and wasting time.

Patrick had left Winchester Football Club five years before I did and now has a whole other life back home in Ireland. I hadn't thought of my time there with him as a reset, but it makes perfect sense. I was resetting from the end of my professional football career and the year that followed of me drinking, partying, and having fuck-all direction. When things went wrong with football, Patrick had warned the transition to a more normal life would be hard, but I didn't get it until I had to live it.

Och. It's been absolute shite.

What's *this* woman resetting from?

Reese is distracted by something across the field, and I take her in, trying to understand why I've found the last five minutes with her exceedingly enjoyable, instead of fake and awkward, as I assumed talking to the parents of campers would be. She's bonnie in a wholesome way, and a spark in her gray eyes tells me she's got more of a story in her. And she definitely checked out my tattoos.

But this stereotypical football mum—like in the American TV shows and movies—is not my type.

I touch my newest ink, no longer sore. It's an intricately drawn football on my shoulder, peaking up from a giant Scottish flag on the outside of my upper arm. I designed it and Ian tattooed it on me, claiming to be impressed by my artistic ability. Ian, a ginger, heavily tattooed bloke who looks tough but spends all his off-work time with his herd of small children, even bought a bunch of my sketches for his tattoo bible.

Drawing has been the only thing that's made me feel good since I left Winchester FC. I can disappear into sketching, much like I disappeared into football, and when I come up for air, I feel more like myself. Two completely different things that both ground me in similar ways. But one I'd repressed since I was a kid, thanks to my parents, who firmly discouraged my artistic bent. They didna care if I had hobbies, or friends, or was happy. And once I was an adult, they hardly talked to me. I was too busy with football, anyway. Now that I'm no longer pro, they want even less to do with me.

But they were right to push me to focus. I've always wanted to play professionally, and if I hadna snapped my Achilles tendon not once, but twice, leading to a doctor recommending I 'retire,' I would still be doing exactly that, instead of losing my spot on the team at thirty years old. I could've played for years more. But now, I gotta figure something else out. Messing around with drawing or tattoos is a secret hobby, not a next career step for someone like me. I can only imagine how people would laugh. That'd give the tabloids something new to talk about, not me drunk in an Edinburgh club.

I almost bailed from this camp multiple times over the past week. I would've, if it werena for my loyalty to David, ex-Winchester FC assistant coach from a decade ago. He now works for a women's football team trying to grow talent to recruit. Maybe I *should've* bailed. I could've gotten back in my car and driven right to . . . ah dinna ken, actually. Where would I go? What would I do? Coaching is the obvious next step for me as an ex-pro footballer. Coaching or being a pundit on sports talk shows, and I didna want to do that. It's been two years. My expiration date is approaching. Pretty soon, people will forget I ever played.

All I've ever known is football. All I *am* is football.

So now I'm here, half-jealous of these talented girls who have their entire sporting careers ahead of them. Half-jealous, half-anxious, half-inspired. Too many halves, I know. I definitely dinna have a future in math-based jobs.

"Reese?" I tilt my head and frown. The pretty pink color and casual smile have drained from her face and she's staring across the field at a couple talking to her daughter. "You alright?"

"Fuck," she whispers, and I raise my eyebrows at the unexpected curse. She shakes her head and sways on her feet. "No, no." Her hands entwine with each other, as if she's trying to warm them up on a cold winter day.

I touch her arm to get her attention. She kinda looks like she's going to faint.

Reese turns to me sharply, glancing down at my hand with a look I canna read, but her eyes are glassy when they return to mine. I already miss her easy smile.

"What are they doing here?" Her voice is low, like she's afraid they'll hear her.

Across the field, Chelsea is now hugging the man, and notably, not hugging the woman with him. The woman who's looking our way.

"Ah dinna ken, hen, who is that?" I cringe. Should I be calling a camper's mum *hen*, which suddenly feels too intimate, too flirty, even though it's not? But she's completely fixated on what's happening across the field.

The couple steps away from Chelsea, who turns our way and frantically waves to her mom. It looks like an SOS signal.

"That's Adrian, my ex-husband, and Britt, his fiancée. My

former best friend." Reese's eyes dart from mine, back across the field, and back to mine. She's swaying again.

"Whoa." Ouch. I impulsively grab one of her linked hands in an attempt to steady her, and now we're connected in some kind of weird dance. "You look like you're gonna pass out. Need to sit?"

"No." Reese keeps her gray eyes on mine and leans forward, moving her mouth toward my ear. I bend down to hear what she's gonna say. There's clearly some kind of crisis going on, but I canna help but notice the softness of her hand in mine, the worn fabric of her sweatshirt, and the way her warm breath breezes onto my ear and neck.

"They're not supposed to be here," she says, inches from my ear, as if she's confiding a deep secret. "Not yet, anyway. Not for weeks."

She doesna lean back, and I dinna move away, enjoying the feeling of her lips so close to my skin. The couple approaches us.

"Just take a deep breath." Her shoulders rise and fall at my words. "Whatever this is, you can do it. But they're almost here."

And with that, Reese's ex-husband clears his throat, and she jumps back from me, breaking our touch. But before she looks at him, she looks back at me, and a brief, grateful smile crosses her face. All sorts of feelings wash over me.

Already, I dinna like this man, but for some reason, I like Reese.

"I can't believe this." The former best friend tentatively smiles at Reese. The woman steps forward and her arms twitch, like she wants to reach out and hug Reese. But she doesna. "I thought you were leaving to go back home today? I thought we'd miss you by a few hours. Did we get the date wrong?" She looks up at the man, forehead creased.

"I changed my flight." Reese's voice is flat, carefully controlled, and a fake smile appears on her face, not getting anywhere close to her eyes. "What are you doing here?" Her eyes flit from one of the newcomers to the other, back and forth, like a mother rabbit keeping track of two foxes near her nest. "I thought the plan was to pick up Chelsea at the end of camp?"

Britt sneaks a look at Adrian. "Yeah, I know, that was the plan. But Jackson got off the waitlist for that sleepaway video game camp. I think I told you about it?"

Reese blinks at her rapidly and shakes her head.

"Well, it's next week, then he goes to Boy Scout camp, then he's on vacation with his dad for two weeks, so it didn't make sense to stay home for him." Britt gnaws on her lip, then tentatively smiles at Reese, her red mouth curling up to reveal straight white teeth.

Adrian clears his throat. "Britt's never been to Scotland, and neither have I, so we wanted to do some exploring. Before . . ." He stops.

Reese flinches so subtly, I almost miss it. A blank stare replaces the fake smile.

Before what? I need to know. Och, I shouldna be in this conversation, but it's fascinating. Do they even remember I'm standing here?

"What about you, Ree? When do you leave? Did your flight get delayed, or . . ."

"August twenty-second." Reese's voice is just a whisper on the warm breeze.

"That's . . . when we leave, too. You're staying the whole time? Since when?" A hopeful smile lands on the woman's lips, and more color drains from Reese's face. "Are we on the same flight back?"

A brief silence descends, and Reese's jaw drops slightly open. They *are* all on the same flight, clearly. Reese must just be realizing it. I almost chuckle, but also want to throw my arm around her shoulders protectively. This woman needs someone on her side.

"We're being rude." The man turns to me. "Hi, Coach. Adrian Whitlock, nice to meet you." Adrian sticks out his hand and shakes mine too vigorously, watching me with a confident but curious look on his face, glancing between me and Reese. "Sorry. We're just catching up on a bunch of new plans."

"Oliver Vass. Welcome." Other people's drama is way more interesting than my own. Nae, this drama is *not* interesting. My job doesna include meddling in the domestic affairs of my campers' parents. Yet it's hard to resist wondering what the real story is here.

"I'm Britt," the ex-friend says to me.

"So neither of you knew the other would be here?" I look back and forth and smile, trying to lighten the mood.

"No," the two women say at the same time, one smiling, one grimacing.

"Well, that must be surprising, aye?"

Everyone ignores me.

"But now that we are, maybe we can do some exploring together. What do you think?" Britt asks Reese, the smile sticking. "Want to grab a coffee or a drink? We have a whole month here all together."

A small strangled sound escapes Reese's throat, soft enough I'm not sure the others heard it. The rabbit just lost track of one of the foxes.

Her former best friend is marrying her ex-husband? They're friends? Only kind of, by the look of it. Britt's face is just so open and hopeful. Reese looks like she wants to sprint toward those green hills and disappear into a herd of sheep.

I feel like someone's nana watching the latest episode of EastEnders.

"Of course. Sounds lovely." Reese's jaw is locked tight.

"Great!" Britt says.

Do they even notice Reese's barely suppressed horror?

"Was Chelsea surprised?" Reese's voice is squeaky.

"Sure was." Adrian stares at his ex-wife with a furrowed brow.

"Mmmm."

Adrian blinks at Reese.

I clear my throat and they all turn sharply to me.

"We're gonna work your daughter quite hard this month. So she willna have too much free time. Are you all sticking around Peebles? Traveling, maybe to Europe? Or down to London?"

I direct the last questions to Adrian and Britt. I'm trying to help, really, I am.

"Well," Britt says and slips her hand around Adrian's arm, then glances at Reese and removes it with a quiet movement. "We're going to make Peebles our home base and spend the month getting to know the area. But we do plan to do a bit of traveling around."

Reese breathes in sharply through her nose.

"You okay, Ree?" Britt bites her lip and pulls at her long braid.

"Yes, fine, thanks. Felt like I was going to sneeze. Must be allergies." Reese shakes her head violently, saying no to something mysterious. Everyone looks confused.

"Hopefully, you'll be able to come to the two family events we have planned, although one's this Saturday and the other's not till the finish of camp. It might be, well, a wee bit boring in between." Am I helping *now*? Doubtful, as Reese's face is getting redder and her fists are clenching and unclenching at her sides. I truly dinna want to witness a murder on day one of camp.

Britt sticks out her red-painted bottom lip and watches Reese.

"Mom!" Chelsea's voice rings from across the field and Reese looks over sharply, relief crossing her face.

"I have to go. We'll talk later." She gives Adrian and Britt a last glance, clearing her face carefully of all emotion in a move she must've practiced many times.

"I'll text you!" Britt calls after Reese, who's already striding away.

A silence falls on the three of us. David's wrapping up with his group of parents and I glance down at a watch I dinna have.

"Anything else you wanted to talk about?" There are so many questions I have, so many things I'd like to clear up about what just happened, but it's obviously inappropriate and none of my business. But damn, the drama. Delightful.

"We're good." Adrian pretends like nothing happened. Britt is watching Reese, her face crumpled.

"She's pissed," Britt mumbles.

"She'll be okay," Adrian says softly, touching her arm. "We didn't plan this. Neither did she."

"It'll be a good chance for us all to reconnect, don't you think?" Britt looks up at Adrian.

I take a small step back. Maybe I can slowly disappear from this conversation and they willna notice.

"Do you have kids?" Britt turns to me.

I freeze in place, unsure of what to say to such a simple question that feels like a punch in the gut.

So I lie.

"Nae. I'm not a father."

"Well, you're lucky in some ways. Life is a lot simpler without kids involved." She slides her hand down Adrian's arm and links her hand with his, this time not holding back on the display of affection. "There's a lot of history between us." She waves her hand toward Reese, who is almost across the field to Chelsea. "And co-parenting makes things hard."

They step away, whispering heatedly, and I feel like I'm going to boke all over my football boots.

Lucas, my son, is the whole reason I came back from Ireland, and at the first opportunity, I lied about his very existence.

A few months ago, when I met Patrick's sister and her two kids —including her ten-year-old daughter, almost the same age as Lucas—I realized I'm missing it all. I missed the first decade of his life because of football and me being a general dobber. Sure, I send them money every month and visit once or twice a year, but it isn't nearly enough. In the summer or around the holidays, I'd show up with some thoughtless gift, or just hand him a few quid. But it's been eighteen months since I last saw him.

I'm not a da to Lucas.

Just because I'm his biological father doesna mean I deserve him. Now all I want is to rebuild my life here in Scotland and figure out a way to get back into his. I'm terrified I'll never be good enough. Who would want someone like me as their father? As things are now, Lucas's mother would never allow me to just drop back in as his da. I'd set fire to that bridge a year and a half ago.

I have to find a way to prove myself. And I will. It's the most important thing.

The *only* important thing.

3

REESE

They are going to ruin my whole reset month.

I really needed this break. The second I saw Adrian and Britt across the field, my insides twisted right back into the knots that had just started to loosen. Wasn't it just my luck that they also changed their flights? If I had only told them my plans instead of insisting on keeping it a secret, I would've known they'd be here. I could've changed my flight. Again. But instead, here we all are.

I'm supposed to be sorting my life out with rest and relaxation and therapeutic Scottish scenery, *not* facing my problems head-on. Who wants to do that? And two on one doesn't seem fair. In hindsight, we've always been an awkward trio, but now that Adrian's switched sides, I see how hard it would have been on Britt once she realized she had feelings for him.

But I can do this, right? I'm at peace with my failed marriage and their future one.

Now that there's enough distance between us, I look back over my shoulder and take them in.

Adrian's wearing expensive jeans and a polo shirt, looking as handsome as ever, tall and confident with freshly trimmed hair and an annoyingly strong jawline. I swear his shoulders have gotten even wider since he and Britt recommitted to CrossFit together. That's where it all started between them. A year before we split, I was supposed to join as well but bailed last minute when I threw my back out.

As always, Britt's gorgeous. She's dressed in a long pink dress with a cute jean jacket over the top, her thick hair braided and laying over her shoulder. I know the dress. We went shopping for it together long before Everything Happened, and even though I prefer leggings and hoodies, we have a similar taste in dresses and clothes. We even used to wear our hair the same way.

I haven't braided my hair in years.

Are they still in love? Looks like it, but I'm not convinced true romantic love is even real. Ever. It's just lust that'll fade away, and then they'll simply tolerate each other. The most significant examples of love I've seen—my parents' marriage and my own—were both washed-out versions of what the movies and romance novels tell me it should look and feel like.

Mom was a mess after our father died, but eventually she was much happier—more herself single then she ever was with Dad, which sometimes makes me think that Stella's onto something with her fiercely independent woman thing. But then Mom found her current husband at one of Chelsea's elementary school soccer games, and she's been the most content I've ever seen her. So maybe my theory on love isn't right.

What I do know is that while losing Adrian was painful, somehow, losing Britt hurt even more.

So when she came to me this past January, *after* I'd given them my blessing, to tell me that her father was really sick, my cold heart thawed just a degree. And when he died a few months ago, I hugged her as she wept, knowing what it's like to lose a father. It hurts, regardless of whether you're fifteen, like I was, or thirty-four, like Britt is now.

In the same conversation, through her tears, she told me she and Adrian were engaged.

Even now, when they've crashed my reset month and are planning their happily-ever-after, I feel guilty for not checking on Britt more often since her dad passed. Her getting together with Adrian after my divorce wasn't technically wrong. And what kind of person doesn't make sure her friend—even an estranged one—is okay after losing a parent?

I hate that I'm always feeling guilty about something.

Chelsea's standing at the edge of the field away from her friends, arms crossed, waiting for me.

"Mom!" She throws herself at me like we haven't seen each other in weeks, not just since yesterday afternoon when I left her at the player barracks behind the fancy hotel outside of town.

Warmth fills me and I accept the hug and kiss her cheek, grateful my teenager is still willing to let this happen. Grateful she still wants me or needs me. I'll take what I can get.

"How was your first night with the girls, sweetheart? And how was your first morning of practice? Everything you dreamed?" I pull away and look at her intently, taking in the high ponytail, headband with the logo of her New Jersey soccer club, and pink cheeks on a makeup-free face.

"Are you serious?" She rolls her eyes so hard, I'm afraid she'll lose them in her pretty head. "You want to talk about soccer?" She re-crosses her arms and juts her chin across the field. "Did you know they were going to show up today?"

"No. Of course not." I will my right eye not to twitch, but I feel the muscle squirm. "You didn't, uh, accidentally tell them that I changed my flight, did you?"

"Mom! No. I swear. I kept it secret, just like you wanted me to. And Dad didn't tell me a thing. Just now, he said he wanted it to be a surprise." The space between her eyes furrows and she looks intently at me.

I cringe. Yeah, I'd asked my daughter not to tell her father I was staying in Scotland. I was going to tell him. Eventually. But really, it's none of his business.

"I know you wouldn't. I just thought it might have accidentally slipped out." I plaster a smile on my face. My eye twitches again.

"Are you okay? Your eye is twitching. And I'm not sure you realize that whatever you're doing with your face right now is not a smile."

"Oh, yes, of course, I'm fine." My stomach turns over as I let my eyes drift back across the field. Adrian and Britt are huddled together and the coach is standing alone, staring intently at his clipboard.

Chelsea sighs loudly, her forehead crinkled. "Is Jackson here? I didn't even ask."

"No, he's got camps and vacation with his dad."

"Oh, right. I'll text him later."

Chelsea had pushed Jackson away during the divorce, sensing Britt was at least partially responsible. But a few months later, Jackson came to hang out with us on Valentine's Day while Adrian and Britt went out to dinner. We watched an inappropriate horror movie, something that Britt wouldn't have allowed. And by the end, Jackson and Chelsea were giggling and screaming on the couch together, immediately friends again.

I was thrilled they reconnected. But she's a teenager, not some little kid I can hide my real feelings from. I know she knows my struggle with Adrian and Britt. I can see it in her eyes. But I need to be a better role model for her . . . so for now, I'm going to pretend she can't see right through me.

"So, you're going to like, hang out with Dad and Britt? A trio of besties, exploring Scotland for a month?"

Horror descends on me. How will I possibly avoid being around them? I'd already agreed to it back there, hadn't I? I'm surprised Britt hasn't texted me already to make plans.

It's okay. I can handle this. I bite back the groan that was rumbling in my throat and take a deep breath. I can show my daughter how mature and wise I am.

Or maybe I should change my flight and flee this place that just a few minutes ago seemed so idyllic?

No! This is my reset month. I can't give that up. I won't.

I can focus on myself without running away, even when obstacles keep popping up in the shape of an ex-best friend. I'm capable of handling all this. I'll act like I'm in one of those motivational posters from the nineties. The one that says OPTIMISM, with a woman staring out at the sea. More appropriate is the one with the cat dangling off a tree that says HANG IN THERE.

"I'm sure I'll see them around. It's a small town. And they want to spend some time together. We're all friends now. It's okay, I promise."

My words sound scripted, and Chelsea knows it.

"Whatever, Mom." She looks at me like I just grew Highland cow horns. "Good luck. I won't have much time to see them, or you. Every meal is a team meal, and I'm sleeping at the barracks . . ."

"I know that, and they know that." I put my hands on her bare arms. "You do your thing. We'll do ours. It'll be great." I tilt my head to a group of girls lingering fifteen feet away. "Are they waiting for you?"

She nods and starts to turn, then pauses.

"Mom?"

"Yes, sweetie?"

"What were you whispering in Coach Oliver's ear? Before Dad and Britt got to you?"

I laugh out loud, but it comes out sort of high-pitched, like the way a hyena would laugh, all bug-eyed and loopy as it's being chased by a lion from the CONFIDENCE poster. Of course, she noticed me talking to her crush.

"Nothing. No hand holding. No whispering in ears. What could I possibly have whispered in that—man's ear?"

I hope she didn't notice the breathlessness in my voice when I said the word *man*. Or the way the air hitched just a tiny bit in my throat.

"You were holding his hand?" She narrows her eyes.

"What? No. Who said that?"

A shadow of a grin crosses her face. "Okay. Whatever." Then she runs off to join her friends.

With a last glance at Oliver, Adrian, and Britt, I quickly follow the girls off the field, turning in the other direction back toward my fish-and-chips-scented flat.

4

OLIVER

"Oliver! Lunch?" David ambles over. "Fish and chips in town?"

I reach for my foot behind my back to stretch my left quad. "Nae. Gonna go ferra run."

"Of course you are, you damn fit lad. How'd you find this morning? You did well with the lassies." David stares at me intently, searching my face. For what? Evidence I'll flee this job, this town, this life? I dinna blame him.

"It was a good morning." I force a big smile.

"Some real talent out there. Who were you talking to?"

"The American girl's parents."

"Ah, Chelsea. She's got some real potential."

"Aye." Chelsea's talent is clear, but the drama with her parents stood out even more.

"Well, be nice to them. Chatting with the parents is the hardest part, really, but we want them to fall in love with our program. So it's a necessary evil." He chuckles.

I nod. "They seem . . . complicated." Reese's face sticks in my mind. I wonder how she's doing now? I wonder where she's staying? Where her ex is staying?

Shut up. It doesna matter. Why do I care?

"Aye. Anyway. See you in an hour." David claps me on the shoulder and heads toward town. I watch him go. It's too bad there's not a coaching spot available at his football club, but he said he'd be a glowing reference for me somewhere else. He's the only person who has faith in me these days.

Well, he and Patrick, who told me to get my arse back to Scotland after I had the revelation that I wanted to be in Lucas's life. I didna do it right away, of course. Even after pestering texts from David badgering me into helping with the camp. He needed an assistant coach. He said he knew I'd be braw in the job. That makes one of us. The only thing I was braw at was playing football.

But maybe I'm good with parents too, nae?

A physical memory of Reese's hot breath in my ear washes over me, and I canna help but grin. My fingers tingle where we touched. I swap feet, stretching my right quad.

I was really hoping she'd lose her cool with them, throw a wee tantrum, but I get the feeling maybe that's not her style. She definitely bit her tongue at the end.

I'd not expected to be caught off guard like this, especially by a camper's mum. I briefly wonder what it might be like if more than our fingers were to touch. A friendly hug, perhaps, or a few more secrets whispered in my ear . . .

I swallow a laugh at my own ridiculousness and release my foot to gently bounce on my toes, stretching my traitorous Achilles tendon, making sure it's completely warmed up, even though I've been moving with the girls for the past few hours.

The best thing about all of this is I've temporarily forgotten about my own drama.

Except I shouldna forget.

I need to stay focused this month. I need this coaching job. I need it so I can get a better one and be the stable human being I must become, not someone messing around in clubs and hooking up with women who dinna care about me, or wasting time in Ireland drawing tattoos, no matter how good that felt.

But as I'm about to take off on my run, my phone buzzes.

It's from Cat.

I dread opening the text and take a deep breath to quell the unsettling in my belly. Lucas's mum's last message to me from when I arrived back in Scotland a week ago runs through my brain like a ticker tape:

CAT

> No, you canna just show up and see Lucas. What do you think that does to him, to have you randomly pop up once a year? Let me think about this.

And farther back, the one that eventually pushed me over the edge and onto a flight to Ireland:

CAT

> Dinna you dare come around ever again unless you've got your act together. He needs someone dependable.

That was after my disastrous visit with Lucas back in Stirling. I'd really fucked things up then. I've read that message a hundred times. I know every word by heart.

My finger lingers over her text, heart racing in anticipation of the message. I've been selfish. Ashamed. Cat thinks I'm a bawbag. My parents do too. And Lucas . . . Who knows what he thinks?

Aye, I've been an eejit, but I'm trying desperately to change. Doesna that count for something? Probably not to Cat. She only knows I've been a terrible father.

I click the text.

CAT

I'm having a tenth birthday party for Lucas on
20 August. You can come. But dinna mess this
up. Come with your life sorted, Oliver. I'm
serious. No repeats of last time.

A gasp escapes my mouth. She's giving me a chance with Lucas? In a month? I can do this. No drama. Life together. I'm working on all of those things.

I roughly run my hands through my wavy hair, which is just long enough to tuck behind my ears.

What *am* I thinking, anyway? In no universe am I father material. Britt just said I'm lucky not to be a parent. Probably because I'm shite at it, and that's instantly obvious to anyone who meets me. She'd immediately accepted that I'm not a da. No one would think that of me.

Another text buzzes in.

CAT

Grant will be there, of course, just like he's
been there for all of Lucas's events for the past
five years, including the last one you showed
up to. I think you know he moved in last
summer. So I mean it—no drama.

Fuck. If I'm the worst father possible, Grant is probably the best one. He's dependable. Has a good job as an accountant, or something. He doesna even have kids of his own. I bet he's always home to have dinner with Cat and Lucas. And in our last annual Christmas phone call, my parents let slip Grant had moved in. They seemed pleased with it, like we werena talking about my ex-girlfriend and *my son*. One big happy family up there in Stirling. My parents had curiously asked what I'm up to. If not football, what would I possibly be doing? Not parenting. Nae. They've never thought I was good enough.

My stomach turns and the familiar urge to flee overtakes me, so

I zip my phone in the pocket of my athletic shorts and take off out of the football field, turning right away from town, passing the lassies' camp barracks at the big hotel, and running on the winding, narrow road without sidewalks.

I push myself. Hard.

I'm a footballer. My professional career might be over, but still, that's all I am. Not a father. Not a boyfriend, not a partner, not even a very good friend. That's why coaching *has* to work. And maybe I can be a part-time father to Lucas. Maybe I can just be his friend. Anything more than I've been would be a start.

I work my way around a turn in the road, almost hoping a lorry will appear in front of me and I'll have to dodge out of the way, as if it was some kind of real-life obstacle course.

Another text buzzes in and I slow down to read.

CAT

Your parents will also be there.

I laugh out loud, but it's without a trace of humor. Of course, they'll be there. I wonder if they are as hard on Lucas playing football as they were on me? They let slip that he's gotten really good over the last year. Or maybe they figured out how to be supportive, instead of punishing a wee boy for not making the top select team. I was ten when that happened, and they didna talk to me for a week. A week! Not talking to a ten-year-old. Is that even legal? It's not like I hadna tried my best. I'd had a bad day. That's all.

The next year, I made the team.

The only good thing they did for me was teach me how to manage my finances, so even after my career-ending injury, even when I was partying and trying to forget who I was, I didna blow my money on cars or houses or foolish things like some of my teammates did. I was *doing* foolish things, for sure, but not with large sums of my money. Better, maybe, or at least better than doing both.

It seems like even back then, my parents didna think I would be the best or longest-lasting footballer. Even though I'd reached the highest level, it was still not enough for them. I never scored enough, never played enough, never made enough money. I wish I could put the memory of their disappointed looks out of my mind. But if being a pro footballer didna impress them, what else possibly would?

My thighs burn, but I sprint down the road anyway. I wonder how hard I'd have to push myself to collapse entirely? Sweat pours down my forehead and stings my eyes. I always had impressive endurance—that's what a midfielder needs. The strength to keep sprinting back and forth, being everywhere, supporting the front, defending the back, stepping into whatever role is needed. Scoring, defending, passing. I could have kept playing, but there were too many younger, better, faster players coming up. The injury was the last straw. My agent couldna find me a placement after I'd recovered, so I hung my head and quietly left the game I love.

Should I even go to this party? How could I? I canna imagine showing up and seeing all of them. Canna imagine walking in with my tail between my legs, head hung low with shame at my absence. Shame at my failures.

But it's also the whole point in my coming home to Scotland. Start a new life here so I can be there for Lucas. It's a test. A life audition. Maybe before the party, I'll hear back from some of the coaching jobs I've applied to.

I need to go. I know that. I want to go. But how will I face Cat, my parents, annoyingly perfect Grant?

And most importantly, Lucas?

I dinna know what he thinks of me. I hardly know what an almost-ten-year-old boy is even like. Will he hate me for not being around?

Why am I bothering with any of this?

I dodge to the grassy side of the road and stop to avoid a tiny, zippy car that leans on its horn when it sees me around a curve.

Partially bent over, I rest my hands on the wooden fence and appreciate the shaking in my thighs that reminds me I'm human.

The twentieth of August. I have just over four weeks to get my shite together before the party. How hard can that be?

A sheep baas next to me and I jump, then laugh. I look around, figuring I'd run a good three miles already, so I set off on a much gentler jog back toward the football fields. I've punished myself enough for one day.

5

___

REESE

Friday, July 22
31 Days Before Departure
Reese's Flat

Comfortable with my laptop on the couch in my fragrant flat, I click through a website staging site I've been revising, finally happy with how it's looking. The user experience and interface agency we work with to build the actual website is in India, my client's in Italy, and I'm here in Scotland, overseeing the whole thing. It's the perfect setup for the summer. I email the link to the client so he can go through each page and send feedback to me on the layout, priorities of communication, and general look and feel of the site.

I send a quick update message to my boss. I've been a project manager with this agency for almost ten years, focusing on website design and digital marketing. She trusts me. I'm thankful for the flexible career she's helped me build, especially since I now only have my income to rely on.

And when I brought up working from Scotland for the summer, there was no hesitation.

"You need this," she'd said, her eyes intense. *"To be honest, I don't want to join one more video call and see your face all tight and unhappy. Like that."* She'd gestured to me with a grimace. *"Life is not only about work. Go to Europe and learn that."*

I know that. I do more than work. I take care of my daughter and worry about my sisters. I check in on my mom and Great-Aunt Evelyn. Sure, maybe I'm still figuring out how to take care of myself, but I'm working on it.

I'm here, aren't I? In Scotland?

In a flat that smells like fried fish and adventure. And I love it. I loved it the second I walked in. It's like I'm studying abroad for the summer as a thirty-seven-year-old woman, complete with class-mates I wish hadn't joined the program.

My laptop pings with a new email—it's the Italian client responding. They will look at the staging site on Monday. Italians don't seem to have any interest in working long hours, or week-ends, or even Friday afternoons.

I close my laptop and wonder what to do with my evening. Chelsea's busy with the other girls and I have nowhere to be. Netflix on my couch? A stroll around the town? The possibilities are, well, not endless, but numerous. My phone buzzes and I grab it, hoping it's Chelsea checking in.

But no, it's a text from Britt. I roll my neck and scrunch up my face, fighting off the wave of unrest that comes with seeing her name.

Now that I think about it, I'm surprised she waited this long to get in touch after the surprise reunion yesterday. Actually, I'm lucky she only sent a text. She'd often appeared at my door with a big smile, an expensive bottle of red wine, and groceries to cook homemade lasagna or another delicious dinner. Well, that was in the Days Before. Now she's so much more tentative around me. If I give her one dirty look, she makes me feel like I just kicked a puppy. How does she do that? She ended up with my ex-husband, but I'm the one who feels bad about hesitating to be her BFF again.

I *could* just not open the text from her. Maybe I'm working late. Or out with new friends, having a pint at the pub. Or, I don't know, asleep at five o'clock on a Friday. But I'm pretty sure I don't have the strength to resist an unread text for long, and if I don't open it now, I'll just stare at my phone all night and wonder.

"Fine," I say to no one. I need to learn some Scottish curse words. I tap open the text.

BRITT

> Hey, Ree. How are you settling in? I'm so excited to be in Scotland. And to spend time with you. What a happy coincidence.

Is it? Can I still have my reset, and give Britt another chance? We could have had so much fun here together, before everything happened. I miss my best friend. And then, there's the co-parenting bit. Britt is living in the same house as my daughter half the time. I need to have a good relationship with her and Adrian, for Chelsea's sake, don't I?

ME

> Thanks for checking in. I'll be working while I'm here, so will be tied up a lot.

That didn't quite come out as friendly as I'd planned. Yeah, I'll be working, but I'm also not planning on putting in a single extra hour, let alone a full forty. Plus, I have more vacation time to use. Those fluffy sheep will be a mere memory in just a month.

BRITT

> Ah, right! I have to check in a couple of hours a week, but am mostly off. Same with Adrian. Maybe we can go on a few adventures together? A day trip on a weekend? Or you and I can grab a coffee sometime?

I remind myself that the most important thing is setting a good example for Chelsea. Not having a screaming fit at Adrian or smashing a cute cat mug. I gave them my blessing to be together. I agreed to let Britt back into my life. I just need to fight through the pain I feel when she asks me something personal and I feel guilty about not wanting to open up to her. Practice will make it easier.

ME

Sure.

There. I screenshot the texts and send them to my sisters, with immediate horrified responses and advice on how many ways I can tell Britt to fuck off. They are not quite on board with the idea of me being friends with her again, and I only keep them in the loop because their explosive reactions validate my confusing negative feelings. However, I will not tell Britt to fuck off. Stella and Maddie know that.

But I have to get out of this flat. Grabbing my phone and a thin raincoat, I leave to explore Peebles.

THE STAIRCASE from my flat to ground level is so narrow, I can't even imagine how the furniture got in there. It must've come in a million pieces and been assembled inside, never to be removed or replaced. Or maybe in through the window with some kind of crane.

I burst out onto the sidewalk, screeching to a halt and looking around. Where, exactly, am I going?

There's a few people in the fish and chips line. A pair of girls around Chelsea's age laugh and push each other, one giggling and shouting the word *moist*. I shudder. *I hate that word too, girl.* Behind them, a man in fancy work pants with a laptop bag talks on his cell phone, maybe on the way home from Edinburgh, which is less than an hour bus ride away.

My stomach rumbles.

If I turn left, I'd head back uptown toward the soccer fields. Turn right, and there are a ton of shops to explore, including a convenience store, the grocery shop, a few restaurants, maybe a pub, and a cafe, if I remember correctly. Now that sounds like a lovely idea. I'll get a coffee. Is it my billionth caffeinated beverage of the day? Yes. Should I not drink coffee after five o'clock in the evening? Perhaps.

Drops of water tap my face, illustrating why I haven't bothered to curl my hair since arriving in Scotland. But it's long and thick and will happily stay straight-to-slightly-wavy in the rain. I close my eyes and breathe in. I came here for a reset, and I'm going to get it. Surely I can do that while also seeing Adrian and Britt a few times?

I dodge people walking along the sidewalk and note a Thai restaurant that smells delicious, a closed bakery with empty pastry racks that I absolutely need to visit some morning, and an upscale baby shop.

Surely, I won't see them that often. And since Britt said they're only working a few hours a week—Adrian is a financial advisor and Britt manages a corporate app incubator—maybe they'll be traveling or otherwise occupied.

Alternatively, Britt will text me daily, trying to get me to be her bestie again. I can see it going either way—most likely somewhere in between. They will be unavoidable.

I screech to a halt just beyond the Thai restaurant and look around with alarm. I didn't even think about where they might be staying. I imagine them popping out of one of the doors nestled in between the shops. They could be anywhere.

"Reese?" A male, Scottish-accented voice interrupts my meandering thoughts.

My eyes focus on the concerned man in front of me.

Oliver Vass.

My insides get fluttery like the eyelashes of a teenage girl, and I take in his blue eyes and crinkled forehead as he examines my face.

"Hi," I say in a wispy voice.

"You look dazed. You're not gonna almost fall over again, are you?" He slips his hands out of the pockets of his jeans, as if to prepare to catch me.

I cringe.

"Definitely not. Sorry about yesterday." I open my mouth to say more, then clamp it shut.

"What are you up to? You look lost."

Like yesterday, his lilting accent captivates me, *you look lost* sounding like *yeh luke low-st.*

"Lost in a daydream," I say.

His eyebrows lift. "A bonnie one, I hope." He moves his hands back to his sides and I follow the movement, my gaze landing on a heartbeat tattoo on the inside of his wrist before he shoves his hands back into his pockets.

My eyes trace up his bare forearms and biceps to his shoulders. A Scottish flag tattoo peeks out from the snug black t-shirt on his right arm.

"Nah. Not really." I cross my arms over my chest, hugging my jacket and thin sweater closer, a small clutch purse in one hand. "Aren't you cold? Because I'm freezing."

"I'm Scottish. I'm used to the cold and rain." He says *Scottish* with a *scote* at the beginning. *Scote-tish.* The fluttering in my stomach grows and I can't help smiling.

"Why are you grinning like that? Are you sure you're alright?" He looks honestly concerned.

I chuckle. "Positive."

"Want to grab a bevy?" He nods his head down the High Street. "Because if we stand here a minute more, I'm going to end up buying fish and chips."

"Bevy?" Confused for a second, I finally realize what he's saying.

"Pint."

"Yeah. Okay." I shrug and try to appear super casual, as if this hot man didn't just invite me for a drink.

"Come on, then."

I dodge the same businessman from the fish and chips line, still talking on his cell phone, now with an overflowing container of french fries—sorry, chips—in his hand, and fall in beside Oliver.

"I smell those fish and chips all day. My flat reeks of it. Actually, I'd be surprised if my hair doesn't as well."

Oliver glances down at me. "You're staying above the shop?"

I nod.

"Let me have a sniff then." He stops walking and turns to me.

"What?"

"Your hair. I'll smell it." He reaches his hand over with a mischievous grin, pausing before touching me, his eyebrows raised with a question.

I snort, then realize he's serious.

"That's kind of weird, but I'm intrigued. *Does* my hair smell like fish and chips? Maybe I can't even tell anymore. Go ahead. Sniff away." Who am I and what have I done with my boring self?

He gently picks up a chunk of my hair, raises it to his nose, and breathes deeply, not breaking eye contact. I have to step closer to him, and he leans down. I'm not short by any means, but he's got to be well over six feet tall to tower above my five-foot-five frame. Everything slows, and . . . Holy hell, what is happening here?

"Nae. You're good. No fried food."

"Fantastic." I sound so weird.

He drops my hair but keeps eye contact. "Pub's right here. The Old Forge."

I go through the door he holds open for me, pausing to look at him. "Just curious. Do you go around sniffing people's hair often?"

"You literally asked me to." His face is deadpan.

"Did I, though?"

He laughs and follows me inside the pub.

The Old Forge is warm, both in temperature and decor, with a traditional wooden bar and a mismatch of tables around the room. The place is three-quarters full of people celebrating a Friday evening.

"What do you fancy? My treat." We approach the bar.

"Red wine, thank you."

Oliver orders my drink, a whisky for himself, and an order of french fries, then pays for it all. We settle in with our drinks—bevies—at a round table along one side of the room, a giant Scottish flag pinned on the ceiling above us.

"Slainte mhath." He raises his glass to me and clinks mine gently. "Scottish for cheers," he translates.

After we put our drinks back on the table, we stare at each other.

What, exactly, are we supposed to talk about now, me and this man who sniffed my hair moments ago? Fine, that'll make me giggle for hours. Days. But now he's looking around the room and I'd bet he's thinking the same thing. What could he and I possibly have in common? He's literally gorgeous, and I'm just, well, me. I clench and unclench my toes inside my black flats.

"So yesterday, you said you're not from here. Are you also living above a random fish and chips shop?" I say, not able to handle the awkward silence.

He assesses me for a second before answering, his eyes roaming my face. Not unfriendly, not uncomfortable, but curious.

"Nae," he says. "I rented a house just outside of town, on the way to the fields. You'd have passed it. It's got bright-yellow shutters."

An image of his house immediately flashes in my mind. It's adorable, with a nice garden, a well-kept porch, and that wooden swing. "I noticed it. An entire house, huh? Here with your family?"

He gives me a funny look. "Nae. Just me."

And with that, I should get out of here and end this painful conversation. I'm sure he has better things to do than hang out with me on a Friday night. I chug my wine until it's almost gone, then suddenly realize it's a terrible idea, as the tangy bite of cheap pub red makes me wince.

"Not the best wine, aye?" He's finished his whisky and eyes my mostly empty glass with an amused glint in his eyes.

"Not really, but it's been a long week. Or, long few days, anyway." The wine may not be high-end, but I appreciate the warm feeling as it settles in my stomach.

"I'd love to hear more about it. That, uh, interaction yesterday at camp was the highlight of my week." He watches for my reaction, and I scrunch my nose. "So another drink? Pints this time? I promise the beer is much better than the shite wine."

I consider. The alcohol is already making this situation less awkward. Or it's covering up the awkwardness, whichever. Why not stay for another? I could use someone to talk to, someone who was a witness, and texting with Stella and Maddie will not be enough for tonight. They're both probably still at work, anyway— Stella almost done with her day in London, Maddie just beginning hers at the restaurant she manages back home.

"Sure. Thanks."

Oliver heads to the bar and I unashamedly watch him go, checking out how well his butt fills his jeans and the way his arm muscles bulge as he moves. I wish I could capture this moment and share it with my sisters, but whipping out my phone to snap a photo right now would be, like, entirely inappropriate. Stella and Maddie have been my best friends since our dad died twenty-two years ago, forcing us to band together to survive the emotional trauma. I didn't have time to keep up with my high school friends, and getting pregnant in college didn't help me keep any friendships from there. Finding Britt when she moved to our town from New York City with her then-husband six years ago was a miracle. A short-lived one, of course. So besides a few mom friends, like my cat-sitter, Marisa, I just focus on Chelsea and my sisters. They're all I need.

As Oliver returns with a pair of pints, I giggle silently, wondering what I am doing here at this Scottish pub, with this random man who claims to want to hear my life story. That might be a stretch, but it's what I'm going with.

"Goan then." He nods his chin at me.

I tilt my head. "Do you want the long version, or the short one?" I sip the first inch or two off the pint.

"Definitely the long version. One hundred percent. Please, entertain me."

I cringe. Telling him about my life would guarantee he won't be attracted to me for long . . . if he is at all. After all, how likely is that? And why would I care? It'd be great to not have to pretend with him. Maybe to have an actual friend here in Peebles. A flash of Chelsea's face appears in my head, if she were to see me sitting here with her coach and crush? That would be messy. But a friend would be awesome. And if he's hot and has a great accent? Even better. No one could fault me for that, not even my daughter.

He rolls his hand in an encouraging motion.

"I'm not sure it's entertaining as much as a showcase of how uncool I am." Anything to make this Scottish hunk happy, I suppose, so he keeps those eyes on me. Just for entertainment. Just for the stories I can tell my sisters later.

"Understood."

"And then you have to tell me something equally boring about yourself, so I don't feel as bad." I'm suddenly completely comfortable with Oliver. I think it was the mindset shift just now—that there's no chance of anything happening, so why not be completely myself?

"Agreed." He smirks. "Now get on with it." Oliver leans back in his chair and keeps his eyes trained on me.

"Also, you have to unequivocally take my side in all parts of any story I tell you. Like, no questions asked, no judgment, just, I've always been in the right."

"Done. Now talk."

I run my fingers through my hair, still damp from the misty rain, and pull it over my shoulder.

"Britt used to be my best friend," I say.

"That rank bitch!" Oliver exclaims immediately, fake shock on his face.

I laugh and gulp from my pint. I might be in trouble with this guy.

Nah.

He is not my type. Really.

6

OLIVER

"Wow." I admit, this drama is fascinating. And I'm not hating staring at this woman's face. She's sweet, funny, and knows how to tell an entertaining story.

"I know. And now, basically, she wants to rebuild our friendship. And it's fine—I said yes. We all co-parent together, anyway."

I make a nondescript sound and Reese narrows her eyes at me.

"What? Are you going to tell me I'm ridiculous for being nice to her, like my sisters do?"

"Oh, I wouldna think of it. It's just . . ."

"She's had a rough go of it. Her ex-husband had an affair with his coworker when he was working in New York City, not long after they moved to town. She was devastated. It was all the late nights in the city, while she was home waiting for him with their son, Jackson. He should've stopped it, should've stopped the coworker from developing feelings for him to begin with." Reese frowns. "That was actually when we got really close." She presses her lips together and pauses. "Anyway, so instead of letting her feelings get out of control for Adrian, she removed herself from the situation. She told us she needed space and walked away."

Reese throws her hands up in the air and waits for my

response.

I scrunch my face. "Hmm."

"There's that sound again. What?"

"Well, it's an interesting defense."

"Defense?"

"You're defending her for stealing your husband."

"No, ha, not really . . ." Reese trails off. "Am I?"

"Well, aye. She removed herself from the situation, but you got divorced, anyway? Then she swooped back in and got with him days later?"

"It was weeks," Reese murmurs, rubbing her chin. "But yeah. I guess that's what happened."

"And then you told them it's okay."

She nods. "I mean, it took me a while to accept it. Like almost a year."

"And after that, you agreed to be friends with her again?"

"Yes?" The skin around Reese's eyes crinkles. "I mean, she gets brownie points for trying to do the right thing, don't you think?"

"I *think* after hearing that, I hate them for you, even if you're not gonna." My pint is almost gone. I'm stress-drinking hearing this story and feel justified in immediately disliking Adrian yesterday.

What I dinna hate is the way being here is making me feel. The whisky, the pint . . . and listening to her.

Reese laughs. "I don't hate them. Really. I'm over it. But I needed some space this month. Just a break from the daily drama of it all. I have to see them at all the school events. I have to co-parent with Adrian. And they're always around. Always." She leans forward and rests her elbows on the table, the v-neck of her sweater dipping between her breasts, showing more curves and skin than she probably means to. Her pint is only a third full, and I suspect she's tipsy.

Fuck. I think she's hot.

"It's possible they deserve just a wee bit of your hate, yeh ken that, right?" There's a twinge in my groin when she grins at me, and my cheeks grow warm. It takes significant effort to keep my eyes on her face, not on her breasts. But then my gaze drifts down to her lips, full and pink.

"Nah. We'll all make it work. For Chelsea." She bites her bottom lip, the very one I'm finding it hard not to stare at.

"That's rather noble of you." I wonder what it'd be like to kiss her. I havena kissed someone since before I left for Ireland and swore off women and football. Now I'm back in Scotland coaching at a football camp and fantasizing about this woman?

Nah is the right word. I need to stop these inappropriate thoughts.

"Sometimes, I wonder if any of it was real to begin with," she continues, and if she noticed me staring at her mouth, I canna tell. "I thought I loved Adrian, but maybe it was just the pregnancy and hormones that got me to marry him so long ago. We were basically kids—I was only twenty-one when I had Chelsea. Twenty-two when we got married."

I feel a twist of jealousy that the man who showed up at camp yesterday got to touch Reese for that long and didna even appreciate it. Maybe he did the right thing—getting married to the girl he knocked up. They'd been right around the same age as me and Cat when I got her pregnant.

Am I jealous?

I shake my head to get the unwelcome, yet pleasant, thought of touching Reese out of my head. She stares and waits for me to say something.

"I'm sure it was real at some point. People fall outta love. It happens." I try to sound reassuring, but I dinna think I've ever been in love. Not with my recent ex. Not even with Cat. Not with anyone. The only thing I've ever truly loved is football.

Even to myself, I sound like a real wanker.

"One more thing." She pauses and breathes in deep enough that her shoulders rise and fall visibly.

"Goan."

She leans forward, as if she's about to tell me some secret. I do the same, until we're only a hand's width apart.

"They're inviting me to the wedding."

"Nae. They canna. They wouldna. Are you fucking kidding me?"

She nods solemnly. "I got the save-the-date invitation before leaving for Scotland."

"Ah . . . ah dinna have the words." Lucas's birthday party pops into my head. At least I have a reason to go to that, even if I'm not particularly wanted. But the wedding of my ex to my ex-best friend? That's hard to even consider.

"I'm not going, of course."

"Nae?"

"Would you?" She waves her hand in front of her and knocks over her pint. Liquid rushes toward her and onto her lap and she gasps.

"Oh, shite." I canna help a touch of laughter from creeping into my voice at the shocked look on her face.

"Damn!" Reese yelps and stands.

"I'll get napkins." I dash to the bar to grab a handful and rush back. The bottom of her sweater is soaking wet, causing it to cling to her stomach, and the thigh of one leg of her jeans is dark with liquid.

I have the incredible urge to wipe her down, to blot her belly and thigh until they are dry. The impulse is ragingly inappropriate, obviously. Instead, I hand her the napkins.

"I'm an absolute klutz," she groans after taking my offering. She presses her stomach and jeans, soaking in the spilled liquid. "Were you laughing at me?" She narrows her eyes and leans over to wipe down the chair.

I ease myself back into mine. "Maybe. You were getting quite insistent over the wedding. I dinna blame you, hen."

She sits back across from me and gives her empty pint glass a yearning look. "I thought you Scottish guys called women lass, not hen."

"Nae, that's just in Outlander, or something a ninety-year-old man would say."

Reese is quiet for a few seconds, then makes a nondescript grunt. "Hen's sweet."

I suck in my top lip, not sure what to respond back.

"Hey, I'm not sure why I told you all of that before. I'm usually not such an open book. And I try to keep my mouth shut around *them*. The one time I let it all out, Chelsea overheard, and it was a disaster."

I take in her flushed cheeks and wide gray eyes and decide I dinna want this night to end quite yet.

"Want a do-over on the pint? Lucky number three?" I nod my head to the bar. Am I trying to get her drunk? Nae. But this is far better than a night out with David or scrolling endlessly through my phone in the empty rented house. It's only a relative thing. Of course a pretty woman is preferable over a sixty-year-old bloke.

She hesitates for a second, considering.

"Okay." She narrows her eyes at me. "But mostly because you still need to tell me something embarrassing or ridiculously personal about yourself, since I just emotionally vomited all over you just now. And yesterday. It's only fair."

She crosses her arms on her chest, unintentionally pushing up her breasts. My eyes widen slightly.

"Aye. So . . . another pint?"

"I'll get them this time," she says, but I leap back up before she can move.

"Too late. I'm on it."

"Then I'm going to the bathroom to try to clean myself up some more."

I force myself to not watch her walk across the bar as I head to the bar to get the drinks.

This woman is not my type. I'm not sure exactly what that is, actually. Taller? Darker? Probably about a decade younger, if I'm honest. Wait. That one who was photographed on my lap that one drunken night out was blond, I think.

Hair color doesna matter. But I've not been with someone like this divorced mum from New Jersey.

I order the pints and barely notice the bartender handing back my card, I'm so distracted by Reese coming across the room.

Now that I think about it, the one woman I've dated who is most like Reese is Cat. Cute, down to earth, and not impressed with me being a professional footballer. *Ex*-professional footballer, that is.

But it's not like there's anything sparking between us, no matter the pleasant warm feeling coursing through my veins or the desire wakening in my core. There canna be. I'm imagining it. We're just two adults passing the time together, having a friendly conversation, no flirting, just a few laughs.

Chanting to myself that this is strictly platonic, I stride back over to the table. I definitely dinna have a developing crush on this woman.

"Slanja . . . what was it again?" Reese clinks my pint.

"Slainte mhath," I correct her with a smile.

She gulps deeply. "So? What's your secret then, Coach Oliver?"

I flinch, still not used to anyone calling me a coach. It's only been two days of camp, after all.

"Uh-oh. What did I say wrong?" Reese's brow furrows.

"Nothing, nothing wrong. I just, uh, never really wanted to be a coach. Never intended to, that is. I wanted to play football forever, which is daft." I grip my glass, rubbing the condensation off with my thumbs. "No one does it forever. But now . . . I mean, it's all I can be. It's the best choice." I touch my new tattoos. "Scotland and football. That's what I am, my only option."

She lets a rush of air out of her nose, following my moving hand with her eyes, her gaze slipping back and forth over my inked biceps. "How can that possibly be true?"

"All I have literally ever been is a footballer. From when I could walk, I played. No one cared if I got good grades or developed any other life skill. Well, besides my parents micromanaging my money, which I suppose wasna the worst thing."

"And? What happened with soccer? Football, whatever?"

I roughly scratch my head. "Do you not ken anything about my past?"

Her eyes grow wide. "Oh, shit. Are you, like, an ax murderer or something?"

"Nae. Dinna be daft." The side of my mouth quirks.

"Thank the lord. Bank robber?"

I roll my eyes and shake my head.

"Any other kind of convicted felon that somehow prohibits you from doing anything that doesn't involve a soccer ball?"

I canna stop from laughing. She grins back at me.

"But yeh dinna understand."

"Okay, okay. So tell me more. What happened to your soccer career?"

"I got hurt." I break eye contact and splay one of my hands on the table, spreading my fingers out wide, then clenching them together into a fist. "And then I recovered and got back in the game. Only I got hurt again. This time, the doctors told me it was too risky to keep playing football, so my club dropped me, even though I was willing to keep trying. That was it. Over. Twenty-five years of soccer, ten as pro, and then I was nothing."

"Oh, damn." Reese reaches over and covers my fist with her hand. Warmth blooms inside me as she moves her thumb over mine. "I'm so sorry."

I look up and meet her eyes, and they're filled with such compassion, I'm frozen for a second. Tears threaten to form. After cold indifference or hostility from so many people in my life, including my parents, having someone—a stranger, really—be so sympathetic to me is surprising.

"It must be hard if everyone's only treated you like one thing, and then overnight you have to become another."

Fuck, that rings true.

I nod. "That's . . . exactly right. And the day I was sacked from the team, my girlfriend dumped me."

"That rank bitch!" She echoes my exclamation from earlier.

"Nae, I almost definitely deserved it." I offer Reese a half-smile.

"Sorry. Keep going." She squeezes my hand.

"I'm not close to my parents, so I didna even talk to them when it happened. It felt like I had no one. So after a year of behaving badly around London and Edinburgh, I went to stay with a friend in Ireland. I hid out for a year."

"Wow. Why'd you come back?"

Bloody hell, what's my answer to her question? There is absolutely no way I'm gonna tell this woman what a terrible person I am for not having a real relationship with my son. Nae. Not when she's devoted her whole life to her daughter. Not when she's looking at me like this—eyes wide and sympathetic—instead of like I'm a pile of rubbish. I dinna want to break this spell.

"Um, I'm trying to, well, connect with my family. Maybe put down some roots again in Scotland. Ah dinna ken, maybe I'll head back to Ireland in the fall." I shrug and try to be casual, but this conversation has turned into anything but that.

She tilts her head. "I think connecting with your family again sounds like a great idea."

"Hmm. Maybe. It feels so difficult." I think of that message from Cat. How much I have to change to get back into Lucas's life. How my parents have no interest in me. How I have to prove myself to everyone.

"I find it so hard, how much pressure we put on our young athletes these days. I try to back off Chelsea, but she's really good and wants to play professionally, so I also want to push her enough that she doesn't lose out on opportunities." Reese leans back in the wooden chair and drinks. Her cheeks are pink from the alcohol, and she's got a dreamy look on her face as she talks about her daughter. "I bet that's what your parents were thinking. Maybe they pushed you so hard that they ended up pushing you away. I imagine they'd love to have you back in their lives."

My jaw hangs open. That's not true. My parents would definitely not love to have me back. But maybe she's right. Maybe they didna mean to push me so far away. Ah, fuck it, too late to fix *that* relationship.

A thought crosses my mind: Cat would love this woman. I bet if I showed up at Lucas's party with someone like Reese, Cat'd welcome me back into my son's life with open arms.

Nae. Yer aft yer head.

"You're a good ma," I say. "I can tell."

She holds my eye contact long enough that I desperately want to know what she's thinking.

"And you're good at getting me drunk." She glares down at her almost-empty pint glass. "Three drinks? I haven't done that in, I don't know, years?"

I laugh again, then finish my own drink. I want another, but I think we better call this a night while I still have good decision-making skills, so I dinna end up making out with Reese in some alleyway.

Not that she'd let me kiss her.

Not that I want to kiss her.

Fuck. Pull it together, lad.

"Walk you home?"

"You're going to escort me back to the fish and chips shop?" She blinks her eyes fake-flirtatiously at me.

"I'm nothing if not a right gent."

"Let's go then." She smiles and pushes her empty pint glass away.

But I swear she looks as disappointed as I feel about the night ending.

7

———————

REESE

"Quick selfie? To commemorate the evening?" Back in front of the fish and chips shop, I sway ever-so-slightly on my feet, taking advantage of the liquid bravery.

Wait, did I ask for a quick selfie or a quickie?

Either one would do, I suppose. I silently cackle.

"What are we commemorating, exactly?" Oliver asks with a completely straight face.

"Uh . . ." I stutter. What, indeed? But there's a weight lifted from my shoulders from talking to someone about all the Adrian and Britt nonsense, and the murky ball of dread in my stomach has shrunk considerably. The amused glint in his eye is a reminder that me and this exceptionally attractive man are only friends. Just acquaintances, even. So I should treat him like a normal human being. Which he probably is, under all those rippling muscles and tattoos.

"Joking." He grins and reaches for the phone clutched in my hand. "I'll take it."

"Thanks, because I'm absolute shit at selfies."

"Well, I'm braw at them, so we make a good pair." Oliver holds his arm out and snaps the picture quickly. I hope I don't look like a goblin next to his beauty.

"There you go. Dinna go posting it online somewhere. I've been in hiding for a year and dinna want to let the tabloids know where I am."

"But do you think I could get some good money for it?" I cross my arms, planning to immediately send the picture to my sisters, not the tabloids. "Or . . . any money for it?"

He narrows his eyes. "Nae. Certainly not. But someone might be interested in the fact that I'm not pissed or with some scandalous woman at a club at three o'clock in the morning."

"I'm not scandalous? Should I be offended?"

"Nae." He holds out my phone and our fingers brush each other when I accept it. An electric tingle runs up my forearm, only partially distracting me from the fact that he thinks I'm not scandalous, and that this somehow disappoints me. "Good night, Reese."

I bite my lip. "Yup. Goodnight."

"See you tomorrow?" He backs away.

"Tomorrow?"

"At the restaurant for the family night? That's supposed to be farewell to the families until the end of camp. Except for you, your ex-husband, and your ex-best friend, of course."

"Which is perfectly logical." I laugh breathlessly. "See you there." He was definitely not asking me to hang out again. I can't believe that even crossed my mind. It didn't, not really.

He smiles one last time and walks away.

Once again, I appreciate his butt and the way his broad shoulders look like they'd hold up the whole of Scotland. I fumble with the lock on the door to my building, wearing the stupidest grin on my face.

I think I might have a new crush.

No! I mean, I think I might have a new *friend*, not a new crush. Not any kind of crush. I'm too old and jaded to have a crush. I do, however, have photo evidence of the evening. I slowly climb the steep staircase and click open my photos.

I moan. It's glorious. I look a little mousy, but not full-on soggy goblin. Oliver's blue eyes pop off the screen and seem to bore into my soul. I immediately text the picture to Stella and Maddie.

A few seconds later, a group video call buzzes in. I push open the door to my flat, kicking it shut behind me.

"Holy hell, Reese, is that the hot soccer coach?" Stella is practically screaming, her background a crowded pub.

I laugh and shrug, making a note to work on my mysterious look and not be a complete open book.

"Yeah. Just a new friend who I had a few drinks with. No big deal." I slip off my black flats.

Stella gasps.

"Hi, hello, it's me, your youngest sister from New Jersey, where it's still a workday." Maddie shakes her head.

"Sorry, Mads!" Stella and I chorus, but neither of us looks exceptionally apologetic.

"I'm so glad you two are having fun with hot men at bars." Maddie's background is the small, windowless office in the restaurant she manages.

"It was really nothing." I stare at myself in the mirror image on the phone, then hide it so I don't succumb to complete self-absorption. "I only sent you that picture to get a reaction."

"Mission accomplished," Stella says. "I'm impressed."

I toss my clutch purse on the counter and fill up the kettle with water from the tap for tea.

"Please tell us how you somehow ended up drinking at a pub and taking selfies on the street with him?" Maddie's brow furrows. She quirks her lips. "I love that for you, but help me understand. That's something *I* would do, not my reliable, responsible big sister."

"I'm not that boring, am I?" I sigh and collapse on my couch as the water heats up noisily. My sisters think I'm incredibly serious and responsible, which shouldn't bother me, but kind of does. I bet no one Oliver dates would be accused of being too responsible. "Did you know that no one uses a microwave to make tea in Scotland? There's not even one in the flat."

"Ugh, Reese, come on!" Maddie groans.

"Really, it's okay that you're boring. Neither of us would have survived our childhoods without you being exactly who you are." Stella nods encouragingly. "But . . . spill!"

"Okay, okay. We ran into each other and went to get a drink. Totally platonic." Sure. But I can still feel the tingly warmth of my skin on his when he told me about his soccer injury, that devastatingly vulnerable look on his face. I suspect he doesn't talk about this stuff often. A bloom of protectiveness sprouts inside me.

"Still . . . When's the last time you got a drink with a hot Scottish guy?" Stella asks. "Scratch that. *Any* guy?"

"First of all, never, second of all, it was actually three drinks."

"You had THREE drinks with him?" she shoots back right away.

"Almost three. I spilled part of one all over myself." I laugh, thinking of how sloppy I must have looked.

As Stella gapes at me, there's a knocking through the phone and Maddie mutes us and turns her head to talk to someone at her office door before coming back on.

"Gotta run, sisters. Keep up the good work, Reese." She stands at her desk. "Oh, I'm heading to see Aunt Evelyn tomorrow with Mom. I'll let you know how she's doing." Maddie blows kisses and clicks off the call.

I make a mental note to text her tomorrow to follow up. Our great-aunt is in her nineties and has slowed down a lot lately.

"I just talked to Evelyn this week," Stella says. "I'm glad she has you and Maddie and Mom nearby." Stella is the closest to Evelyn, even though she's so far away and only goes home to New Jersey twice a year. They have a special bond. We're quiet for a few seconds, just the loud bustle of a busy London pub buzzing behind her. "Anyway. Girl, tell me more about this soccer coach. I need details."

"He was really easy to talk to, actually." I grab a mug from my cabinet and linger next to the kettle. "I just pretended he was a normal person, not a super-hot ex-professional soccer player. Which basically means nothing to me anyway, so whatever."

That's not completely true. Professional soccer means a lot to my daughter, and these coaches are important to her future as an athlete.

"And since you're a super-hot, successful, single woman, that's exactly how you should be thinking of him." Stella's stepped outside of the pub and is on a main London road. A red bus zips behind her, followed by a steady stream of black cabs.

"I'd just gotten that text from Britt about meeting up." My insides squeeze. "And I needed some air."

Stella huffs. "You didn't talk to him about all that nonsense, did you?"

"Course I did." The kettle boils loudly and clicks off. I pour steaming water over a Scottish breakfast tea bag nestled in the bottom of the mug, then add a splash of milk and two spoonfuls of sugar. "Honestly, you know I'm not trying to get with him. But I could use some kind of friend here if I'm going to survive the month."

Sucks that it went from my reset month to my just-get-through-it month.

"Stupid Adrian. This is why you should never have gotten married."

"Stella. I got married because I got pregnant. Do you think I shouldn't have had Chelsea?"

"Don't be dramatic. I'm super thankful for my niece. But you didn't have to marry that dick. Whenever people get married, they just roll over and give up their dreams."

I'm certainly not going to defend marriage to her, not

tonight . . . or ever. But Stella seems extra spicy about the topic this evening.

"I know you hate marriage." I attempt patience. "I get it. I'm a divorced, almost-middle-aged woman. You don't have to convince me how much that *institution* sucks." I bite my lip and tilt my head into the camera. "Hey, is everything going okay with Ben? Cause this kind of feels like it's not all about me."

We met Stella's good-looking, outgoing English boyfriend last weekend when we were visiting her in London. He was nice enough, but there was something off in their interactions. I wonder if she's told him about her views on marriage and love. That would be a fun conversation to witness.

Stella's face darkens. "It's totally about you."

"Okay. Fine." I scrunch my face and sip from my steaming mug. The tea is perfectly hot—only slightly scalding my tongue— and perfectly sweet. I open my mouth to say something else about Ben, but Stella shakes her head in warning. "I believe you, okay?" I don't believe her.

"Anyway. Maybe you're right about having a friend in that town."

"Exactly." I slide down onto the comfortable couch and kick my feet up on the coffee table, mug nestled on my belly.

"But maybe you should also hook up with him." She leans close to the phone, so it's zoomed in on one of her black-lined eyes, fake-innocently blinking a million times.

I groan. "Not this Scottish fling thing again, little sister. You know that's not my style."

"Yeah, well, neither are selfies with hot men on the street." She shrugs. "Was he wearing a kilt? Jesus, but I love men in kilts."

"No, Stella, he wasn't wearing a kilt to the pub. Also, and I cannot emphasize this enough, it would be seriously inappropriate for me to hook up with my daughter's coach."

"Eh. It's Europe. Things are different here."

I burst out laughing. "Are they?"

"What are they gonna do? Kick her out of camp? Spread rumors at school about you? Good. You could use some better press. This is your month, even if Adrian the dick and Britt the bitch showed up."

"I don't hate them anymore. Adrian's not a dick, and Britt's not a bitch. Okay?"

To my sisters, this is a black-and-white situation, but my reality is firmly in the gray. It's more complicated than a simple *they are wrong so therefore I hate them*. I wish it were that easy.

I let Stella go back to her Friday night out and lean my head back into the couch, the mug of tea still warming my hands, a smile lingering on my face.

I'm here to get space from my life in New Jersey. To reset how I think about myself and my future. To ground myself in what's important. And most importantly, to set a good example for Chelsea as a strong, independent woman who doesn't let people get to her. And I'm not about to let Adrian and Britt showing up ruin that for me. I'm thrilled to no longer be married to Adrian. And they make each other happy, which makes the home where Chelsea lives half the time a better one.

Still, there's that stubborn dark cloud inside me when I'm around those two. I've forgiven them. I've given their relationship my blessing. I loved them both so much. They're here. So am I. I'll have to deal with it.

Have a fling, Stella and Maddie say. As if it's that easy. Oliver was looking at me with more than a passing interest tonight, but there's no way he actually wants to make out with me. I can only imagine what his ex-girlfriends look like. Probably tall and blond and skinny. Young. Broody. I'm sure they're gorgeous in selfies, with effortlessly posed limbs, giant doe eyes, high cheekbones, and perfectly plump lips.

Definitely not a late-thirties, imperfect, far-too-open soccer mom.

I send a quick text to my daughter to say goodnight. Not for the first time tonight, I wonder what she'd think about me hanging out with her soccer coach. She'd probably be angry, or jealous. Humiliated that her mom is making a fool of herself. I swallow. Would it be better or worse than her father getting engaged to another student's mom? Better, surely. It's not like anything that happens here would last beyond a few weeks.

Why am I even thinking of that nonsense, anyway?

Chelsea responds back with a smiling emoji and a selfie with some of the girls in her room.

Tomorrow is Saturday, the first free day I'll have had since arriving in Peebles, so I'll do some exploring. It'll distract me from thinking about the evening event, where I'll have to once again face Adrian and Britt.

And Oliver.

8

OLIVER

Saturday, 23 July
28 Days Before the Birthday Party
Bella Italia Restaurant

I honestly forget whose parents I'm even talking to. David was not joking when he said that dealing with the adults would be the hardest part of camp. Luckily, everything is easier after a few drinks, and I'm stationed at the bar for that very reason.

This particular father is more interested in asking me about my time at Winchester FC than his own daughter. The mother looks bored and lays her hand on his arm.

"I think we're hogging him, darling," she says with a posh English accent. "Surely there are other parents around who want to ask him about their *child's* football skills." The last bit's a tad sarcastic, and I bite back a grin.

"Right, right, absolutely." His eyes widen and he looks around, where there are not actually any parents waiting to talk to me.

"Come on, then." She pulls on his arm. "Thanks for your time, Coach Oliver. We'll see you in a few weeks." They walk toward the exit, her whispering in his ear.

I take a deep breath and scan the room. The dinner of pasta and fresh-baked bread has been cleared, and the young lassies' tables are empty, as they'd quickly escaped to do something else.

Reese is seated by the exit, looking completely miserable with Adrian and Britt. That woman—Reese—has lived rent-free in my head since I left her in front of her flat last night. Thoughts of her filled my mind—during my run, at the shop, when I woke from my afternoon snooze, and while I browsed online for new coaching job openings. I can't get her out of my head.

There's a couple on the other side of Reese, and she glances over at them. Even I can see the plea in her eyes to be included, but they are deep in conversation with each other. Britt touches Reese's arm. Reese jumps, as if she's spotted a spider crawling on her body. She forces a smile and nods at something Britt says.

This woman needs help.

Reese glances down at her empty glass and her eyes light up. She holds up the drink as if to tell her former best friend, see here, this glass is empty, therefore I have to leave the table.

I chuckle to myself and keep my eyes trained on her as she exchanges words with Britt, then pushes back from the table and strides toward the bar. And me.

Her eyes meet mine and she pauses about a meter from me, an exasperated smile landing on her face. This one is real, not like the forced smile she'd given Britt a minute ago. Something moves in my chest.

"You couldn't save me? Pulled me away for some soccer emergency or something?" She closes the gap between us and stops in front of the bar. "An urgent discussion on Chelsea's passing skills? Or the future of her sporting career?"

Why didn't I think of that?

"Och, apologies. I thought maybe you were enjoying yourself." I focus intently on looking casual, but my arms suddenly go stiff and awkward and I fear she can see right through me. Why is my heart racing?

"Fuck, no." She sighs deeply and leans against the bar next to me, shutting her eyes for a second. "Sorry for all the swearing. I'm not sure why they are bothering me so much tonight." She's wearing a black tank, an open form-fitting gray sweater, and dark-blue jeans that hug every curve of her body.

Not that I care about what she's wearing. But bloody hell, she looks hot.

"Swear all you want. Makes me like you more."

Her eyes fly open and she grins at me. Again.

"I'm supposed to bring them back drinks." She slides the empty glass on the bar and rubs the sides of her jeans. "Of course, I finally find my escape route—because you weren't going to help me—and Britt won't let me go. She asked for refills, just to ensure I don't slip away." She mumbles the last part mostly to herself.

"I've failed you. I'm so sorry." I lift my hand to the bartender. "Two shots of vodka, please."

"What? They don't want shots."

"The shots are for us."

She laughs, a surprised smile lighting up her face. "I don't need a shot."

"*Everybody* needs a shot sometimes." I wink at her and feel like such a dork, but she keeps smiling at me. "Especially everybody who's sitting at a restaurant in Scotland with their ex-husband and ex-best friend."

"Fine. But it's been a few years since I took one. Like, maybe a decade. Or two."

"You're in for a treat, then. Shots taste even better when you're older, I promise. And it'll help with the whole . . ." I subtly lift my hand in her ex's general direction. ". . . thing."

The bartender slides over the filled shot glasses and I push one toward her. What am I doing? Trying to get her drunk . . . again?

"If I puke, it'll be on your shoes."

I laugh. "Deal."

Reese taps my shot glass, then throws back approximately a third of the liquid before making a distressed face.

"That is awful."

I slam my empty glass on the bar. "You have to do it in one go, hen. This is not a sipping vodka. It's a crappy Italian restaurant in Peebles, Scotland. Remember the red wine at The Old Forge?"

"Damn, I do. Okay." She throws back the rest of the shot and shakes her head violently. "Gross."

"But you feel better, right?"

She pauses and quirks her mouth to one side. "Yup. I suppose I do." She smiles and it goes right to her eyes.

"Your lesson of the day is that alcohol solves every problem. Even that one." I nod to her abandoned seat.

"You're a wonderful teacher, thank you. Like some kind of sage." Her face is transformed as she flirts with me. Aye. That's what's happening here.

"I've trained for years on the art of being a wise one."

"Amidst your soccer training?" Reese runs her hand behind her neck and tilts her head.

"Football. And aye. It was my side gig."

"Mmm. Makes sense."

This is the most fun I've had all night. The parents are thinning out, and no one threatens to interrupt us.

"I guess I should get their drinks and go back." She glances back at the table.

"Nae, you absolutely shouldna get them drinks." I touch her arm gently. "And you are not going back there. I canna let that happen. It'd be irresponsible of me. They're like a pair of crocodiles and you're a wee duckling."

She laughs again, this time louder, and leans into my touch. Another bloom of warmth springs up inside me.

Across the room, the sound of Reese's laughter attracts attention. Adrian watches with a furrowed brow, and Britt whispers in his ear. He's got that same look of curiosity—and maybe slight annoyance—on his face that he did yesterday at camp when I steadied his ex-wife as they approached. Reese hasna noticed.

"You'll never believe what she—Britt—just told me." Reese leans forward and her hair slips over her shoulders. She's curled it tonight in gentle waves that I'm tempted to touch. Maybe I should ask if she's still worried about smelling like fish and chips. I reluctantly remove my hand from her arm.

"Goan," I say instead.

"We saw that couple across the room." Reese nods her head to a now-empty table. "With the baby? They're gone now. Anyway, she got this wistful look on her face and told me she wants to have a baby with Adrian after they're married. It was like she was asking my permission or something. Can you believe that?"

My jaw drops open. I can barely get an invitation to my son's birthday party from Cat, yet Reese's ex-husband's fiancée is discussing weddings and babies with her?

But after being around her for a few days, I get it. I'd want to confide in her as well. I'd want her approval on my life decisions.

"Did you tell them to fuck off? Please, tell me you told them to fuck off."

"Hardly." She gets a faraway look in her eyes. "I mean, we're friends, right? And it's not like it bothers me, not really, but . . . Anyway, I nodded and said congratulations."

"Bloody hell, Reese. You need a bodyguard. Or a life coach. Or something. You are too nice."

"I'm not too nice. You should hear the awful things I think."

"Aye, do tell."

She gives me a withering look. "Pass."

I chuckle. "How about this? For the rest of tonight, I'll protect you from those wankers." I throw my arm around her shoulders, the vodka shot and two pints giving me the absolute balls to suggest that someone else needs a life coach besides me.

She looks up, nestled in the crook of my shoulder, and a tingle runs up my spine. She feels perfect right here. Next to me, her body against mine. I feel grounded, settled, and not like a total fuck up.

Suddenly, I have the best idea ever. It's pure dead brilliant. In fact, it'll go down in history as The Moment Oliver Was a Genius.

Up this close, my eyes drift over the light smattering of freckles on the bridge of her nose and cheeks, which I'd not noticed the night before at the pub. Her eyes are as gray as the Scottish sky. And her hair is as soft under my hand as I'd remembered from the hair-sniffing incident.

"Well. Thank you. I never thought I'd be the person who needs protection from an ex-husband and an old friend, but, alas, here we are."

I grunt and glance back over at them. "Are we calling her a friend?"

"Yeah." She shrugs.

"Well. Either way, they are incredibly interested in what is going on over here."

"And why a random dude has his arm around me?"

"Och, I'm not so random."

She starts to turn her head back toward the table, but I stop her with my finger, gently touching the soft skin under her chin. Her cheeks immediately turn a shade of pink rose. She trains her eyes on mine.

"I have a proposition for you."

I ken I shouldna do this. It canna end well. There's neigh a human in the whole of Scotland who would advise me that this is what could be considered a good idea. But I'm gonna do it. Because I'm a selfish basturt.

She blinks and bites her lip. "I'm listening."

9

REESE

I am in so much trouble.

I stare into Oliver's gorgeous eyes, memorizing the curve of his high cheekbones and the gentle slope of his nose, leading to smooth, luscious lips.

Pressed up against him in a, um, completely platonic way, my whole body is short-circuiting. And now he has a proposition for me? Is it for him to take me back to his house and ravage me in a hundred different ways until the light of dawn creeps in . . . at, like, four o'clock in the morning, because the sun rises at an ungodly hour here?

His finger lingers under my chin, sending sparks down my neck to my core.

No, definitely not that option. Surely not.

"Hear me out, alright, hen?"

I nod, basically unable to speak, or swallow. His eyes dart down to my throat.

"Let's pretend to be dating."

"What?"

That is so far from what I thought he was going to say that I let out a giggle. Actually, I didn't have a clue what his proposition would be, besides my singular-night-of-passion daydream.

"Ah ken, but listen." He keeps his eyes on me and nods subtly to Adrian and Britt's table.

"Listening."

"They canna stop staring at us. Between that and what you've told me, I think it's safe to say they are somewhat obsessed with you, Jersey."

My heart lurches. The man has a nickname for me.

"I can be your . . . bodyguard." He removes his finger. "Clearly, you've already agreed to be friends with them again. One big happy family, aye? But if we pretend to be together, I can be your excuse not to spend quite so much time with them while you're here. Say Britt asks you to meet up for a best friend coffee date. Oops, sorry Britt, you're busy with me instead. Yeh ken?"

I blink approximately a billion times, my heart thudding so loudly in my chest, I can hardly process his words.

"And if you do have to cut aboot with 'em, maybe I can be there, too. A bit of a buffer."

"Cut aboot?"

"Aye. Hang out, in American." The corner of his mouth twitches in amusement.

"So you'd be my . . . boyfriend?" My voice is scratchy, and I wish I had a drink to wet my throat. Another shot, maybe. "You're suggesting that we pretend you're my boyfriend?"

"Aye. It'll get them off your back." He shrugs. "You'll be on your own again when you're back home, but here . . . I can help."

I glance back at Adrian and Britt snuggled up together, all happy and cute. Britt smiles at me tentatively. I can't undo what I've already agreed to, and I won't. It's too important. I know they're committed to being relentlessly kind to me, likely hoping I'll forget the past. Britt has apologized again and again. And Adrian is, as always, calm and logical. They know being a good mom to Chelsea is the most important thing to me. But it's so hard.

I look back at Oliver, who is studying me. I mean . . . it could work. A squeak escapes my throat as I consider the one-sided agreement. Wait. What's in it for him? I narrow my eyes at him.

"But why would you do that? Are you even allowed to, um, fake date the parents of campers?"

He makes a face. Clearly, he has not thought through this terrible, amazing, ridiculous plan. "Ah dinna ken. There's no rule book. I never signed a paper saying I'd behave myself. I just showed up when David asked me to. I should probably check that he's even gonna pay me."

My eyes search his face. Fake date this man? It's a reckless, wild idea. But maybe it's a way to take back my reset month and turn it into an adventure. It's better than me snapping at Adrian and Britt —again—and destroying all the progress we've made so far.

The more I think about it, I realize it's a really mature, reasonable way to handle this situation. It makes perfect sense.

"Here's the deal." Oliver puts his hands on my shoulders and turns me fully toward him. "I need someone to come with me to a, uh, family event in a few weeks. It's an important one."

"Your parents will be there?" A ball of something that must be sympathy knocks around in my chest. He'd said he's here to make things right with his family. That resonates with me in a deep way.

He hesitates, then nods. "Aye. If I showed up with someone like you, it would make things so much easier."

"What does *someone like me* mean?" I twist my lips. That doesn't sound particularly positive.

"Nothing bad, I promise. Last time I saw my family, I was a complete rager. Hungover, rude, unhappy . . . That was eighteen months ago. They're giving me another chance." He drops his hands from my shoulders and runs them through his hair. A wavy chunk bounces back in front of his eyes. "*You* have your shite together."

I laugh. "Do I?"

"Aye, Reese. You do."

"I'm such a mess that I came here to reset my life."

"You're not a mess."

"But you think I'm boring, right? I'll bore them into getting along with you?"

"Nae. You're anything but boring. But being with you would give me credibility. Make me not look like such a dobber. A loser."

My lips twitch into a smile. "You are not a loser. You got hurt playing soccer. And now you're figuring your life out again." I have to clench my fists to not reach up and push the curl off his forehead and assure him he's worthy of the life he wants.

He grunts.

"Okay. I'll go with you to the party. And pretend to be your girlfriend, because somehow that'll help you with your family." This is happening? I can't wait to tell Stella and Maddie. They'll be so proud.

"Alright." A hint of an insecure smile crosses his face, and it makes him look incredibly vulnerable. Did he think I'd reject him? How has anyone rejected this man? My insides squeeze at the turn of his lips.

"But I don't need you to pretend to be my boyfriend in the meantime." I shake my head. "Honestly. That part is kind of ridiculous."

He can't possibly really want to do that. I'll help him out with his party, but fake dating otherwise? It's too much.

"Oh nae, I want to do it. No offense, but your ex-husband's face makes me crabbit." He pauses. "Really annoyed."

I crack a smile. "He's not so bad."

"No more defending him." Oliver's eyes lock with mine. "You wanna have your whole reset month here in Scotland? Let me help give you that. It might not be exactly what you imagined, but it'll be something."

"Okay." I rub my hands on my arms, entranced that he remembered why I came here to begin with. "Let's do this. You and I will pretend to date, so I don't get stuck hanging out with Adrian and Britt all month."

"Aye." He nods and grins.

"And I'll come with you to that family party."

"That would be brilliant."

I want to ask more about this party. Why is he so scared to go by himself? His parents must be terrifying, yet he wants to make up with them? What will I be facing when I get there? I search for a clue, but he's staring at me as if he's peering right into my soul. It doesn't matter why he needs me there. I'm going. And in return, he'll help me survive the messy web I've woven with Adrian and Britt and Chelsea. I can't change my mind about being friends, but I also can't handle spending the whole month hanging out with them. This is the perfect solution.

"Should we shake on it?" I try to act light and casual, like this is an agreement I make every day with a hot Scottish soccer player.

He holds out his hand.

I bite my lip and take it, acknowledging the swirling in my insides when our skin touches.

What on earth have I just agreed to?

10

OLIVER

Monday, 25 July
26 Days Before the Birthday Party
Banks of the River Tweed

I wander twenty minutes out of town along the River Tweed to get to a spot that feels right. I already took my long run during the camp lunch break, and arriving back at my house at four o'clock in the afternoon was going to leave me with too much alone time.

Too much time to think about Reese and this fake dating chaos I'm creating.

I lean back against a giant oak tree, my legs bent in front of me, a blank sketchpad perched on my knees and a pencil balanced in my hand. I'd bought them at the stationery store on the way here, unable to resist the fresh start of a clean notebook and a sharp pencil.

When I left Ireland, I told myself I'd focus only on coaching and Lucas. But I need this. To stay grounded. Focused. Because *this* feels like coming home, even more so than arriving back in Scotland. The weight of the pencil in my hands is like an anchor holding me in a safe harbor. The hypnotic sound of lead on paper soothes me as the live beauty in front of me starts to appear on paper.

I trace the lines of the old railway viaduct, the river running fast beneath it. There's a sign to continue walking to Neidpath Castle, so I add that in.

Most preschoolers draw stick people and kindergarteners draw rainbows and cats and dogs. I kept going, eventually in secret, after my parents found me *sketching* a football at age eight instead of *studying* one. They let me know, using condescending language no child should hear, how much they disapproved.

Not long after I made the top club team—the one my parents gave me the silent treatment for not making when I was ten—there was no longer time for anything besides football. I spent every free minute watching old games, analyzing the strategy behind each move, identifying mistakes and opportunities, and taking notes. The only drawings I did after that were like those in a playbook.

But this. This continues to feel good, even if it's once again a secret.

A couple in their fifties strolls past, hands linked. I flip the page of the sketchpad, leaving the landscape image unfinished, and sketch an entwined pair of hands from the mid-biceps down, adding details like tattoos on the one arm—not of football—and a more delicate wrist of the other one. It doesna look quite right.

I pause and run my hand roughly over my face. Next time I'm with Reese, I'll have to take a good look at her hands.

Or not, because this is a fake relationship. Who cares what her hands look like? I can google women's hands. That'd do just fine.

But I dinna pull out my phone.

A family walks by, two parents and a boy with a small white dog on a leash, the animal's joyful barking disturbing my thoughts. The three of them are much more animated than the older couple, and I can't resist capturing a quick and rough sketch of it.

I flip back to the landscape page and add more details. The

yellow wildflowers growing by the bank of the river, pops of bright color in the green carpet of grass. The dark shadow of the oak tree reaching out over my head and the walking path, darkening the green grass beneath me. I'll have to buy some colored pencils later. Then, impulsively, I draw a fresh outline of a boy standing on the edge of the water, back facing me, hoodie sweatshirt on his body, hair short. I'm completing the stone on the archways of the old bridge when the family with the dog passes back along the path.

My phone tells me I've been here almost two hours. I lost track of time, so I snap a picture of the sketch of the boy and send it to Patrick before I get ready to head back. He, better than anyone else, knows all the different sides of me: footballer, artist, absentee father . . .

He responds immediately:

PATRICK

Brilliant. Seen Lucas, have you?

I lift my shoulders, stress contracting my muscles.

ME

Nae. In a few weeks.

PATRICK

Good. That drawing would be a wicked tattoo.

Huh. Interesting idea. The boy needs work, but I'm in no rush. I want to get it perfect.

My fingers hover over the keypad. Do I tell him about Reese?

Instead, I search for local tattoo parlors. There's one fifteen minutes away in Interleithen. I wish I could ink it myself, but most people canna tattoo their own bodies, and besides, Ian hadna let me touch a needle. Not that I'd asked. It's one thing to draw with pencil on paper, an eraser always available, and quite another to permanently mark someone's body. You dinna just decide one day to try out being a tattoo artist.

When I showed up in Ireland a complete disaster, Patrick directed me to his couch and gave me jobs to do. He let me tend bar at his family's brewery. Introduced me to Ian. Patrick didna force me to talk about football. He hardly mentioned the game, aside from us watching matches together. He never brought up coaching. He never tried to make me do anything, except head back here once it was clear that's what I wanted to do. Needed to do.

It still seems impossible to reinvent myself, almost two years later. Just because Patrick did it doesna mean I can.

Especially with Lucas. How can I become a parent, just like that? If I havena been able to do it so far, what are the chances I can turn it around at this point, when the kid is heading into the teen years? I wish it came naturally to me, like it had with Cat. She'd committed her life to Lucas the second she found out she was pregnant. I, on the other hand, stayed away.

I was a wanker.

So I guess I deserved to be dumped the very second Kendall, my ex, realized my latest injury was career-ending. We'd been dating for almost a year, so it should've hurt more, but she never loved me, and I never loved her. We were each other's accessories. I'm sure she barely noticed my absence.

My stomach turns thinking about facing my parents, Cat, and Lucas. At some point, I need to tell Reese about Lucas and what she'll witness at the birthday party in just over three weeks. I'll have to give her some time to digest it all. So not the day before, but surely I dinna have to admit anything yet? How will I confess to her I hardly know my own kid? She's like Cat: sacrificing her life and structuring her existence around her child.

The exact opposite of me.

I'm not nearly good enough for Reese. Good thing we're just fake dating, because this way, I can *pretend* I'm good enough. I can be someone else. Someone she might like. Someone good enough for her to call her boyfriend.

Opening my email, I steel myself for my daily job search status check. Usually it's tumbleweeds in here.

I scan my inbox, glossing over promotional emails and other junk, then breathe in sharply. There's one promising subject line: *Assistant Coach Position at Crenshaw FC.* I click through, expecting a rejection, hoping for something more.

From: Karla Smith
Subject: Assistant Coach Position at Crenshaw FC

Hello Oliver,

We were intrigued by your application for our open coaching position! As we assess all the applicants, can you please answer the following screening questions?

- *How would you describe your coaching style?*
- *Why would you be a good fit at Crenshaw FC?*
- *Who do you consider the most inspirational football player of all time?*

We'll be in touch soon.

Kind regards,
Karla

A sense of relief washes over me. Even if coaching isn't my dream, it's encouraging to make positive progress in the pursuit. What else would I do, when football is all there is to me?

I follow the link after Karla's signature to the club website. The relief is replaced by dread. Ah, yes, I remember reviewing this last week. The tagline plastered on the website: *We're Scotland's Upstanding, Ethical, Family-Oriented Football Club.*

Shite. None of those things sound much like me. I'm a disaster and a drifter, neglecting my family for a decade. That's not the kind of club representative they're looking for, I bet. What would I say if they asked about my personal life? My son? My parents?

It'll be an uphill battle to prove myself.

I tuck my notebook under my arm and stand to stretch, slowly heading back to town along the deserted path, thinking about how to answer Karla's questions. I can easily make up my coaching style, with a whole three days of evidence to back me up, and the question about how I'd fit is a fluff one I can fake my way through.

The last one? Easy. Lionel Messi, the Argentine forward.

As a kid, I dreamed of being remembered in history like Messi will be. He's had an incredible career, even leading his national team in a World Cup win. But that's not to be for me. I think I've finally accepted my professional football career as it was—unremarkable relative to legends like Messi. Even so, I did get to live a dream most footballers never get to.

Still, it's time to move on, get out of my head, and get into the present. And the present is telling me I need to get my shite together. Reese's face pops into my head. I wish she could help on the job front, too, not just Lucas's party.

11

REESE

28 Days Before Departure
Reese's Flat

What. Have. I. Done?

Fake dating? What am I, in some annoying rom-com? Those are completely unbelievable. That never, ever happens in real life. Honestly. Fake dating is the most ridiculous trope. *Real* life is about responsibilities and being a good role model for your child, both of which I am definitely not projecting at the moment.

I freeze in the middle of a lap around my tiny flat, which basically involves a loop around the couch, a dodge into the small kitchen, a quick circle of the table, then spinning to do it again. It probably takes about eight seconds. Every other lap I dart down the short hallway to my bedroom and bathroom to spice it up.

"Oh, lord." I rub my forehead as I start it again, passing the bedroom for the twentieth time, focusing on my current nightmare. What happens if Chelsea discovers I'm fake dating her soccer coach? I'm not sure she'd even believe it, but if she did, what would I do? What would I say? I need some kind of plan, but most importantly, I can't let Chelsea find out. So I need to add another layer of complication to this situation: secrecy. Only that defeats the purpose of fake dating Oliver, doesn't it? Unless we can keep it from everyone except Adrian and Britt. The four of us would have to promise to keep it a secret.

What's the point in it all? Sure, I'll have some buffer from Adrian and Britt for the next few weeks. But in my real life, they are everywhere. There's no hiding in Sharontown, New Jersey, where our lives are entwined at school and at home. So why make an absolute disaster of things while we're in Scotland?

On the other hand, I can't ignore the tumultuous roll of my insides at the thought of hanging out with Britt here in Peebles. Or being dragged along on day trips as their third freaking wheel. She's already asked about meeting up this weekend with her and Adrian.

But, dammit, we have no real fake dating plan. Oliver randomly mentions a family party and throws out *let's pretend to be dating*, and we shake on it. Like, an actual handshake, as if we're business associates.

Now what?

Here's the thing. There are too many details that we haven't worked out. I'm a planner—a huge planner. That's how I run my work life. I build a website layer by layer. I design digital advertisements one element at a time until it all comes together into something impactful. That's why I'm successful. I don't wing it.

My phone buzzes in my pocket, making me screech to a halt in my kitchen. Maybe it's Oliver.

I groan and chide myself for being so embarrassingly eager. I know it's not Oliver as we don't even have each other's numbers, which is another element of absurdity about this situation. I don't know my boyfriend's phone number. Because it's all fake. He's fake. We're fake.

I lean on the counter and check my phone. A photo of Peanut Butter sitting on a keyboard pops on the screen, along with a text.

MARISA

Hey girl. PB's helping me get some work done.
He's doing great. Thought you might need a fix.

"Aw." I make a sad face and wish it was my keyboard he was disruptively sitting on.

ME

Remind him who he belongs to.

MARISA

He says he belongs to no one. How's
Scotland?

I turn and lean on the counter with two hands, dipping my head and closing my eyes. I consider telling her that Adrian and Britt showed up. She'd be shocked and horrified, but she tends to bite her tongue when it comes to them. The school world is a small one, and Marisa and I have never talked openly about how my marriage ended. But she must know. I'm sure *everyone* knows.

ME

Amazing, gorgeous, rainy, delightful . . .

MARISA

And not New Jersey?

ME

Bingo.

I slide my phone back into my pocket. I've got, what, less than a month in Scotland before I go home and force Peanut Butter to let me pet him? Surely I can make it that long.

It's just a few weeks.

Days, really, to pretend to date Oliver. We just have to not completely screw it up. How hard is it to fake date someone?

A memory pops up in my mind, one that'd been lingering there since Saturday night. When I was around thirteen years old, I overheard my parents fighting. They'd separated once for six months, but got back together for us kids, as Mom tells it now. That night, my younger sisters were asleep, but I sat at the top of the stairs leading to the second floor, hidden from my parents with my back against the wall, listening to their argument. My mom had angry-whispered something to Dad that I'll never forget: *Try harder to fake it. For the children. You need to make them believe you want to be here.* It had been devastating at the time. Dad didn't want to be there? Since then, I've realized that being a parent and an adult is a lot more complicated than simply not wanting to be somewhere.

But Mom's words still ring in my ears, and something lights up in my brain. Huh. It's not enough to tell Adrian and Britt that Oliver and I are dating—we need to go all in. It can't be subtle. We have to make them buy that it's real.

It can't look fake. Not even a little bit.

Shit. I need to talk to him about all this. I know this is more than he signed up for, but I need to know that he's all in.

I dash to the small bedroom and look in the mirror, running my hands through my hair and rifling through my makeup bag. Sure, it's fake dating. But it's early in our fake relationship, so it makes sense that I'd put some effort into how I look. I tell myself that as I apply black eyeliner, which contrasts with the gray of my irises, and sweep dark mascara on my lashes. I haven't had one video call all day, so I hadn't bothered with makeup yet. I pull a chunky sweater over my head—summers in Scotland are not what they are in New Jersey—and head out the door.

I stride down the High Street until the shops and restaurants thin out, toward the soccer fields and his house. I know exactly which one it is, the cute stone house with the yellow shutters and dreamy front porch, the one I noted was out of my price range.

My breath hitches when it appears on my right. It's bigger than I first noticed, wider in the back and deep. Far larger than my house in New Jersey.

"Is he keeping his whole family here?" Then I bite my tongue when I remember he's estranged from his parents. That's his whole problem. But the dude must have some money leftover from his pro days. I doubt the soccer camp is funding this place.

Standing at the end of the cobblestone path to Oliver's front door, I pull my hair over my shoulder and breathe deeply three times, trying to calm the pounding in my chest. I wish I could have texted him to warn him. What if he's with another woman? Or sleeping? Or just . . . busy?

I twitch my lips and glance longingly back the way I came. Probably could've shown up at camp tomorrow instead. That would've been easier. But I'm here, so might as well not be chickenshit.

I march up the walkway and onto the porch, noting the lovely cushioned swing and tempting rocking chairs not visible from the street. I knock, not letting myself hesitate again.

"Guess he's not home. I tried," I say to no one and spring down the steps after waiting for five seconds. When I'm barely two steps from the porch, the door creaks open behind me.

I freeze and wonder if maybe I can dive into the bushes. Maybe he won't notice me, kind of like when little kids play hide and seek and only cover their faces.

"Reese?"

He definitely noticed me.

I wipe my face of what I imagine is a look of pure panic and slowly turn. All the breath disappears from my body at the sight before me.

Oliver poses in his doorway, one arm leaning up against the doorframe, his hair wet, gray sweatpants low on his hips, no shirt covering his magnificent chest.

A weird sound squeaks out of my body, and my jaw hangs open. Tattoos adorn both biceps: the Scottish flag I'd seen on his right arm, but above it is a soccer ball draped over his shoulder. A full jersey with the #11 is drawn on his left bicep with another ball, and a giant bear on his chest, the claws reaching up his neck.

So that answers my earlier question. It *is* a full bear.

I can't rip my eyes from his abdomen. His muscles are tight and detailed, his shoulders wide, and all I want to do is to run my hands over the ridges and valleys of his body. My face burns and I cannot get a single thought straight in my mind.

Oliver clears his throat and crosses his arms on his chest, now leaning a shoulder against the doorframe, a knowing smile on his face. Has he practiced that move? Surely he has. It can't be natural.

A soft moan threatens to escape my chest. He switches the way his arms are crossed, and his forearm muscles twitch. Ahh. What is wrong with me?

"Alright?"

Guess he noticed me eye-fucking him.

"Hi. I, uh, am just, um, I needed to see you, I mean, talk to you, *talk* to you." Heaven help me. Please. "So I came here. I found the house with the yellow shutters. I mean, I knew where it was, but then you told me, and I came here."

Oh no. No, no, no. Like I've never seen a hot, shirtless man before? But I'm actually not sure I have seen a man quite like this. At least not close up. Adrian was pretty fit for a financial advisor, but even all that CrossFit didn't get him pro athlete ripped.

Reminds me, I fucking hate CrossFit.

"Well, you found me." Oliver raises his eyebrows and grins. "Wanna come in?" He gestures back into his house.

"Lord, no." I can only imagine what would happen if I went inside. Where he was just recently naked, in the shower, like, completely without clothing. My eyes drift down again. I shake my head violently.

Focus, Reese. Why am I here?

"Listen, I was thinking, like, a lot. A lot lot. Kind of freaking out, if I'm honest."

He steps out of his house onto the porch. "Why are you freaking out?"

"Why? Why are you *not* freaking out?" I take a deep breath. "Okay. Here's the thing. Fake dating, while a great idea, is also, like, against everything I believe in, or at least everything I'm trying to role model for my daughter."

"Are you backing out?" His brow furrows and he uncrosses his arms, slipping his hands into the pockets of his inappropriately snug sweatpants, edging the waistband a bit lower, revealing more of that v-shaped muscle that leads right to . . .

Sweet baby Jesus. How much does he work out? He doesn't even play soccer anymore. Does he just do a thousand crunches a day for fun?

I close my eyes to break the spell. "No. I mean, I don't think so."

"Good. You had me worried there for a minute, Jersey."

My belly tightens pleasantly, and I open my eyes to see him smiling broadly. I clear my throat too loudly and try again to explain. "But I don't think it can be really fake."

His eyes open wide. "Well, that's intriguing." He steps back as if to let me walk past him through the open door. "Sure yeh dinna want to come in?"

Yes, I'd very much like to see the inside of his house, but no, I'm definitely not going to do that.

"I'm good out here. I don't mean we'll actually date." The words rush out of me and end with a high-pitched giggle. "I mean, it needs to be convincing. It can't look like I'm faking it. Like I'm desperately trying not to hang out with Adrian and Britt."

My mind wanders off, and Oliver fades to the background. I'm not trying to avoid Adrian and Britt. Not really. I'm just trying to keep to my original plan. To get some space. Figure myself out. And not look pathetic doing it.

"Whatever you say, hen. So what are you suggesting?" His

voice brings me back, and there's an involuntary squeeze between my legs when he calls me hen.

I clear my throat. I have to get my mind out of the gutter.

"That we have to actually get to know each other. Not just in front of other people. They'll never buy it."

He tilts his head and quirks his lips. "Goan."

"Let's hang out. Talk a little more before we have to, like, perform in front of them. Then it won't look so fake."

"I can get on board with that."

"You can?"

He nods.

Well, that was easy. "Great. And we need a fake breakup plan. Your family party is in, um—"

"Twenty-six days," he says without hesitation.

"Right." I blink. He's been thinking about that. "And I leave Scotland in twenty-*eight* days. So the natural question if we are dating—er, fake dating—is what happens after that?"

"The answer is obvious," he answers immediately. "We live in two different places. Even though it's quite sad to have had such a delightful summer relationship end so suddenly, I dinna think anyone will be surprised."

"A *fake* relationship." I narrow my eyes at him. "But you're right. Long distance would never work." I shake my head aggressively. "My whole life is back in New Jersey. And your whole life is . . ."

"Here in Scotland?" He shrugs his gorgeous shoulders.

"Exactly. So we need to really go for it. Like, we just couldn't help ourselves, even though there's an exact expiration date for our relationship."

"Our fake relationship."

"You got it now." I let out a rush of air. "We need a real breakup."

He chuckles. "If you insist."

I smile back, but my insides are swirling. He must think I'm a loser, but that ship sailed before I showed up at his doorstep. He knows the truth. I've shown him my weird true colors already. I might as well throw myself into the fakeness of this relationship.

There's a lack of logic there that I can't quite identify. I work through it in my head. I really believe that most people are faking it in their relationships, at least once the initial infatuation wears off. Look at my parents, after all. But Oliver and I will just do that from the start, so we'll both be clear on where we stand.

It's perfectly logical.

"You're a unique person, Reese Hart."

"Thanks, I think?" A warmth blooms in my chest, radiating out. He takes a few steps forward and leans a shoulder against the porch pillar.

Fuuuuck he's hot with these poses. I bet he's in some kind of hot soccer player calendar. My cheeks bloom with warmth to match my chest.

"Are you one hundred percent sure you don't want to come in? We can start to, uh, get to know each other now. This place has a fancy espresso machine."

"First of all, what makes you think I'd like a fancy espresso machine? Second of all, no thank you. Not now. Not tonight. Not in your house."

"Would you not like a fancy espresso machine?" He gives me a lopsided grin.

"I would like one, but that's beside the point."

He grins and runs a hand through his damp hair. "How about later this week? The Old Forge?"

"Perfect."

"Thursday night, Reese?"

"See you there." I suppress a shudder at the way he says my name. Somehow, it's even sexier than when he says *Jersey* or *hen*. "Oh, and maybe I can have your number so I don't have to show up at your house again?"

Because this has been an absolute disaster. We need to do

everything in public and via text. That'll keep me safe from whatever is hiding behind that front door. Like his shower. And his bed.

"I quite like the fact that you've shown up here, but aye, I guess that makes sense." He reaches into his pocket and pulls out his phone. "What's your number?"

I give it to him.

"I'll text you so you have mine."

"Perfect. Great. It's a date. Fake date. Fake."

Fighting the urge to run, I turn and casually walk away, tripping on a traitorous cobblestone on my way to the sidewalk. When I'm out of sight from his house, I let out a loud groan.

"Oh no," I whisper to no one. "I'm such a dork." I think I'll be replaying my horrific awkwardness back there for the next ten years.

My phone buzzes.

OLIVER

> I now know an espresso machine impresses you, but do you always prefer coffee over tea?

ME

> What?

OLIVER

> You said we should get to know each other.
> Might as well start with the basics.

I bite my lip. He's right. And this should be much easier, talking to him without having to focus on not ravaging him with my eyeballs.

ME

> I prefer coffee, but I do enjoy a good cup of too-sweet tea.

OLIVER

Noted. Just tea for me.

ME

How do you deal with mornings without the extra caffeine? I don't understand people who don't drink coffee.

OLIVER

I'm sorry to disappoint you. I also enjoy an Irn-Bru on occasion.

ME

Irn-Bru? Sounds made up.

OLIVER

Ah, an Irn-Bru virgin, are you? I'll introduce you to it at some point. Your turn.

I shuffle down the sidewalk toward town, hardly paying attention to where I'm going, a goofy smile cemented on my face.

ME

Favorite color? Mine's blue, like a bright sky blue.

OLIVER

Mine's sky-colored too, but gray. A Scottish sky.

I look up to cross a street. I'm going to have to keep this under control. This casually beautiful man is not into me for real. And I'm not into him.

And even if I did like him, I can't go there. He's Chelsea's soccer coach. He's five years younger than me. He lives in Scotland.

He's out of my league.

I desperately need to go meditate for like two hours to get the image of him leaning shirtless against his doorframe in gray sweatpants out of my mind.

If only I knew how to meditate.

My phone buzzes again.

OLIVER

Did you have any pets growing up? We had a
dog named Mince Pie. He was the best.

ME

We had a cat. A tabby named Muffin.

Three dots dance on my screen.
I think I'm in trouble.

12

———

OLIVER

Thursday, 28 July
23 Days Before the Birthday Party
The Old Forge

In only one week, this woman has gotten to me. I lean against the cushioned bench and scroll through the text chain on my phone.

ME

What's your favorite animal? Mine's a bear. Like my tattoo.

REESE

Oh, you have a bear tattoo? I never noticed.

ME

You've seen me without my shirt on, remember?

REESE

I don't remember that at all. Doesn't stand out in my mind.

I guess mine's a cat. They don't bother
pretending to like you.

ME

Says the woman who has a fake boyfriend.

REESE

Hush. My turn, but first, a warning: I googled
get-to-know-you questions for couples.

ME

Bloody hell. Of course you did.

REESE

What's your greatest fear?

ME

Spiders.

REESE

Oh, come on. My fake one is heights, but my
real one is that I'm afraid of not setting the right
example for Chelsea.

ME

Why would you think you dinna set a good
example for Chelsea? I'm sure you do.

REESE

I'm kind of a mess. That's why I fled to
Scotland for the summer.

Fuck. She just opens her heart right up.

ME

How's that working out for you?

REESE

Answer the question, please.

I type a response, even though she'll be here any second.

ME

Being nothing but a footballer. I'll be taking no follow-up questions.

Those are just the last few texts from today. There are so many more. I'm careful with my responses, trying to keep it surface level, revealing as little as possible. I'll tell her about Lucas after we get to know each other better. Next week. There's a stabbing in my gut as I think about keeping my son a secret. I canna tell her the biggest thing driving me. Not yet. I like the way she looks at me. I dinna want it tinged with disappointment at finding out what a terrible father I've been. She thinks she's setting a bad example for Chelsea? Ha. I'm the *worst* example for Lucas.

Unfamiliar excitement runs through my veins as I eye the door. I feel like a kid with a first crush. From the second she walked away from my house on Monday night after stuttering her way through her get-to-know-you proposition, I've had a smile on my face. I loved the way her cheeks grew pink as her gaze drifted over my torso. And the way my body ignited under that gaze.

She definitely saw my bear tattoo.

It's just a game, and in a lot of ways, it feels exactly like that. I shouldna let myself be so attracted to her. But goddamn, it feels good to have her attention.

Reese appears in the doorway, the rush of air from the outside lifting her hair off her shoulders for a beat. She's a vision in jeans and another tight, thin v-neck sweater hugging the curves of her breasts. She's curled her long hair, and it settles on both shoulders like waves of a dark ocean crashing down as the door closes behind her. And when she meets my eyes, her cheeks spring pink circles, just like on Monday.

I grin as she approaches, not even attempting to play it cool.

"Hey." Reese slips into the chair across from me.

"Hallo."

The corners of her mouth turn up at the edges and her eyes crinkle adorably.

"This for me?" She reaches for her pint.

I nod. "Now that yeh ken how bad the pub red wine is, I thought you'd want to stick with beer."

"Perfect, thanks."

"Slainte mhath." I raise my glass to clink hers. "Careful now."

She purses her lips at me. "I don't normally spill drinks all over myself."

"Aye, of course not."

Our gazes lock and we take each other in. We're on a whole new level from the last time we saw each other. For instance, I now know the last time she cried was the night Adrian and Britt arrived. I told her I dinna remember mine, but I do. It was in Ireland, after I met Patrick's nieces and realized I was fucking everything up by hiding from Lucas and the world.

"So," she says after drinking deeply. "We have a lot to cover." She moves her pint in slow circles.

I burst out laughing.

"What? Don't we?" Her hands settle and the spot between her eyes crinkles.

"We do. Aye."

She's nervous. About being here with me? After the hundred texts from this week? But I get it. I've been thinking about seeing her again. Every day at practice, I scanned the bleachers, hoping she'd come to watch Chelsea, but she never did.

"First of all . . ." She drinks again. "Breakup date."

"You're dumping me already?"

She tilts her head and gives me a withering glare.

"Take this seriously, please."

"I am. I promise. Fake breakup date."

A pained look settles on her face.

"Alright?" I ask.

"I'm sorry. I've never done anything like this before. I mean, this is ridiculous, isn't it? You and I pretending to date so I don't have to spend the next three weeks being miserable?"

Her words throw me. "Ah dinna ken." I shrug. "People fake relationships all the time. They just dinna ken it."

"Exactly!"

"Exactly what?"

"That's what I think. Everyone's faking it, even if they don't think they are."

I narrow my eyes, trying to follow her train of thought. "Wait. You think *all* relationships are fake?"

She nods.

"That's savage." I've not been in what anyone would call a healthy relationship, but I at least believe they exist. For some people. Not for me. "What about your parents?"

"Pretending. For us kids."

My eyes widen. My parents don't have an inspiring marriage, but they're perfect for each other in a cold, distant way.

"Sisters?"

"Stella's dating some English guy, but I don't buy it. And Maddie's always been a mess with men."

"Aunts and uncles?"

"Not much extended family. My great-aunt Evelyn never married and seems super happy despite it."

"Wow."

"And us." She waves her hand back and forth between us, overly careful not to hit the pint glasses. "If we can convince everyone this is real, then that will solidify that even the realest-looking relationship could be fake."

"Och. You're dark, yeh ken?"

Her lips curl into a smirk.

"Right. Enough on that." She shrugs and grabs her silver letter C necklace, jingling it against the thin chain. "Three weeks and three days from now—it's a Sunday—that'll be our fake breakup date. It's the day after your family party, and the day before we leave to go back to the US. It doesn't have to be dramatic or anything, but we need to be able to explain it."

"Well, that'll be easy," I murmur. "Like you said on Monday, you're going back to New Jersey, where you have a job and a life. And I'll be here, doing whatever it is I'll be doing."

"Exactly. Although maybe you need to sort that out, huh?" She raises her eyebrows.

"Maybe. But that's another topic altogether."

"Fine, we'll save that for later. So we break up because of the distance. People should buy that. It's not like long-distance relationships ever work."

"Nae."

She nods her head aggressively. "Everyone will understand it was fated to end right from the start. But what about your family? Will they buy it? Will that even help you if you bring me to the party, I meet everyone, then disappear forever?"

"Hmm." It's definitely a plot hole. They'll all love Reese, almost definitely more than they love me. How could they not? And then they'll hear how I fucked it up again. Honestly, it would track. "Well, I could tell them we're gonna try long distance, and then eventually I'll say we broke it off."

Her face falls. "That would be worse, wouldn't it? Trying to do long distance and then failing? How depressing to think it might work, and then it doesn't."

I lean over and cover my hand with hers, loving the sensation of our fingers touching. "Hey, Jersey, no need to be sad. It's fake, right?"

She laughs. "Right. Duh. So that's set." She eyes our hands but doesna move to separate them.

"Did you have any other rules in mind?"

"Yeah." Reese crinkles her nose and drinks from her pint. "I think . . . I think we need to keep it a secret."

I furrow my brow and lean closer to her, pointedly looking around for eavesdroppers. "How's that gonna work?" I whisper.

She glares at me, and I bite back a grin.

"I've been freaking out about what Chelsea will think. I'm not sure which is worse—that I'm dating one of her soccer coaches, or that I'm *fake* dating one of her soccer coaches. Especially you."

"What does that mean?"

"She worships you."

I frown. "She doesna act like she worships me. She's far less giggly than the others, actually."

"Really?"

"Aye."

"Still. I want to be a good role model for her. And if she finds out, she'll think that all I care about is myself. Or what her father thinks of me. Or avoiding Britt."

"You should care about yourself."

She pulls her hand away from mine and sits up straight as a board, ignoring my last comment. "So first, I want to keep this whole thing a secret from Chelsea. Second, I don't want anyone to figure out we're faking this, so even if she finds out, she'll think it's real."

"That's quite complicated." This is why I'm not in relationships with women. Too many layers to understand. But seeing her clutch her pint and bite her lip fills my chest with . . . something. Ah dinna ken what. But I dinna want to run away. Not from this woman who is prioritizing how her daughter feels above all else, but also putting in understandable defenses around her own heart.

"I know. Want to bail?"

"No, ah dinna wanna bail, Jersey." For once in my life. "We'll be *together-together* in front of Adrian and Britt only. Otherwise, we're just friends."

She lets out a big breath. "Thank you."

"But you'll have to figure out how to keep it from Chelsea. Can you get Adrian and Britt to keep it a secret? So Chelsea doesna find out?"

She groans. "That's a problem for another day."

"Sounds like one." I pause and run my hand over my cheek, wondering how she'll take my next question. "Are we touching?"

"What?" Her eyes grow wide and flit down to the table, where our hands were just linked.

"We need to further define our terms and conditions. When we're with Adrian and Britt, pretending to be dating, are we touching each other?"

She literally gasps, then laughs, then realizes I'm not laughing. I blink and keep my face deadpan serious.

"Right. I suppose we are," she says slowly. "Like, we'll do things that people in relationships do in public. That's it."

"People do lots of things in public."

"You know what I mean."

I nod. Ah definitely dinna ken what she means, but it feels like this is as far as she wants the conversation to go right now. Are we allowed to hug? Kiss? Or would that be crossing a line? A very tempting line.

"How'd we get together? A drunken night at The Old Forge?" I suggest helpfully.

"Ohhh. You're right, we need to have that story straight. Okay. Let's think. The first time they saw us together was last Thursday at camp. Then we ran into each other on Friday night . . ."

"'Twas a good night."

"It was." She's blushing. I might be, as well.

"That had to be the night. We ran into each other. Had drinks. And, um . . ."

"Had a shag?"

Reese throws her head back and cracks up, and I'm distracted by the creamy skin of her neck and the way she finds me funny. "I mean, do they need that kind of detail? But yeah, sure, that's what happened."

"Look at you, coming to Scotland for the summer and having yerself a fling."

"Hmm." She smiles at me. "Maybe this will be fun."

"Why not, right? We can have a few laughs while also telling your ex to fuck off." I swig from my pint.

"We are not doing that." She sighs and looks lost in the few seconds of silence that descend on us.

"Yeh dinna have to let them into your life, yeh ken?"

"I do, though," she says. "I have to co-parent with Adrian. I know you don't get that part of it, but sometimes you have to sacrifice yourself for your kids. That's what I'm doing by keeping a good relationship with them."

My stomach squeezes. She's right. I dinna understand. Just because I fathered Lucas doesna mean I'm a real parent. I probably willna ever be. Right now, I canna even admit he exists.

"Besides, I gave them my blessing. And I told Britt we could try being friends again. I used to love her like a sister."

"Whatever you say."

"What about your parents?" she asks, ignoring my comment. "I know you said you're not close to them? But you want to be, right?"

I scoff, then rein in my attitude. She thinks I want to rebuild my relationship with my parents, so I should keep the hostility to a minimum. "My parents are perfect for each other. They are . . . distant. Da always wanted to be a professional footballer. He was good, but not pro good. So he pushed me hard, when he thought I could make it. But it was only about football, not about me." I clench my jaw. "Even when I was pro, he criticized every game. Every touch. I stopped talking to him, didna answer his texts. And when I got hurt, he was so angry. And when I got hurt *again* and lost my spot on the team? It was like I'd personally betrayed him."

"That's so awful." She scrunches her cheeks.

"Havena talked to them much in the past, I dunno, five or seven years. Only once a year or so." They've all been one big happy family without me in Stirling. Ma, Da, Cat, Lucas, Grant. None of them need me, nor do they want me.

"I'm surprised you even came back here, just to make things

right with your parents. Do you have any other family?" Reese looks thoughtful. Trying to figure out what I've left out of the story. She's perceptive as well as bonnie.

"Ma grew up in Fife, but everyone's in Stirling now." I shake my head, but dinna answer the last question. I canna truly answer it without lying, so that'll have to do. "Back in Ireland, I'd gone to a family event with Patrick, the friend I stayed with. His sister was there with her husband and their daughters." I leave out that the oldest girl was almost the same age as Lucas. "And I realized I needed to sort through my past before moving forward in life. So that's what I'm here to do."

I throw my hands in the air. Fuck. That was a lot more truth than I'd planned on sharing. But at the same time, not nearly enough.

Reese stares at me for a second, searching my face. I pray she doesna push me for more information. I'm not sure how I'd explain this further without confessing about Lucas. Instead, she stands and moves around the table, perching on the bench next to me, one leg bent so she can face me. Her presence makes my heart beat faster and louder. She grabs my hand with both of hers.

"What are you doing?" I ask, and it comes out in a whisper. Maybe I could tell her about Lucas now. Maybe this is the right moment.

"Practicing, I guess." Her voice is equally wispy, and she searches deep into my eyes. "But also, I want you to know that I think you're brave to find that out about yourself. And to come back here to deal with your past and make up with your parents."

Our hands tingle together and she moves hers slowly around mine, the friction between our skin like sparks. My eyes drift down to her lips, and I consider leaning down and kissing her. For practice. But something tells me that would be too much. Too much for this moment, and maybe too much for our fake dating, no matter how tempting.

Och, fuck. I can't ruin this moment with my inconvenient truth.

"Well, you're a natural at this," I say, ignoring her comment on my personal journey. I throw my free arm around her shoulders and pull her close to me. Her legs straighten out and our thighs touch. She hesitates for a second before leaning her head against my shoulder.

"Think we look like a real couple?" She slides her closest hand onto my thigh. "What if I do this? Too awkward?"

Fuck me.

"Aye." I swallow hard and ignore the stirring in my chest to her words and the response in my groin to her touch. "That works."

"Are you free Saturday?" she asks, her head still against my shoulder.

"Yes. Want to hang out again?" I need more of this woman.

"Adrian and Britt want me to go to Melrose Abbey with them. Have you been? Chelsea has a day trip somewhere else with the campers that day." She moves her head and looks up at me, her lips mere centimeters from mine.

My stomach squeezes, and I fight the urge to pull her onto my lap. Why does this feel so natural?

"I went a long time ago. But I'll go with you."

"Excellent. It'll be our coming-out event."

"It's a date." I pick up a chunk of her hair on her shoulder, and gently run my fingers through it. Her eyes flutter and her pupils enlarge.

"One more rule, Oliver Vass."

"What's that?" I respond, hoping she brings up kissing or lap-sitting or something that'll get me even closer to her.

"No trying to get me to fall in love with you."

I grunt and chuckle, uncomfortable with how much I'd like that. "I wouldna think of it."

"Good. Because you can be quite charming, you know."

Och, Reese Hart, but so can you.

13

REESE

Saturday, July 30
23 Days Before Departure
Melrose Abbey

Britt's eyes are burning with curiosity when Oliver and I join them at the back of the short line to get into Melrose Abbey.

"Morning," Oliver says to the pair.

"Hi!" Britt chirps. "Did you two . . . come together?" She looks at me, then Oliver, then Adrian, begging us with her eyes to answer this question and all the other unasked ones.

"Yup, sure did!" I infuse over-the-top cheerfulness into my voice.

"Well, thanks for joining us, Coach." Adrian nods at Oliver and avoids eye contact with me.

"I'm so glad we're getting to hang out together. Isn't it gorgeous here?" Britt waves her hand in the air. She takes a step toward me, and I have a vision of her linking her arm in mine and whispering personal questions in my ear.

I glue my elbows to my sides and murmur in agreement, plastering a smile on my face.

We pay for tickets and wander into the magnificent archways and stones of what is supposedly the most famous set of abbey ruins in the country. What Britt said is true: the abbey is stunning. And today, the bright blue skies, warm air, and rare sun streaming in through the ancient empty windows create a dreamy atmosphere.

Adrian and Britt walk ahead and I slow my pace so Oliver and I are a solid ten feet behind them.

"I'm so glad you're here," I whisper and slip my hand around his arm, much preferring the solid presence of him versus Britt.

"My pleasure. And Britt canna be bothered about your friend-ship at the moment. She wants to know *why* I'm here." He looks down at me and grins. Just then, Adrian glances back over his shoulder and the movement draws my gaze. He quickly turns to face forward again.

I pull myself closer to Oliver. It had never occurred to me that the way to shield myself from Adrian and Britt might be with another human being. After the meltdown I had with Adrian ages ago, I've been so busy trying to act like a mature, accommodating, logical human being. Keeping the peace. Rebuilding relationships. Maybe all I had to do was get a boyfriend.

Britt slows her walk and in two seconds, we're right behind them.

I fumble for my phone and pull up Google, where I'd already done a search for Melrose Abbey. "1136 AD." I continue scrolling. "That's when this place was built."

"Mmm-hmm. Fascinating." Oliver nods, a big, exaggerated up and down movement of his chin. I press my lips together to hold back a laugh.

"Can you imagine?" Britt stops and spins around to face us. She's wearing a bright-yellow sundress and strappy flat sandals, as if we're out for a day on the Jersey Shore boardwalk. The color emphasizes her perfect olive skin tone. I'd judge her for going tanning, but I know it's the natural color of her skin. The woman wears SPF 50 sunscreen every day, no matter the season. She's infuriatingly perfect.

"There are no buildings this old in America," she says matter-of-factly. Britt's eyes land on our linked arms, and Adrian finally turns around. My hand tightens on Oliver's arm under their judgment. So I go back to my phone.

"Google tells me the oldest buildings in America are from the 1600s." I scroll through the search results.

"Why dinna you have a wee search for the oldest building in Scotland, Jersey?"

I chuckle and tap the question in. "Oh, wow! That's really old."

"Goan then. Tell us."

"Apparently there's an old stone house from, uh, 3500 BC in Papa Westray, which is one of the Orkney Islands." I look up at Oliver and shake my head. "All of that feels made up."

"The world isn't centered around America, yeh ken." He raises his eyebrows.

"I never said it was!" I poke him.

"Ouch!"

"Oh come on, that didn't hurt. And I'm not that kind of American. I'm well-rounded. My sister lives in London, remember?"

Oliver laughs and my eyes flit down to the smooth skin of his neck, covered with the bear claw tattoo.

Adrian clears his throat. "Let's keep walking, shall we?" Adrian grabs Britt's hand and gently pulls her along. It takes her a second to drag her wide eyes away from us.

I completely forgot we weren't alone. We were . . . flirting in front of Adrian and Britt. I stifle a snort of laughter.

I go back to scrolling, keeping my hand tucked in Oliver's elbow. "Honestly, this is remarkable. Have you been to the Orkney Islands? They are in the middle of nowhere north of the Scottish mainland."

"Nae, never been. The Shetland Islands are up there, even further out in the ocean. It's quite remote, but people do live there. I knew a footballer once who grew up there."

"I better close this browser before I fall down a research hole filled with remote Scottish islands." I slip my phone back in my pocket.

"We should get a picture," Britt says to Adrian, nodding toward a wall with incredibly intricate masonry.

"Oh, let's go this way," I mumble and pull Oliver down another pathway, having no desire to take cute travel photos of Adrian and Britt so she can post them online and get a billion likes. I'd rather walk straight into the cold Scottish sea.

Oliver goes along with me, glancing down expectantly. Once we're out of hearing distance, I slow and look up at him. "You were right. This is perfect."

I look over my shoulder to confirm Britt's watching us and whispering into Adrian's ear. For once, *I* have the juicy thing going on. I slide my hand down Oliver's arm, going slowly to appreciate the hard curves and valleys of his muscles, and grab his hand.

"Did you call me perfect? Nae the first time I've heard that."

I roll my eyes and scoff, but get distracted when he entwines our hands, linking one finger at a time. A delightful shiver runs up my arm. It's only because I haven't held hands with a man in literally years. That's all. My body is that desperate for affection, even fake affection. Kinda pathetic, but I don't really care right now.

"I didn't call you perfect," I say, my voice breathless.

"Didna you?" He stops and turns to me, grabbing my other hand, as if we're about to sway together to a slow song. "We can give them a few seconds to take this in." He glances down at our hands and I follow suit. They're kind of beautiful, linked together. His fingers long and thick, mine long and skinny, no rings on either of our hands. His heartbeat tattoo prominent on the inside of his wrist, my heart-shaped formation of freckles on my right hand. He'd told me via our text conversation that that tattoo's meant to remind him of what's worth living for. Originally, that was soccer.

Now, he's not sure.

I'm unable to stop staring at the ink. I like that one because it can change meaning over time. What would be important to me now and also when I'm fifty? Eighty? Only Chelsea. But Oliver's heartbeat tattoo is just a reminder to keep life in perspective. To know what's important and let the rest go.

There's some kind of moral there relevant to my current situation, but I can't quite grasp it. Perhaps when I figure it out, I'll get my first tattoo. Oliver squeezes my hand to bring me back to earth.

"Let's go that way." He nods outside the walls. "We wanna give them something to think about, but just a wee bit at a time."

"You are disturbingly good at this," I say. "Have you fake dated before?" I let him lead me outside the crumbling walls and away from prying eyes.

"Nae." He squeezes my hand, not dropping it, even though I'm sure they can't see us anymore.

"Me neither, if you can believe it." He snorts in response. "Hey, I could've, you don't know."

"Aye. It's possible."

I follow him through an archway and down a short stone path.

"I remember coming here on a school field trip as a kid. There are sculptures somewhere. Ah. Here we go. A bagpipe-playing pig." He pauses and gestures to the funniest little statue. "Oh, and over there, hobgoblins."

"I love it." I drop his hand for a second and reach for my phone. "I'm going to take a picture so I can send it to Chelsea." I snap one and send it off. She adds a heart to the photo right away. I'm thankful there are no follow-up questions, like who I'm with.

"Want me to take one of the two of you?" Britt's voice rings out from behind us.

I startle, and Oliver chuckles.

"She's like a ninja," I whisper.

"I know you're selfie-challenged." Britt smiles brightly at me, a genuine smile on her face.

It's true. She's remarkably good at selfies, and I'm remarkably bad at them, even though I'm taller and my arms are longer. She knows just the angle to take the most flattering photo of herself and others. We have about a billion selfies taken together from our years of friendship, and I can instantly tell which ones I took and which ones she did.

Adrian takes me and Oliver in, brow slightly furrowed, looking confused and uncomfortable. Like he's not sure how to feel. I can see that. He's spent the past two years feeling guilty for what happened between us and with Britt, and now he's not quite sure what to make of all of it.

His discomfort feels good.

I open my mouth to say no to the picture offer—my fake boyfriend is also good at selfies—when Oliver jumps in.

"Actually, a picture sounds lovely." Oliver hands her his phone and turns to me without letting go of my other hand, cute crinkles at the corner of his bright eyes as he grins at me. "Why not?"

My breath hitches.

"Mmm-hmm. Sure." I nod and turn to ease myself into the nook of his shoulder, so glad we practiced this at the pub so I'm not feeling the sparks between us for the first time here, in front of Adrian and Britt. Like the other night, I fit perfectly in the curve of his shoulder. I slide my arm around his waist.

Britt takes a few photos before stepping forward to hand Oliver his phone.

"I know you used to be a professional soccer player." She stays close to him. "I'm always trying to get Jackson to play sports. He's all about video games and Boy Scouts, but he agreed to play recreational soccer in the fall. I don't know how it's going to go, considering he hasn't played since he was in second grade. Any tips?"

What's her game here? Jackson is not a sporty kid, which is no big deal. He's involved with a ton of other clubs and activities. Why push him into soccer?

Oliver obliges, talking to her about training and the basics to become a strong player. All things easily accessible on the internet. Or from Chelsea.

Adrian steps next to me. "Hey, Reese," he says.

Oh no. Directly talking to me?

"Hello," I manage to mutter, darting my eyes to Oliver, who doesn't seem to notice my predicament. "Since when does Jackson play soccer?"

Adrian shrugs. "I'm not sure he's actually signed up for the fall. I think Britt's working on it."

Britt's gotten Oliver to step away with her. It's a trap.

"How's your time here going?" Adrian's eyes are intently focused on mine, searching for a clue.

"Wonderful, thanks for asking." I give him a bright, fake smile. "I've been working during the day, taking walks, exploring Peebles, seeing Chelsea when I can . . ." I glance at Oliver, chickening out from mentioning him. But Adrian follows my gaze and looks back at me with curious eyes.

"Glad you're enjoying yourself. I know Britt really wants to hang out with you when you have time."

"Yeah, sure, of course."

"Thanks for not freaking out about us showing up. I can't believe we both changed our plans and didn't tell each other about it."

"Mmm, that was quite the surprise."

"Once Britt found out Jackson would be gone for most of the month, I really wanted to come see Chelsea. A month seemed like a long time to be away."

Adrian's a far better father now than he was when we were married. It's like he realized he'd have to make an actual effort to have a relationship with his daughter. He and Britt really have created a warm, loving home for Chelsea and Jackson. I'm grateful for that.

My stomach twists.

But I also resent it, especially when they're all together at Britt's house, and I'm alone at mine. Being divorced is complicated.

I sigh. "I'd hate to not see Chelsea for a month. It'll be hard for Britt to be away from Jackson for that long."

He nods. "Yeah, she's handling it well so far. They FaceTime every night. He's texting with Chelsea a lot, too."

Why are we having this conversation? Am I supposed to go get friendly coffees with Adrian now, as well as Britt? I shift my weight from one foot to the other. "Well, we better—"

"And I wanted to see if you'd thought about coming to the wedding," Adrian interrupts. "Did you get the save-the-date? Invitations won't go out for a while, but we wanted to get it on people's calendars."

The wedding.

"Yup. I got it."

Oh yeah, I got the save-the-date invitation. In a reaction much like the time I screamed at Adrian after he told me about him and Britt, I set it aflame on my stovetop. Literally. I found the fire wand that I use to light candles and watched gleefully as the thick cardstock turned to ashes. The fire alarm went off. It felt so good. I mean, I put it on my calendar first, of course. I'm not a monster.

I can't believe they invited me. How dare he? How dare *she*?

I know how they rationalized it. We're all friends now. One big happy family. Wouldn't it be weird if you didn't invite one of your friends to your wedding? The mother of your child? Someone who used to be your best friend?

"I haven't decided," I admitted. It's the honest truth. Should I go? It feels like something an unhinged human being would do. I tilt my head. "Would you go to *my* wedding?" My words have a bite to them, and he looks surprised. I smooth over my expression. "Sorry, didn't mean that to come out like that. But would you?"

He sighs, like I'm so exhausting to deal with. "Chelsea would love it if you came. So would Britt."

Does Chelsea really need me at her dad's wedding? She's going to be a high school junior. I'm not sure she'll even notice I'm there. And Britt needing me feels narcissistic. Sure, if she was marrying anyone but Adrian, I'd go in a heartbeat. I'd probably be the maid of honor. That muddy river of emotions rises inside me. These are two people I loved—love?—marrying each other. Two people who were really important to me. Why *wouldn't* I go to their wedding and be with my daughter?

Because it still feels like they both betrayed me. Even though they didn't.

I swallow, then try to breathe, then open my mouth to say something back. Nothing comes out.

"Think about it. For Chelsea?"

"Fine," I say.

"Good." Adrian's face clouds over. "Also, what's going on—"

"May I have Reese back?" Oliver appears in front of us just in time, like a gorgeous knight in shining armor. I've never been so freaking happy to see someone's face. Britt lingers behind him.

Adrian looks Oliver up and down, his eyes resting on the tattoos adorning his exposed arms, the bear claws reaching up out of the neck of his t-shirt.

The bear claws, which *are* attached to a bear body. I know that, as I got to witness his chest in all its glory, including the ridges of his abs and the v-shaped muscles leading into his gray sweatpants. Desire surprises me by twitching in my core.

With Adrian still staring at him, Oliver looks at me and winks.

"Yes, yes you may," I say, and Oliver grabs my hand and pulls me back toward the abbey, leaving Adrian with a slightly gaping mouth. "You saved me, but I could have used you, like, five minutes earlier."

"We werena even apart for five minutes."

"Exactly. He brought up their wedding. Then, just when you walked up, he was going to ask about us."

Oliver grins at me, leading me around a curve and away from the happy couple. "I'll be faster next time. Let me make it up to you. I wanted to show you this nook. We might find it suitable."

"What nook? Suitable for what?"

But then, I find out.

Oliver walks me backward against the tall, towering side of the abbey, into a shallow space that fits me perfectly. The stone is hard and cold against my back, but a flush creeps over my entire body as Oliver leans one hand above my head against the rocky surface, his arm bulging with muscles.

"They'll trail us," Oliver says, his voice low and raspy, his pupils growing large in the shadows of the ruins, something intense and overwhelming pulsing from his body.

"Mmmm." I can't get a word out as my heart is beating louder than a bass drum. His mouth is inches from mine, and right now, I couldn't give a shit about Adrian and Britt.

He glances down at my lips.

"Reese. We didna specify exactly what was in the terms and conditions of this fake relationship. I tried to bring it up, but you didna answer me." His voice is low as he slides his other hand slowly behind my neck and into my hair, causing tingles to travel from that spot to every nerve ending in my body. I'm trapped between him and the stone walls. Deliciously trapped.

"Just . . . normal stuff," I manage to say. "Remember?"

His hot breath is directed right at my mouth. I can't seem to catch mine. He runs his thumb along my jaw and then gently touches my bottom lip. I'm pulsing everywhere. The world fades around us, and I want him to kiss me. Touch me.

Please, Oliver, something, anything.

Worried I'll melt into a puddle at his feet, I reach out for his sides, slipping my hands over his shirt and around his midsection, grounding myself, but also inadvertently pulling his hips closer to mine.

He responds by stepping forward until our bodies are touching lightly. Every part of him is hard, and the desire for him to press against me is overwhelming. I imagine what it'd be like to have him in this position if we were alone. My body responds again, and there's an intense ache between my legs I haven't felt for a long time.

"Like kissing?"

"Yes, please."

"Thank fuck."

I tilt my face up even closer to his and he bridges the gap between us, touching his mouth to mine.

His lips are soft and gentle and as soon as they make contact, I want more. Sparks shoot from our mouths to my chest, right to my core, and I press my body forward so it's tighter against his.

He lets out a groan and pulls his head back.

"Bloody hell," he murmurs, eyes darting from my eyes to my lips.

I lean forward to kiss him again, desperate to feel his tongue in my mouth, when movement catches my eye, and the back of Britt disappears around a corner.

"Oh, that was Britt," I gasp, and the temperature between our bodies decreases a few degrees. Only a few, though. *Holy shit.*

"Perfect." Oliver steps back, the connection between our bodies severed. He's got a mischievous glint in his eyes.

That was just a performance for Adrian and Britt? Did I imagine that his desire was as strong as mine? There was something there, not just a show kiss.

I breathe deeply and smooth my hair to make sure I don't look like I was just ravaged in the middle of some old ruins. Even though I was.

"They definitely saw us. That was . . . quick thinking?"

He laughs and holds out his hand. "Just setting the story in motion. Maybe he'll stop asking you about the wedding if he's fixated on us."

I take his hand. "Again, you're pretty good at this."

He blinks at me, a soft expression I can't quite read crossing his face.

"I'm a good actor. I guess it's a new skill I'm developing. For you. For this. Maybe I'll put Fake Boyfriend on my CV." He waves his other hand around and I follow him back to the main part of the abbey. "Wanna check out the museum?"

I nod, trying not to let his words feel like a stab to my heart. Of course, he's just acting. That's what this whole thing is. It doesn't matter that his body responded to mine, and it doesn't matter that besides his kiss filling me with insta-lust, there was a warmth glowing in my chest. That means nothing.

This is fake. He knows it, and I know it.

What have I got myself into?

14

———

OLIVER

Oh, bloody hell. I think I took that too far. I know I did.

I'm a good actor. Is that what I said to her? Made it sound like I was only doing it for show, so Adrian and Britt would see.

I'm such a wanker. I didna miss the look that crossed her face. Disappointment? Annoyance? Or something else entirely?

Her hand is nestled in mine like it belongs exactly there, and I lead her into the museum, not planning on paying attention to the displays.

That kiss. My groin still aches at the thought of it. And it was only a passing kiss on the lips. I didna get to feel her tongue touching mine or slip my hands around her waist and under her shirt.

I try to focus on the old book in front of us. Reese is quiet. What's she thinking? I definitely surprised her. Shocked her, even, but she seemed to get into it without hesitation. I guess she's an even better actor than I am.

It wasna just my body that responded. Seeing her against that stone wall, looking up at me with her wide eyes . . . I could have stood like that all day staring down at her. Fuck Adrian and Britt. I didna even know that they could see us, no matter what I claimed.

But if she's uncomfortable with what happened, I need to know. So I can apologize and not do it again.

Still . . . I'd really like to do it again.

Reese pulls me toward the next display.

"Hey." I tug on her hand until she turns to me, her cheeks immediately flushing.

"Are they watching us?" Reese's eyes dart over my shoulder.

"No, Jersey, they're not in here." We linger in front of a strange assortment of extremely old cooking pots, not nearly as impressive as the grave of the heart of Scottish hero Robert the Bruce, just outside. "I think I, uh, surprised you back there."

"The kiss?" she practically whispers, eyes laser-focused on me, the word floating in the air between us like a flower petal drifting from a magnolia tree.

"The kiss."

She pulls her hand from mine and tugs on her long waves, pulling half her hair over each shoulder. The room darkens as clouds cover the sun and the light streaming in from the windows dims.

"A little surprised." She sucks in her bottom lip, distracting me. I canna read her expression.

"I'm sorry. I hope I didna cross a line." I know I did and I'm not sure I'll be able to get that kiss out of my mind, regardless of what she thinks of it.

Then a shy grin settles on her mouth, the very mouth my lips were connected to mere minutes ago.

"I'm glad you kissed me."

And with that, the sun fights its way back, and the room brightens.

"Good. Me too." I throw an arm around her shoulder. "And it'll give them something to talk about."

She grabs the hand hanging off her shoulder.

We wander around, clinging to each other and laughing at every little thing we see. Eventually, inevitably, we stumble back outside and into Adrian and Britt again.

Britt's got her obvious curiosity plastered across her face, and Adrian is still casting his questioning looks at Reese.

I want to fucking punch that guy. What right does he have to look at her like that, after losing her so spectacularly? And then getting with her best friend? Guilting her into attending the wedding, using their daughter as an excuse? I dinna care that Reese is mature and accepting of the situation. I hate it.

I dinna let go of Reese's hand. We're going all in with this.

"You guys want to grab a bite to eat?" Britt checks out the time on her phone.

I look down at Reese and catch the quick flinch in her cheeks. Fuck, no. I'm not letting this happen. Even if it would mean I get to spend more time with Reese.

"Oh, I canna stay longer. I need to get back and take care of a few things," I say, even though it's mid-afternoon on a Saturday. "You ready to head back, hen?"

Reese looks up at me, a smile in her eyes but not her mouth, although a twitch at the corner gives her approval away.

"Sure."

Reese looks obviously relieved. Who wants to continue with this charade of friendship? No wonder she's exhausted. No wonder she needs a reset.

"Bye," Britt calls as we stride away.

Reese dives into the right front seat of my car and slams the door shut, then swears when she realizes she's on the wrong side. Instead of getting out and walking around the car like a normal person, she wiggles over the middle console. I slip into the driver's seat, biting back laughter.

"Alright?"

She's leaning her head against the headrest, eyes closed. "That was . . . a lot."

I watch her, memorizing the curve of her neck, the way her lips are perched so perfectly on her face, her long eyelashes linked together, separating when she opens them and swivels her head.

She reaches her hand out for mine. No one is watching, but I dinna hesitate to grab it. My eyes dart down to her lips. I can still feel her hips against mine when she ran her hands along my sides in that stone nook. Heat rises to my neck.

"Yeah. Thanks for today. It was almost fun messing with them."

"Almost?"

"Definitely fun, I mean. A billion times more fun than if it were the two of them versus me, without you there to save me from wedding conversations."

"You're not gonna go, are you?"

She shrugs. "I don't know."

"Ah dinna ken why you'd even consider it."

Reese blinks at me and squeezes my hand. "It's a mom thing."

It's like a punch to my gut. I'd never understand a ma thing. Or a da thing.

Because I'm a sham. A liar.

"Well, maybe I'll fly to New Jersey and be your fake date to the wedding."

Her jaw drops. "Not a half-bad idea."

"But we'll already be fake broken up from our fake relationship, so . . ." I wait for her to suggest we dinna break up at the end of camp before she leaves. But she doesna. It's a daft idea.

I put the car in gear and head back toward Peebles, but it's not long before Reese's phone vibrates with a text.

"It's Chelsea. She's going on a ghost tour of Peebles with the girls tonight."

"That sounds fun. Better than getting pissed at the pub."

She gasps. "Shit, you don't think they're drinking, do you?"

I glance at her briefly in the passenger seat before turning back to the winding, narrow roads. "Nae. They're good girls.

We're all looking out for them in town, including the bartenders at The Old Forge. They have a curfew and strict rules. They're safe."

"Just another thing I didn't totally think through when we came here."

We pass by the girls' barracks on the right, my house on the left, and I pull into a spot in town in front of the fish and chips shop.

"What if she finds out?" Reese squeezes her hands together. "About us."

"Well. What would you say if she did?"

Reese's eyes widen. "That I'm a weak, sad example of a human being?"

"Nae. Try again."

"That I was so desperate to escape her father I found a fake boyfriend?"

I sigh. "Once more."

"That I'm an adult and can fake date whoever I want?"

"I reckon that's the closest we're gonna get today."

Reese laughs.

"Listen, Reese. Chelsea's a strong, fierce, sixteen-year-old lassie. I'm sure she can handle knowing her mother has a life outside of her."

"With the soccer coach she was obsessed with for weeks before we got here?"

I raise my eyebrows. "Was she, now?"

"The one that all the girls probably have a crush on?" She raises *her* eyebrows.

"She's the least likely to have a crush on me, from the way she acts."

"Is that supposed to make me feel better?"

"Aye."

Reese offers me a smile and looks out the front of the car, a regretful look settling on her face.

"Look at me." I reach over and cover her hands with mine, like she did the other night when I opened up about my childhood.

Reese stares down, slowly flipping her hand over so that ours are entwined together, like the messy story we are weaving. She takes a breath and lets it out as a long sigh, then looks over at me.

"Chelsea willna find out from us. And the best you can do is tell Adrian and Britt to keep it to themselves. They shouldna have any need to talk about us with her. Of course, they don't seem to respect boundaries, so . . ."

"Boundaries are not one of their strong points."

"I've noticed. But even friends—if that's what they are—have boundaries." I shake my head, amazed I'm once again giving another person life advice. "Just tell them to keep their mouths shut. Offer it to Britt as a best friend pinky promise."

Reese chuckles. "She might like that."

"No one will find out. And if they do, no one will be able to tell we're faking it. We're gonna get an award for this performance." I think of the kiss. That was anything but fake.

She nods once, but I'm not sure she's convinced.

Right. We need more practice.

"Have any free evenings this week? We can have another get-to-know-you night."

A smile replaces the regretful look.

"Good idea. I have plans with Chelsea on Monday, and a few late calls with the US on Tuesday."

"Wednesday?"

She nods. "That would work."

"Wednesday night it is. I'll come with dinner. We'll talk about . . ."

"Our entire lives?"

"Aye, Reese. Whatever's left to talk about, anyway."

Internally, I object. I dinna want to talk about myself. I certainly dinna wanna tell her about Lucas yet, which seems like a bigger secret each time we're together. But I promised myself I'd tell her about him the next chance I could, and this—right now— would be the perfect time. Shite. Okay. I can do this.

Reese's eyes roam my face and land for a few seconds on my lips. I swallow and it makes a too-loud sound.

"So my flat on Wednesday?" She sucks in her upper lip. I doubt she's trying to be sexy, but fuck, she definitely is.

I nod. "With wine. How about a cheese and cracker spread?" I look out at the busy Peebles High Street, not able to stare at her tempting mouth any longer.

"Wine and cheese? That's quite possibly the perfect dinner."

"See? That's something else I know about you now. Your favorite meal. And I happen to be an amateur cheese connoisseur."

"Are you?"

"Aye." I nod.

Is it a terrible idea for me to come to her flat? When we're alone with each other? With alcohol? And the memory of that kiss still lingering? Maybe. Do I care? Nae, I absolutely do not.

"Hey—"

"Well—"

We both start talking at the same time.

"Go ahead," I say.

"I was just going to say, I'll see you later, Oliver."

"Me too. It's been fun." I grip the steering wheel.

Her hand rests on the car door handle for an extra beat before she disappears from the passenger seat and then through her door.

I pull out my phone.

ME

Favorite childhood memory? Mine was an away tournament when I was twelve. Another family took me and three other boys. We had our own hotel room and stayed up inappropriately late, laughing and doing reckless shite. We broke a lamp, one of them fucked up his ankle doing a flip off the bed . . . it was like I had brothers.

I pull away from the curb and toward my house, arriving just three minutes later, practically screeching to a halt in the driveway so I can get to the text she'd already sent me.

REESE

Halloween when I was ten. Stella was six, Maddie was four. We dressed up as cookies. I was a rainbow sprinkle cookie. My mom was milk and my dad dressed up as . . . a napkin. My parents seemed so happy. Not at all like they were faking it. Mom was smiling, Dad wasn't withdrawn.

I get out of my car, my chest filling with warmth. Three dots dance around on the screen as I slowly climb the steps of my front porch.

REESE

My turn. Where would you live if you could choose anywhere?

ME

I've always wanted to spend time in Australia. Maybe one day. You?

REESE

Scotland's pretty beautiful so far.

I unlock my front door and kick it shut behind me.

How different would this be if she were in Scotland permanently? There'd be a potential future. But maybe the expiration date on this (fake) relationship is why I'm more and more attracted to her as I get to know her. Because it's something I canna have.

Aye. That's it.

But I shoulda kissed her goodbye just now.

A secret fake relationship. Fuck me.

I click through on my phone to the picture Britt took of the two of us. Reese is pressed up against me, my arm resting around her shoulder. She's so beautiful.

Despite our ruse, I think she's the realest person I've ever met. She knows who she is, and it's not just one thing. She's a sibling, always texting her two sisters. She's a mum, always thinking of Chelsea first. She's got a career. She's adventurous. She's not sleeping through life, even if she thinks she's confused and needs a reset.

She's brave and ballsy and so damn hot.

I change quickly into running clothes. I need to sweat out the intense feelings swirling inside me.

Because I really want to get to know her better. And there's nothing fake about that feeling.

15

———————

REESE

Wednesday, August 3
19 Days Before Departure
Reese's Flat

I flit around my flat, fluffing pillows on the couch, wiping down the counters, rearranging the canisters just so. Why do I care what Oliver thinks about my rented flat? I don't, not really, but the swirling nerves inside me won't let me sit and relax while I wait for him to arrive. And text him.

ME

> Favorite ice cream flavor? Anything with a lot of chocolate and peanut butter for me.

OLIVER

> Eh, I don't eat ice cream.

ME

> Who doesn't eat ice cream?? I don't think I can fake date you anymore.

This afternoon, I had another conversation with my sisters,

trying to convince them we are *fake* dating. I failed miserably. Then I moved to the storyline that it's only a summer crush. A fling. I'll die on that hill.

But now Stella's sending me endless memes of hot, shirtless Scottish men in kilts. The world has a thing for that, apparently, and now I'm picturing Oliver in a kilt, which is not a useful image in my brain.

Her latest text buzzes in, just to me.

STELLA

So, just to summarize the current situation, you're "fake" dating this ripped, tattooed, ex-pro soccer player just to avoid one-on-one time with Adrian and Britt?

ME

For the tenth time, yes.

STELLA

And they've seen you two together?

ME

Yes.

STELLA

AND THEY SAW YOU KISS IN SOME ROMANTIC DARK CORNER IN THE RUINS OF AN ANCIENT ABBEY?

ME

Also, yes.

STELLA

And—final question—he's coming over tonight. WITH WINE?

ME

Once more . . . yes.

I lean against my kitchen counter and let out a half laugh. This conversation is a trap.

STELLA

Because you need to get to know each other better so it's not obvious it's fake?

ME

My god, woman—the answer is yes.

STELLA

But you feel SOMETHING for him, no? So it's not really fake?

My fingers hover over the keypad. Do I?

ME

Stop shouting at me, please. It's nothing. Honestly. I've hung out with him three times. Let's not make a big deal out of this.

STELLA

You know how ridiculous that sounds, right? Of course I'm going to make a big deal about this.

ME

I have to go. He'll be here any minute.

STELLA

We're talking soon and you need to tell me everything.

I send her a kiss emoji and turn my phone over on the counter.

What am I doing? I have some kind of feelings for Oliver, but I've known this guy for two weeks. Is it just lust? Probably. Is it guilty pleasure at having a hot man pay attention to me? Surely. The way he looks at me, like he could just eat me up, makes my mouth water. The way he reads me . . . The texts he writes . . . We've continued our conversation over the past four days. A hundred texts, easily.

I know he loves autumn because of the way the leaves crunch under his feet, and that he's always wanted to see the fall colors in America.

His answer to my question on whether or not he wants kids was simply: *maybe someday.*

I've held nothing back, and at this point, he knows me better than most people. At least, he knows more random facts. Like how I hate the word moist and that I can't stand to have my feet touched.

He's kissed me.

"Oh my lord," I say to the empty room, closing my eyes to recall the feeling of his lips on mine. My heartbeat accelerates.

I want him to do it again. Tonight.

In the time between the kiss in the abbey and now, I've decided I want more. More of his lips on mine. He might have surprised me last weekend, taking control . . . but tonight? I'm going to make sure it happens.

Who am I? I had the nerve to dismiss it to Stella just now. *It's nothing,* I said, but that feels like a betrayal, even though Oliver will never know. Stella would go feral if I told her that something more might be stirring inside me. I can't let her know what's really going on.

What *is* really going on?

My phone buzzes on the counter.

OLIVER

At your door.

"Calm down," I order myself, words that have worked on no one, ever. With a last deep breath, I jog down the steps and open the door to the street and find a smiling Oliver waiting for me against the backdrop of Peebles's High Street.

"Hey." My eyes take in his striking beauty. His hair is still wet from a shower and the persistent light rain. His cheeks flushed from the walk over. Those dark lashes reaching over crystal-blue eyes. He's got a reusable grocery bag hanging in the crook of one arm and a bottle of red in the other.

"I have alcohol." He lifts up the hand with the wine. "And I brought cheese, crackers, and Scottish treats." He moves the bag toward me like an offering.

"Ohhh, sounds amazing." I can't stop a goofy grin from creeping on my face, even as tingles run up and down my body just looking at him. "Come on up." I step back and let him climb the steps ahead of me.

I give myself an internal pep talk as I follow, staring at the way his ass fills out those lucky-as-hell jeans. My pep talk starts with: this man is a friend. A sweet, admittedly smoking-hot friend. That's all. A friend who has taken the time to get to know me and be there when I need him. I needed something else to fixate on besides Adrian and Britt, and even if I haven't been able to avoid them, some of the thick mud around my feelings for them has thinned. What's underneath the murk? I'm not sure yet, but I feel stronger. More confident.

What Oliver is not: my boyfriend. Sure, Saturday's kiss left me desperate for more, but it was all for show. The man is out of my league. And he's not what I need in my life, at least beyond this summer.

He's doing his job beautifully. Exactly what we agreed on. *Almost* exactly. Maybe he's improvised a bit. On my lips. One more kiss won't hurt, will it? And maybe just a test to see how his hands feel on me?

Oliver steps into my flat and walks right to the kitchen, placing the bag on the counter.

"I bought a lot of Irish cheese. It's basically all I ate for the past year in Ireland."

"Sounds amazing." I open cabinets until I find the big wooden cutting board, then grab a few knives from the block.

"But first, Irn-Bru." Oliver slides an orange-and-blue can out of the bag, a mischievous grin on his face. "Beloved by all Scots— well, most, anyway—and known for its delightful orange and blackcurrant flavors. Two glasses, please." He cracks the can open.

"Right, of course." I grab two short glasses and he fills each halfway with the carbonated beverage that looks like Orange Crush, the disgustingly sweet soda from my childhood.

"Goan then. Try it." His eyes are wide.

I pick up the glass. "This is important to you, huh?"

"Of course it is. It's Irn-Bru." He's dead serious and I bite back a laugh.

I sip, unable to suppress a slight gag.

Oliver narrows his eyes. "Delicious, right?"

"It's even worse than it looks. It tastes like orange-flavored mouthwash. Do adults drink this? Or just children?"

Oliver gasps and clutches his heart. "That hurts. Irn-Bru is a Scottish delicacy. It's a fantastic hangover cure, if you must know. And it's going to be a real problem if you dinna embrace it."

I slowly slide the glass along the counter toward him. "You can have mine."

"Americans. You think just because it's banned from being sold in the US, you can tip up your nose at it."

"It's banned in the US?"

"Mmm. By the FDA, apparently, is what I've heard. Moving on." Oliver turns back to the bag and pulls out a packet of short-bread, then turns to me. "I dinna suppose you also hate short-bread, do you? How about puppies? Do they disgust you as well?"

"Oh, no, I definitely love shortbread and puppies. Does that make up for the . . ." I nod my head at the offensive orange beverage on the counter.

"No, but it's a start." He sighs like he's deeply disappointed, then continues to pull out packages from the bag. "Three different Irish cheddars. You have to try all of these. I picked up a blue cheese as well." He examines the label on one of the wrapped chunks. "And blueberry Stilton. This one's outstanding."

"So you're a soccer player, a coach, *and* a cheese connoisseur?" I stand next to him and unwrap the hard Dubliner cheese, cringing at my awkwardness.

He glances down at me with another of those mysterious looks, his mouth quirking into a gentle smile.

"Eating a lot of cheese is an easy way to become an expert."

"Tell me more." I touch his arm and push gently. "What other secrets do you have? What have you not told me?"

He rips open a box of crackers and spreads them on the cutting board, not looking at me.

"There are grapes and chocolate, too." He pulls out a bunch of red grapes and hands them to me. "Cadbury, of course. None of that Hershey's garbage."

"Whatever you say." I drop the fruit into a small colander and run tap water over it. "Surely there's something else you're holding back from me? Some secret skill? Are you a chocolate connoisseur as well?"

"Hmm. Well."

"Well what?" I flick the running water off.

"I draw, too." His voice is quiet and unsteady, as if he's making some big confession.

"Draw?" I turn to him. That's the absolute last thing I expected him to say after our playful teasing, but he nods, confirming I heard right. "What do you draw?"

"Lots of things." He opens another package and shakes out a different kind of cracker. "These are like biscuits. Good for the soft blueberry cheese, since both are sweet."

I lean my butt against the counter and watch him arrange the cheeses and crackers just so, his fingers flitting over them, separate knives slicing through the different chunks.

It might be the sexiest thing I've ever seen.

"Should I open the wine?" I have to at least try to get him to tell me more. He must want me to know him better. Why else would he tell me he draws?

Oliver grunts but doesn't look up, so I locate the corkscrew before removing the aluminum wrap and rotating the spiral into the cork. I guess I'm not the only one who's been keeping steel bars around their heart. But with the way his parents held him at arm's length—who only talks to their adult child once a year?—and how the people around him disappeared when he lost his spot on the team, I can empathize with the way he's protected himself. Why open yourself up when it's practically guaranteed you'll get hurt? People will show their true colors and you'll be alone again, stuck in a situation where you can't even get away from those who hurt you.

Or maybe that's just me.

The cork pops with a satisfying sound.

Oliver stops messing with the food and turns to me, freezing in the line of my intense scrutiny.

"I've always drawn. From the time I can remember. But my parents never encouraged it. They called it a waste of time." He turns and opens the cabinet between us, finding wine glasses on the first try.

"Go on." I pour us each a generous portion. We clink and drink before he continues.

"I, uh, would sketch here and there up through when I was a preteen, basically in secret as my parents thought it was silly. But once things got really intense as a teenager, I stopped. And when I went pro, I forgot all about drawing. Football was all I had time for. There was nothing left afterwards."

I blink and wait for him to continue. He's staring at a point over my shoulder, where there's nothing interesting to look at, lost in his thoughts.

"I drew a jersey and ball shortly before I got hurt." He pulls up the left sleeve of his t-shirt to reveal the inked jersey above the soccer ball.

"It's gorgeous." My breath catches. I'd seen it before, of course.

"The tattoo artist did an amazing job." He runs his hand along the details of the ink and examines the image like he's never seen it before. I'm mesmerized at the sound his hand makes running over his own skin. Would it sound the same against my skin? Would mine against his? A warm shiver creeps up my spine.

"You're very talented." My voice catches.

"Ian said I was," he murmurs, lost in his own world.

"Ian?"

He glances up. "Um . . ."

He's considering whether to tell me something. I just know it. I swallow and wait for his decision on whether he trusts me or not.

"Ian owns a tattoo parlor in Ireland. I stayed with Patrick and worked a bit at his family's brewery, but also spent time at Ian's. I drew a lot of tattoos, and he started selling them to clients. He'd give me a commission when clients chose them. Before I left, he bought a bunch of designs off me."

"That's amazing. See? You're so good, people pay to get your work tattooed on their bodies forever."

"Maybe." An electric current crackles between us. He keeps his eyes trained on me and unconsciously licks his bottom lip.

I move forward and close the two-step gap between us. My belly is heated from the sips of red wine and lack of food.

"Can I look?"

He nods, an almost imperceptible movement of his chin.

Feeling like I'm moving in slow motion, I reach for his other arm, pushing his sleeve to his shoulder with one of my hands and running the other along the ink. His breath catches as I lightly touch his skin. Aware of the reaction I'm getting from him, I keep tracing the flag slowly, hoping he doesn't sense the fluttering of my insides.

Our eyes meet, mere inches from each other. "Are you going to get any more tattoos?" My voice is a whisper and I leave my hand resting on his bicep, even though it has no right to be there. All thoughts of being responsible, a good example, the perfect co-parent, fly out of my head. Tonight—this—is about me and Oliver. It feels delightful to be selfish. To touch him.

"Ah dinna ken." He makes a noncommittal movement of his

head and looks from my eyes to my lips. "I never talk about drawing. No one knows, except Ian and Patrick." His voice is deep and soft, as if he's telling me another secret.

I suck in my top lip, shaking at the connection between us.

"I was thinking of getting a tattoo, but I'm not sure what to get. Or where I should get it." I move my finger slowly on his arm.

"You want a tattoo?" He tilts his head, a flame sparking in his eyes.

I shrug, doubling down on my impulsive statement. "Yeah. I don't know what yet. Something meaningful."

"Well . . ." He takes my hand and turns it over in one of his, then traces the inside of my wrist with a finger. "This is a popular place to get a first ink. Like the one I have."

My skin burns at his touch. "I could do that." I swallow. "Where else would you recommend?"

Oliver examines my face, still touching my wrist. "There are lots of other places." He moves one of his hands to my collarbone, pushing aside the open sweater I'm wearing over my tank until one side of it hangs off my bare shoulder.

He runs his fingers along the sharp ridge of my collarbone and I breathe in at his touch.

"Or here." He draws circles on my shoulder, then moves to the top of my bicep, pushing my sweater farther down. "Here, too."

I feel a pulsing between my legs and I'm wet, my body yearning for more of his touch. I don't think I've ever wanted someone as much as I do Oliver right now. Not for years. Never, really. But I know this is what I want. It's what I need. To feel desired, wanted, touched.

By this man.

I tremble and will my body to stay still. I lick my lips and he watches the movement of my tongue.

"How about lower?"

"Lower?" his breath hitches.

I nod my head. "Show me where else. With your fingers."

16

OLIVER

Oh, fuck.

What is she doing to me? My cock is so hard, aching to be released from the confines of my clothing. The woman is asking me to touch her. Literally making me show her where on her body she should get ink, and so far, she's not satisfied with her wrist, her collarbone, her shoulder, or her arm. *Lower, she says. Fuck.*

Her cheeks are flushed and she's licking her damn lips, just centimeters from my face. I push her sweater off her other shoulder until it hangs off both of her elbows. I'm obsessed with her pink skin and that look on her face.

How'd she get me to tell her about sketching tattoos? It's a secret I was going to hold close to me forever, but yet, here I am, just casually telling Reese on a random Wednesday evening. I coulda just not told her. She was teasing me about Irn-Bru and cheese and then it all came out.

She didna make me feel weird about it, or self-conscious. In fact, it was the opposite. She makes my hand yearn for a pencil and a pad of paper. Not now, of course. My appendages have better things to want to touch at the moment.

I trace my fingers down her arms and try to think with the

head that's attached to my neck. She straightens her arms and shakes her sweater off, letting it fall onto the kitchen floor.

This is Reese.

This is the woman who I've spent two weeks getting to know. Who's made me laugh via text and in person. Who I'm protecting from her twat of an ex-husband and backstabbing ex-best friend. Who doesna give a fuck that I was a professional footballer, and that I'll never be one again. Who is willing to come with me to Lucas's birthday party, because she knows it's incredibly important to me.

Who doesna even know about Lucas.

A voice inside me says I shouldna do this. *Dinna go down this path. Not with her. Not when she doesna even know the truth.*

"What about my hip?" Reese's voice is low. She tilts her head, and when I dinna move right away, she grabs my hand and moves it to her side, pulling up one end of her tank top to expose her skin and pressing my hand against her bare hip. Her confidence pulls me in.

"Reese." Her name is a question on my lips, but I rub my hand in a circle on her hip without waiting for an answer, running my fingers just under the waistband of her jeans.

"Is that a good place?" She puts her hands on my chest and moves them up to my collarbone, then to the sensitive spot at the base of my neck, touching the bear's claw that peeks out. She tugs the neckline of my t-shirt down to get a better look. "Who did this one?"

"I—" My voice squeaks, so I clear my throat. "I got that one in London five years ago. Took three different sessions, hours each."

"That must've hurt." She traces her fingers over the top of my shirt where the rest of the bear is inked, surprisingly accurate to the animal's edges and curves. Has she been thinking of it since that day she showed up at my house? Just the thought that she might've been fuels the blue flames in my center.

Fuck. Who knew a woman tracing her finger on my shirt could turn me on this much?

"Nae." I stare at her face as she stares at my chest, my hand still rubbing circles on her hip. I'm feart to be the one to push this further, no matter how much I want to. She's gotta lead the way. I dinna want to take advantage of her or screw things up.

Och. That's a new one for me.

"Can I see it all?"

"You want to see the whole bear? Again?"

"I absolutely want to see the whole bear again."

Fuck, this woman. I'll do anything she asks right about now, so I pull my shirt over my head and drop it on top of her puddled sweater on the kitchen floor.

"Beautiful," she says, and runs her hands over my pecs.

"You could also get one on your back," I say, knowing I'm about to lose my mind if I dinna get to touch more of her.

"Show me where, Oliver." She looks up, her eyes hooded.

I slowly turn her around, missing the sparks of her hands on my bare chest. "Here." I move her hair over one of her shoulders and touch the base of her neck. "But you wouldna be able to see it." I link my fingers in the straps of her tank and bra together, slowly pushing it down off her right shoulder. Then I draw a circle on the back of her shoulder.

Reese's body lifts and lowers with deep breaths.

"Or here." I lower my lips to her skin and gently kiss the spot just below. She visibly shudders and arches back toward me.

I pull her hips against mine, letting her feel my hardness, then I return my mouth to her shoulders, nuzzling into her neck.

"You could do the other side instead. Or matching tattoos." I bare her other shoulder without looking, then move my mouth to the same spot, treasuring the salty taste of her skin. I should stop. I lift my mouth with the intention of doing just that, but she rubs her ass against my groin. Fuck. She leans back and the feel of her bare shoulders against my chest is like a wildfire being fanned by persistent wind.

I run my hands down her sides and slide up her tank to expose her lower back, our hips still moving against each other.

"Women love getting tattoos here . . ." I circle my fingers on her lower back, watching our connected hips push against each other.

She reaches back and grabs my hands, pulling them around the front of her so she can press against me completely. I slide my hands from her belly up her bare skin, stopping at the bottom swell of her breasts, dragging my fingers just below, my thumbs skimming within a centimeter.

Reese takes my hands and moves them up and over her breasts, arching against my hands. I breathe in sharply. She wants this. *Fuuuck.* My breath quickens and I tug down the layers of her tank and bra so my hands can cup the naked curves. I circle her nipples with my thumbs until they grow hard under my fingers.

"Oliver . . ." she murmurs and grinds against me, her head leaned back against my shoulder.

Any more of this and I'm going to lose control. Would that be such a bad thing? I havena touched a woman in a year. But this isn't just any woman. I canna just fuck her and leave her. I willna do that. I willna mess with her life any more than men like Adrian have already done.

I stop moving my hand and withdraw it, immediately regretting the motion. She turns around and faces me, and seeing the look on her face nearly makes me come. Her eyes are dark, her lips moist from licking them. She takes my hand and moves it back to her breast, round and full and overflowing in my hand. I stare at my hands on her body, and I'm fucking trembling, like a teenager touching a woman for the first time. But the sight of her is gloriously unbearable.

"Jersey," I say, holding back a groan as I get even harder, if that is possible.

"What?" She's breathless and her gray eyes are boring into mine, pupils wide with desire.

"Are you sure about this?"

As a response, she slides her hands around the back of my neck and pulls my face down to hers, pausing just before our lips can touch.

"Are you?" Her hot breath bounces off my lips.

"Fuck, yeah, Reese, I'll do whatever you want. But . . ."

I'm sure. Sure about what? Ah dinna ken. Sure that I want her. Bloody hell, aye, I want to feel all of her bare skin underneath my hands. I want to touch her everywhere, explore her body with my mouth and my fingers. I want to be inside her. I want to see what she looks like when she comes.

Reese freezes, leaning back so our eyes meet.

"Oliver. When you kissed me at Melrose Abbey, you woke something in me."

My breath catches in my throat, because I feel the same way.

"And I want more of that feeling."

I'm tempted to say something, to make this deeper, confess my secret, let her know me. But it terrifies me.

"Well. Who am I to deny you?" I say instead.

She smiles and moves her arms from around my neck. Then she takes my hands and puts them on her ass, pressing one hand on each cheek, pushing my hands harder against her, grinding our hips together more.

"Then kiss me."

But I pause for another second. She just told me everything and nothing at the same time. What if she's just getting caught up in the moment? What if she regrets this tomorrow, and it messes everything up between us?

I dinna want that. I spent a decade not caring about how my actions affected other people, especially women, and it got me nowhere except alone. It was only about fucking and disappearing as soon as possible, mostly unsatisfied, or having a lonely, empty-feeling relationship with some girl.

It's wild I'm hesitating, since I'm literally in a fake relationship with Reese. It's even wilder that I'm comparing her to Kendall, a woman I dated for a year.

But Reese wants to know who I am. This woman, who is rubbing herself against me and begging me to kiss her, has peered into my soul. I've not let her in, of course, because I know she'll bail when she sees the real me.

And we're just pretending. But . . . this feels a lot like *not* pretending. I'm confused and I want to stop thinking so hard.

Without another thought, I press my lips against hers. She moans and flicks her tongue into my mouth. I move my hands from her ass up to her lower back, then slide my hands down under her jeans and underwear, slowly, until I have her bare ass cheeks in my hands. I massage and squeeze until she's groaning into my mouth.

I need her naked. I feel myself losing control and take a deep breath, pausing for a second against her mouth.

"Alright?" I whisper.

"Mmm." She slides her hands between us, and my eyes follow the movement, heart beating even faster. She unbuttons her jeans first and pushes the flaps aside, then reaches for my fly. I sharply inhale as her fingers feel the desperate bulge pressed up against the zipper.

"Stop asking me questions," she murmurs, gliding her hand up and down the ridge of my cock, jeans and boxers still between us. "I want your mouth on me."

I dinna think I can breathe. The sensation of her pressure on me is so intense.

"If you keep touching me like that, this will be over before it starts," I say.

She huffs and pulls her hand away reluctantly.

We're doing this. My body's taken over and there's nothing I can do to stop myself from touching her, unless she tells me no.

My hands still on her ass, I shift one around until my fingers nestle in the hair above her clit.

She inhales sharply and practically mews at me as I slide a finger between her legs. Fuck, she's so wet for me. I rub her with my thumb and gently stroke her with one finger. She's grinding against my hand, and I slip one finger inside her slowly as she moves against me. Reese pants into my mouth, then licks my lips and caresses my tongue with hers.

I add another finger and pulse slowly, gently, until her hips move faster against my fingers. I cover her bare breast with my other hand, pinching her nipple just enough to get her attention but not enough to hurt.

Fuck, I wish I were inside her, but this is almost better, having this hot woman fuck my fingers.

I rub harder and harder and she grinds against me. She's gonna come, she's almost there, I know it.

She moans and I feel her insides pulse hard against my fingers as more liquid pools in my hand. I almost come with her, pushing my cock against her thigh.

"Oh my god," she says when her body stills. "That was so good."

I pull out my fingers, enjoying how fucking wet she is. That was, without a doubt, the most turned on I've ever been at someone else's orgasm.

I kiss her swollen lips and close my eyes, then they spring open when her hand slides against my stomach, into my boxers, and directly around my cock. She retreats for a second, then reaches between her own legs and comes out with her fingers glistening wet, returning to stroke me.

"Oh, fuck," I say and pulse through her fingers.

"I want you inside of me," she whispers, pulling me away from the counter and to the couch, never breaking the pumping motion.

"Are you sure?"

"While I appreciate the continued request for consent, you need to stop asking me. I said yes. What else can I say?" She pauses in front of the couch and pulls her tank top over her head, unsnaps her already askew bra, and flings it off.

I stare at her—red nipples tight, waves of her hair partially covering one of them.

She steps forward and pushes down my jeans and boxers, then gently shoves me onto the couch after I step out of them. Reese wiggles out of her jeans and underwear, swearing under her breath while doing a little dance to get naked. I lay back and watch her, memorizing every curve on her body, the arch of her hips, the wet glistening between her legs as she climbs over me. I reach for her breasts, pulling her to me so I can wrap my lips around her nipple.

She moans and lowers her wet center down to rub against me.

Usually I'm the one in control, but she's like a freight train I cannot stop.

"Shit," she says, not stopping her back and forth movement.

I release her nipple from my mouth and look up at her hooded eyes, unable to stop a moan.

"What, Jersey? Dinna stop."

She blinks. "I have no intention of stopping, unless you don't have a condom."

"I've got one." I reach down into the pile of clothes on the floor for my wallet, still in the back pocket of my jeans.

"You carry a condom in your wallet?"

"Do you not want my wallet condom?"

"I definitely want your wallet condom." She sits up and grabs the condom from my hand, ripping it open with her teeth and shoving it on me efficiently, as if she does this every day.

I lean back and close my eyes, groaning with the building tension in my body.

"I want you on top of me," she demands.

With barely a flinch, I grab her ass and flip us over so she's underneath me.

"Reese." I tease the tip of my cock on her clit. "You're so fucking hot right now." I slide my hand down her body and guide myself in.

She gasps and looks right into my eyes, rocking gently against me. I have a terrifying thought that we're exactly where we should be. That this is perfect. Me and Reese.

"Harder," she says, thank fuck, and I comply, pumping in and out, watching her face, watching her build toward another orgasm, controlling my own desire to make sure she's ready before I am.

Just when I'm sure she's going to come, and sure I canna hold on a second longer, her mouth drops open and she yells out. My own orgasm explodes and my eyes roll back in my head.

Her body tightens around me again and again as waves of pleasure engulf both of us, then she releases me and I drop down on my side next to her, pulling out, balanced on the couch with my ass hanging off the edge.

"Oh, fuck," she says, eyes closed.

I watch her. I'll never be good enough for her. But while she lets me, I'll try.

I trace the curve of her breasts with a finger, down over her stomach, resting on her hip.

"Here. This is where you could get a tattoo." I circle the spot on her hip, much lower than I touched before.

When she opens her eyes and turns to me, I see something new there.

"I don't know what that was, Oliver, but it was incredible." Her expression is soft and vulnerable.

"You're the one who said it has to seem real between us. Well, now we've *really fucked*. They'll be able to tell just by looking at us."

Her face clouds over. "Yeah. Exactly."

Shite. I've said the wrong thing, but ah dinna ken how to fix it.

"Really, though. That *was* incredible." I slide my hand along her jaw and touch her lips with my thumb. "*You're* incredible."

"Yeah?" She stares at me, the cloud lifted, but I can't read her expression.

"What, you dinna believe me?" Fucking Adrian. I guarantee he did not appreciate this woman like he should have.

"Mmm. I believe you. Now, let's go eat cheese and chocolate and shortbread."

"And drink wine and Irn-Bru?"

"You keep the Irn-Bru, I'll stick with wine."

We both stand and pull on our clothing. She brings the cheese board over to the couch and I refill our glasses of wine at the kitchen counter, leaving the fizzy orange drink behind. I dinna take my eyes off her. Did that just happen? It was the most connected I've ever felt to a woman while having sex. When she comes back in for the crackers, I grab her around the waist and pull her body against mine.

"Jersey. Alright?" I ask, praying she says yes. That her eyes tell me she has no regrets.

"Sweet baby Jesus, what did I tell you about asking me that?" She places her hands on my chest and looks up at me, warmth in her eyes and a sweet smile on her face.

I laugh and lean in to kiss her, pausing before our lips touch to search her face again, wondering if it actually is okay. My attraction to Reese has exploded over the past weeks. I'd not planned to give in to that desire. But there was no way I could resist her orders to touch her, kiss her, fuck her.

I close my eyes as our lips touch, feeling myself stir again for her.

"Okay," I murmur. "I willna ask you that again."

But I have so many other questions.

17

REESE

Thursday, August 4
18 Days Before Departure
Reese's Flat

"Oh. My. God," I whisper for the hundredth time today. My computer screen glares at me, too bright, and I barely see the social media ads that I've been designing this morning for a client, this one based in the US. Luckily, these don't require a lot of brain power. The client, who recently launched a new over-the-counter heartburn treatment, wants to test a series of ads, creating combinations of the image, tagline, and call-to-action to see which one performs best.

That feels kind of like what I'm doing. Testing out different versions of myself to see which one I like the most. When I'm with Chelsea, I'm the mother version of me. With Adrian, the ex-wife. Britt, former best friend. With Oliver . . . a lover. And I really like this new role. It's so different, the feel of it like a foreign fabric on my body, soft and warm, a little edgy.

But it's also dangerous. I'm playing with fire, my racing heart and fluttering stomach feeling uncomfortably out of control.

I nibble on a decadent piece of millionaire's shortbread, which is shortbread with a layer of caramel and soft chocolate on top. Also on my plate—courtesy of Oliver's early morning run to that bakery on the High Street—a dark chocolate and currant scone and half a buttery, which is basically a delightfully squished croissant.

I can't believe that all happened last night. I can't believe how I acted, like someone else had taken over my body as I let Oliver ravish me on that very couch, the one right over there, looking so innocent in the light of day. My eyes bulge with a flesh-colored flashback. Did I rip the condom wrapper open with my teeth? Surely not. That doesn't sound like something I'd do.

But it does sound selfish. What kind of mess am I making for myself? And Chelsea? *That's* how I break my years-long dry streak? My cheeks flush and I breathe noisily in through my nose and out through my mouth. I touch my collarbone, one of his suggested spots for a tattoo, and run my hand down my chest to my hip, where he ended up.

I'm having a hard time regretting it. Maybe my sisters were right, and I *do* need a fling with a hot Scot.

But this is more than that. Isn't it? That vulnerable look in his eyes last night when he confessed to me about drawing as a kid. He chose *me* to confide in, practically trembling as he shared the details. All I can think about is his open honesty. How real he is being with me, even in our fake relationship.

About that.

I bite my lip. No one was watching last night. There was no need for us to have sex to *build chemistry*. So why did it happen? Why did I instigate tracing his tattoos with my fingers, and then sticking my tongue down his throat? I was absolutely determined. Was that fair of me?

I press my lips together in a barely contained grin, searching again for regrets but coming up empty. The *it's nothing* from last night's text chain with Stella seems extra-ridiculous now.

My phone illuminates next to my mouse and I snatch it up. Text message notifications assault my home screen. One from Oliver and one from Britt. I click on Oliver's.

OLIVER

Thanks for an amazing night. x

I feel a twinge between my legs that reverberates up into my chest. I pushed him out the door early this morning. Waking up next to him was almost too intimate. He swung back around twenty minutes later with treats, a goofy smile on his face as he practically skipped away from my door.

ME

I can't stop thinking about it.

What I want to say is: when can we do it again?

I drop my phone on the counter too roughly and it spins away from me, but I can't resist grabbing it again when it lights up with Oliver's response.

OLIVER

I'm entirely too distracted to be teaching teenagers complicated football plays.

ME

That's why you get the big bucks.

OLIVER

Good reminder. I'm not sure David's paid me yet. Or if he plans to.

I run my hand through my hair and bite my lip.

ME

So. What's your least favorite food?

OLIVER

Pineapple. No particular reason, and no
followup questions.

ME

I love pineapple! How can you hate it? Mine's
mushrooms, because they're a dirty fungus.

OLIVER

I love mushrooms.

ME

Gross. I can't hang out with you anymore. At
least I have a reasonable explanation as to why
I hate mushrooms.

OLIVER

What? Okay. I hate mushrooms too.

Laughing, I click through to Britt's message.

BRITT

Hey you, want to meet for coffee this morning?
We've been here for weeks already and haven't
gotten to catch up.

I lean my head back and close my eyes. I have to talk to her about keeping this thing between me and Oliver secret, which I meant to do after the Melrose Abbey trip last weekend. Only I never got around to it. And maybe this new version of myself will finally be able to calm the unrest inside of me when I see her and Adrian. It's time to truly let go and embrace our future as co-parents.

I tell Britt I'll meet her in twenty minutes. Am I ready for this? I guess I'll find out.

THE PEEBLES BEANS is only a block past The Old Forge. I float down there, distracted and grinning like a high school kid who just got into their top college choice. Britt won't ever suspect I'm faking this thing with Oliver. I'm not that good of an actor, and I'm sure my giddiness is all over my face.

I attempt to paste a normal look on before opening the door to the cafe. The welcoming aroma of rich coffee beans invades my body in the best way, the clatter of ceramic mugs and the whirring of grinding machines music to my ears. Everything about this place is wonderful, but Britt sitting in the corner waving at me triggers alarm bells in my brain.

I lift my hand and get in line for coffee before joining her. I need a minute to think. Even without Adrian beside her, my discomfort with Britt is even worse than before. What the fuck? So much for feeling more at peace with the situation.

"Ree, I got you one!" Britt calls. She gestures in front of her at a second steaming mug.

Guess I don't get my minute.

"Thanks," I say, sliding in across from her.

"Vanilla latte?" The corners of Britt's eyes crinkle, her painted lips curling upward into a warm smile.

"Perfect." I attempt to smile back. Britt and I agree on a lot. We always have. We like the same music: nineties grunge. Same favorite coffee: vanilla latte. Best weird movie genre: dinosaurs eat everyone. It was why we were such fast friends when she moved to Sharontown with her ex-husband. And it wasn't just how we got even closer during her divorce. It was the hikes we'd take together in the nearby mountains on a cool fall Saturday morning when Jackson was with his dad. We'd laugh each time we'd show up for coffee or at Target looking like sisters, her the short blond one, me the taller brunette, our hair in matching thick braids.

We went through so much in the years we'd been friends. Which is why it's so hard to untangle this messy web of feelings.

Maybe in time, it'll get better. It's only been two years since Adrian and I split up, and eighteen months since they got together.

"Hey, so how are things? I feel like you have a lot going on right now." Britt smiles sweetly at me and sips her latte.

She wants me to confide in her, talk like the true friends we used to be. But whenever I try to get myself to engage with her on more than a surface level, the thick steel door to my heart slams shut.

It's because she's marrying my ex-husband. Duh.

There's no other way I can explain it. Even if she didn't technically steal him from me, even if she did the 'right thing' by pushing us away before anything happened, even if she waited until the divorce was final, and even if she'd do anything for me (besides give up Adrian), she still chose him.

It's now them on one side, me on the other. What a mess.

But today, I'll give her a little of what she wants, so she'll give me what I want. Secrecy about Oliver.

"Well, things are going amazing with me and Oliver." My cheeks grow warm with a flash of what we did in the kitchen last night.

"Oh, yeah?" Britt leans in. "This is so edgy of you. To, like, throw yourself into this thing with Oliver. Can we call it a Highlands fling?"

"We're in the Borders, not the Highlands."

"Yeah, yeah, whatever. But a Highlands fling sounds better than a Borders fling." Britt laughs and I cannot stop myself from laughing with her.

It feels good—and also awful—and I struggle to rein in my negative thoughts, which are fighting their way back to the surface.

"Anyway," I say when we both quiet, backing down from the unexpected bonding moment. "There's not much to tell. It's all new, of course."

There's actually *so much* to tell, if only she was my best friend for real. But she's not.

Before everything happened with her and Adrian, there was an incident. Looking back on it, I should have seen it as the red flag it was. It wasn't even a thing. Just a weird feeling. On Christmas Eve the year before the divorce, Britt and Jackson came over to our house, like they'd been doing for years. Chelsea and Jackson were playing cards at the dining room table and the adults were in the family room drinking wine and listening to Christmas music. I went into the kitchen to restock the appetizers tray, and I peeked back into the family room a minute later, meaning to ask if either of them needed their wine refilled. Britt had moved from the small couch to sit beside Adrian, facing him with one leg tucked under the other. She had a hand on his knee and was leaning in, smiling and telling a story about the project she'd been working on. His shoulders were turned toward her, but I couldn't see his expression. There was nothing overtly wrong with the situation. Really. It was two close friends talking.

But the look on her face.

There was something there. Something that niggled at my belly, that made me hold back from calling out to them. I retreated into the kitchen.

At the time, I shook it off. But before heading back into the family room with the food and a fresh bottle of wine, I remember thinking that Adrian and Britt were always so excited to talk to each other, so interested in what the other one had to say. That was normal, though, right? Married couples tend to run out of things to talk about, but with friends, it's different.

In hindsight, it wasn't nothing. How did I let that happen?

"New is exciting." Britt nods her head.

"Mmm," I murmur. "But I wanted to ask you—and Adrian— to keep this between us. I don't want, uh, Chelsea finding out and getting the wrong impression."

She tilts her head. "I don't know, Ree. As fun as the idea of a vacation fling is . . . Chelsea might kind of take it badly if she finds out what's going on. When we mentioned our Melrose Abbey trip,

Adrian had to actually lie to her about who was there with us. We didn't know what she knew."

I breathe in sharply. Shit. Maybe I shouldn't have texted Chelsea that picture of the hobgoblin statues.

"Oh. Well, I'm sure she didn't notice anything off."

But I know Adrian must be pissed about lying to Chelsea. Damn.

"Maybe you're right. But we still worry about her." She gnaws on her lower lip.

I bite my tongue to stop myself from bringing up how badly Chelsea had taken it when Adrian and Britt officially got together. The hypocrisy in their worry over this is overwhelming.

"As her mother, of course I worry about her, and I appreciate you doing so as well." I choke out the last words, but they're true. "I'll be more careful, I promise. Thanks for covering for me."

"Sure." Britt pauses and sips from her latte. "I'm happy for you, though." She smiles and I believe her. She's never wished anything bad on me. She's always been supportive.

"Thanks, B." My old nickname for her slips out and her eyes widen with surprise. We sip lattes in silence for a moment.

"What about Oliver's son? Has he told him about you two?"

The room starts slowly spinning.

"Son?" My voice is too loud in this small cafe. "Oliver doesn't have a son." I don't have enough air. Where has all the oxygen gone?

Britt frowns, a wave of concern settling on her face. "He . . . has a son. It's kind of easy to find online. Haven't you googled him?"

No, I was making a point *not* to google Oliver Vass. No. There is no way he left something that important out of our conversations. It's impossible. We've told each other so much over the past few weeks. I know . . . well, less about him than he knows about me. I'm definitely the one oversharing in most of our conversations, going deeper, more personal.

But I asked him directly if he wants kids and he'd said: *Maybe someday*. That was a lie?

"Reese? Are you okay?"

How many times had he asked me if I was okay last night? I can still feel his hands on my jawline, tracing my bottom lip, gripping my bare ass. All the text messages. All the things I'd told him. And he kept this from me?

Did he think I'd never find out? I'm so confused. But it doesn't matter. None of this is real, no matter how it felt last night.

"I'm fine," I say, my voice flat. "I knew. Obviously. He's keeping it quiet, so I was just covering for him." The lie comes out easily and I try to wipe my face of emotion. Britt narrows her eyes, as if she's trying to understand my logic. "Why'd you google him, anyway?"

Britt shrugs. "He's Chelsea's soccer coach. They're spending a lot of time together."

Of course. That's so reasonable. I should have looked him up as well. I swallow hard and fiddle with my phone, turning it over out of habit. There's a text from Oliver.

OLIVER

I canna stop thinking about you.

"Shit." I don't mean to say it out loud, and Britt's eyes open wider. My acting abilities suck. I slam the screen face down on the table, feeling sick to my stomach.

"I didn't mean to pry, Ree. But . . . when I asked him if he had kids on the first day, he said no."

I can't stop myself from flinching.

"He lied, which is so weird. Why would he want to keep his son a secret?" Britt continues talking. "I'm sorry if I'm getting too involved. But I'm worried. I just want us to be a happy, blended family. You, me, Adrian, Chelsea, and Jackson." She pauses, her hand twitching on her mug, as if she wants to reach out to me. "We both know how hard the tween and teenage years are on kids.

His son is around ten. Remember ten? Right before all hell broke loose with puberty and social drama?" Britt crinkles her eyes. "And if Oliver's not worried about that, if he's lying about being a dad, then . . ."

So much for her being so happy for me. Or is she only looking out for me, like a true friend should?

I think of Oliver saying he's only a soccer player, and that's all he'll ever be. That he escaped to Ireland, then came back to deal with family issues. How he was so desperate for me to come to the family party with him. Is his *son* going to be at this party? *Oh, shit. I bet he is.* When the hell was he going to tell me?

It all has new meaning now. I lean back, keeping my hands a safe distance from Britt's. I think about his stories about his cold parents, his lonely childhood, the rejection he's faced as an adult. A stab of sympathy for him flares inside me, melting away one small sharp edge of the hurt at being lied to.

No. He left out something huge. Too huge. What else might he be hiding?

I look at my phone. "Oh, wow. I have a call in fifteen minutes. Better get back to my flat." My voice is high-pitched as I push back the chair, its legs making a loud stuttering sound against the wood floor.

"What are you two going to do once Chelsea's camp is over and we all go back to New Jersey?" She leans in and tugs at her braid.

"We haven't gotten that far. I guess we'll break up. I'll be fine. I always am." Fine seems to be the word of the day. I abandon Britt and what's left of my vanilla latte, striding out through the glass front door, away from her. The rain falling from the gray Scottish sky brings me back to reality.

The whole point in fake dating Oliver was to protect me from the prying eyes and ears of Adrian and Britt. But all it's done is make Britt feel bad for me. Worry about me.

The exact opposite of what I was going for.

And the worst thing is, she might be right. I'm in way over my head.

This thing between me and Oliver? All fake. Multiple orgasms last night? Unreal. We're just pretending. Just like all romantic love. The only genuine love I feel is for my daughter, my sisters, my mother, my great-aunt.

"Dammit." I dodge walkers on the busy sidewalk of the High Street.

How could he lie to me like this?

On my way up the steps to my flat, I slow down and finally do an online search for Oliver Vass. It's time. So many results pop up. I scan the first page, clicking on a picture of him in a tuxedo with a gorgeous woman.

I know so little about him. He's a stranger, no matter what happened last night.

I close the search. We've barely started, but this thing between Oliver and I might already be over.

18

OLIVER

Friday, 5 August
15 Days Before the Birthday Party
Football Fields

I examine the messages in my text chain with Reese, looking for a reason as to why she's stopped responding . . . the last one especially.

I canna stop thinking about you.

Was it too much for her?

I texted her a few more times after that. Even tried calling last night. That's a huge deal for me. I dinna do phone conversations voluntarily.

What'd I do wrong?

Now it's Friday afternoon, and she's also not shown up at practice. I keep glancing at the bleachers, to the point where David has asked me who I'm waiting for. I havena told him about Reese, but yesterday at camp, he asked me why I was smiling like his five-year-old granddaughter with an ice cream cone.

I pass the ball to Chelsea for the one versus one speed and reaction drill we've been working on all afternoon. She's good. She wins the ball nine times out of ten, easily the best player we have here. And she seems happy and well-adjusted, laughing and having fun with her new friends and football, which is far better than I was doing at her age. I bet she doesna need to be managed so delicately. She could handle the truth about what her mum is going through. But what do I ken? Like I'm parent of the year over here?

David blows the whistle and gives the lassies a pep talk, reviewing the week's work. I stand next to him for moral support, trying to pay attention to how he motivates the team. When he dismisses them for the weekend, the girls wander off in a few groups.

"Cards tonight?" the talented French goalkeeper with Chelsea suggests. "Or are you seeing your maman?"

Chelsea shakes her head and I listen for the response as their voices fade away across the field. "Nope, not tonight. Let's get the others to play after dinner."

So Reese isn't seeing Chelsea. And it's not like she's with Adrian and Britt. Sure, it's still probably the workday, but something's wrong. I fucked up somehow.

Wednesday night is all I can think about. The way her soft skin melted under my hands, the way her tongue moved in my mouth, the way I was whole while inside of her. I've never felt closer to someone. David was right. Yesterday I couldna wipe the grin off my face. But after texting all morning, adding to our addictive get-to-know-you game, it stopped abruptly.

I need to ken what happened.

As the lassies disappear from the fields, I know what I need to do.

I STOP at my house to take the fastest shower of my life. I'm not even trying to get her back in bed. I just want to know what's in her head. Still, I shouldna smell like a day of football.

Am I panicking for no reason? I pause inside of my front door, hand on the doorknob to head out to Reese's flat, and think.

My brain's empty of ideas, just a giant vacant room with flashing red lights. I canna see straight. Canna think of what I did. Maybe she's not even mad at me. Maybe she's simply busy with work.

But too busy to text me back? Fuck it. I gotta go.

I'm at her house in less than ten minutes, standing outside the street entrance to her flat. Which . . . willna help to knock on, as the actual door is up a flight of stairs.

Instead, I text, taking the chance that she'll acknowledge me if I'm physically standing here.

ME

I'm at your door. Can I come in?

It feels stalker-ish, but I need to do something to get her attention. At first, there's nothing. I wait an entire sixty seconds, pondering what my plan B will be, but ending up in the same empty room of my head. Just when I'm about to bail, the bolt slides to unlock, and the door clicks open.

Reese stands in front of me, hands on her hips, looking every bit as angry as I suspected. But she also looks devastatingly vulnerable, the corners of her eyes crinkling in a cringe.

"What happened?" I have no idea what I've done, but it sounds just like me, pissing someone off—usually a woman—and having no clue why. In the old days, if I'd tried hard enough, I could figure it out. The difference is I've never really cared. But with Reese, I do. Likely too much.

She expels air from her nose and crosses her arms.

I want to pull her in my arms and kiss that angry look off her face.

"Why don't you come in?" She steps back and lets me walk past her into the building.

Once inside, I stop and turn to her, at a loss. Are we still faking this? Is it fake? Is she . . . fake mad at me for fucking up our fake relationship in some way I don't even know?

Bloody hell.

I'm totally confused, but she stomps up the stairs and I follow, feeling as if I'm a baby gazelle following a predator to her den.

She stops just inside the door to her flat and turns to me, letting me pass, but clearly not welcoming me in for a cuppa.

"Reese," I say, barely stepping inside. "I'm not sure what's going on right now. Why are you looking at me like you're furious with me?" Every muscle in my body is clenched and adrenaline courses through my veins, muddying my thoughts and triggering an urge to flee this place.

Her eyes bore into mine and she's sucking on her top lip. Worried and angry. Deciding if I'm even worth the trouble of a fight, probably.

I should save her the time. I'm not.

I've never been worth it in relationships. Cat let me walk out the door and never once tried to get me to come back. I'm not good with women. It's like the father thing—I'm not made for it. Not made to be a boyfriend, either. I'm not—

Oh. Shite.

There is one major secret I've been keeping from Reese.

"You have a son," she whispers, just as the realization crashes over me.

"Fuck." I run my hand roughly over my face. That's what's wrong. The adrenaline fades away and I want to sink to the floor and bury my head in my hands.

"Why didn't you tell me?"

"Ah dinna ken why I didna tell you about Lucas . . . I'm so sorry." I squint my eyes shut, but when she doesna immediately tell me to fuck off, I open them again.

"Lucas," she says when I'm looking at her again, then nods. Her creased forehead smooths at the sound of my son's name, then clouds over again.

"I meant to tell you. I was going to tell you Wednesday night. I'd promised myself I would." I swallow the lump in my throat, the lump that represents every relationship I've fucked up by not doing the right thing. Keeping secrets, fucking up priorities, not giving a shite about the other person's feelings.

"But you didn't." She looks down at her feet and lets out a silent sigh, her shoulders lifting and falling.

"I didna tell you because I couldna. Couldna bring myself to ruin what's going on with us. I know that's fucked up. I was going to tell you, I *had* to tell you eventually. Reese . . ." I trail off, again wanting to run out of here, knowing there's no fixing this. I've ruined it. "I'm not a da to him. I'm not anything to him. Nothing. Just some wanker who sends money to his mum. And you are such an absolutely amazing mum to Chelsea. The opposite of me. I couldna bear to tell you the truth. That I'm nothing. Just a footballer. That's it." I squeeze my eyes shut.

"Dammit, Oliver." Her voice is distant, beyond the wall of pain that surrounds me when I think about Lucas and exactly who I have *not* been to him. What I've missed. Ah dinna even *ken* what I've missed, because I dinna even ken what it means to be his father.

I keep my eyes closed and clench my fists at my sides. I know how this ends with Reese. Hell, I know how this ends with Lucas and Cat. With me disappointing them. I'll never be who Cat needs me to be to get back into their life. I'll never be a good father.

I've gotta get out of here before Reese completely rejects me. This is just another reminder of how much I've failed at being a decent human being.

"I'm not even a footballer anymore. I'm a summer camp coach. *Assistant* coach. I'm nothing." I open my eyes and train them on the floor, then take a step backward toward the still-open door, fists clenched at my side, muscles ready to run back to my place alone.

"Hey," she says, the edge faded from her voice. "Forget soccer for a minute, okay? Do you want to be a father to Lucas?" Reese takes two steps toward me to close the gap between us. Her hands slip around my fists, gently encompassing them, stopping me from stepping outside the door.

The soft contact jolts me out of the dark, self-pitying hallway I was retreating down. Reese's gray eyes are locked on mine intently. They're wide and dry . . . but there's no anger left. I nod so subtly, I'm not sure I even moved my head. It hits me how easily my son's name came from her lips.

"Yes," I whisper. "But I canna." I pull my hands away and take another step back, away from her, away from this woman I've already disappointed. I have one foot out the door. "I'll leave you alone now."

"Don't you dare leave, Oliver Vass." Reese grabs my hand again and drags me inside and toward the couch, spinning to kick the door shut with her heel.

The fuck?

Dumbfounded, I follow her and let her push me down. She sits next to me, facing me. Only it's not nearly the same vibe as when we collapsed on the couch together on Wednesday night.

"Were you really just going to walk out in the middle of this fight?" She puts her hands on either side of my face to keep me looking at her. It's the sweetest of gestures.

"Fight?" I'm not sure what is happening right now, but I sure love it when she touches me. It's like a lighthouse, leading me home when our skin makes contact.

She groans, exasperated, sliding her hands off my cheeks, taking her time at my jaw. "Yes. That thing that was just happening. That conversation, argument . . . heated discussion. Whatever you want to call it. You don't just, like, give up and walk out. Especially since you had the balls to show up to begin with."

"You dinna?" Fuck, I need to stop parroting her, but I feel like I'm living in some kind of alternate reality, one where people care about other people and dinna bolt when they're not exactly who we want them to be.

"Listen to me, Oliver, you big, dumb, gorgeous beefcake. You are not just a soccer player. *Footballer.* Whatever you want to call it. Do you hear me? Who pounded that into your head? Your parents? Coaches? I'm freaking pissed at them. A soccer player isn't your *identity*. It's something you did, do, whatever. Something you loved. A job. And maybe it's over now, and that's okay. You are a man. A son. A father. A . . . lover." She traces her hand along my left forearm.

Oh. That's where I should get my next tattoo. Maybe one of my son, maybe the drawing of him standing on the banks of the River Tweed. Or something else. The thought of a tattoo that represents anything besides football hitches my breath.

"Maybe you haven't been there for Lucas up until this point. But I'm certain it's not too late to be in his life. You can do this. I know it."

I lean forward and drop my head into my hands, curling down low between my legs.

How is it that this woman believes in me? Could she be right? Could I be more than a footballer? Suddenly, the room's too bright, the traffic from the High Street too loud, but Reese's hand on my arm is like an anchor, keeping me from drifting away.

I'd been terrified of what she'd think of me when I told her about Lucas, but here we are, and she hasna run away. In fact, it's the opposite. She's refusing to let me go.

Ah dinna ken if I can face the fact that I might not be who I thought I was. Were my parents wrong? And maybe other people are right? People like Patrick, Ian, David.

And Reese.

19

———————

REESE

Part of me is so angry that I could wring Oliver's gorgeous neck. He didn't think I could handle the truth about his son? I can handle it. I've had a lot of practice with difficult truths.

Watching him next to me, I'm devastated. He's a broken man. Someone did that to him. His parents. His mentors. People who should have been supporting him, building him up, but instead, told him he was only one thing. Even I know—am still learning—that I am one person who plays multiple roles, none of which define me completely. I was never just a mother, or an ex-wife, or a sister, a best friend . . . even if it sometimes feels like that. Oliver's helped me realize I'm more. I can be more. So can he.

"I'm still coming with you to that party. I'm guessing Lucas will be there."

He nods and lifts his head from between his legs to look at me, his eyes as light as a clear summer day.

"It's his birthday party."

There's raw emotion radiating off his face, reflecting on me, burning my skin like the rays of the sun.

I tuck a leg underneath me and touch his back to take some of that emotion and absorb it.

"Okay. We can handle this together." I rub a circle on his t-shirt, moving my hand with his breathing.

"Reese . . . ah dinna ken that I can be a father to Lucas." Tears shine in his eyes. "I'm terrified of being a bad da, like I've been so far. What if I try to be good, but I just canna?"

"Hey, Picasso. Listen up."

At that, Oliver's mouth gives a tiny quirk. Did I just come up with my nickname for Oliver? Yup, sure think I did.

"I'm listening."

"Who knows that they can be a good parent? Nobody. You just have to show up. That's the only thing I know for sure about parenthood. Be there when your kid needs you. Don't run away because you're scared."

Inside, I'm twisting and writhing. Maybe I *don't* have to be a perfect role model for my own daughter. Maybe I should follow my own advice and just be there for her instead of obsessing over being flawless. Will that be good enough?

And maybe that means that I don't have to be friends with Britt again. I don't have to be the easygoing co-parent, accepting the vision she has of us all being one big, happy, blended family.

Oh, shit.

Relief courses through my body like a warm, gentle ocean wave. With an imperceptible shake of my head, I take that thought and shove it back into the hole it crawled out from. I'll deal with it later. Or never. Right now, I need to focus on Oliver.

There's a silence between us, where our locked gaze is so intense, it feels like we've both been sucked into a black hole, endless and all-encompassing.

"Thank you," he whispers.

I shrug and turn my lips up. "It's all part of the agreement."

"Reese . . ." Oliver shakes his head and turns his body toward me.

My phone rings on the coffee table, where I left it when I first saw Oliver's text about being downstairs. There's no way I'm going to disrupt this conversation. No way. Except, when I look over, it's Chelsea's name dancing across the screen.

I glance at Oliver, devastated to interrupt whatever he was going to say to me. "It's Chelsea. I have to answer. I always answer her calls."

I can't read his face, and as I slip into the kitchen to talk to my daughter, he leans back against the couch, eyes shut.

"Hey, sweetie, everything okay?" My voice is almost a whisper.

"Why are you whispering? Are you in a library?"

"Nope. Not in a library."

"A church?"

"Definitely not a church, either."

"You sound weird. Why do you sound weird?"

"I've said, like, ten words. Why do you think I'm being weird?" I stifle a laugh. Nothing gets past this girl. I should keep that in mind. "I'm in my flat, being totally normal. You just don't usually call, so it kind of threw me." I lean against the counter and attempt normalcy.

Oliver gets up from the couch, drawing my attention. What if he walks out? What if I've said too much? But he strides down the short hallway and ducks into the bathroom.

"Okay, whatever. Speaking of weird, I saw Dad and Britt today. She was acting so strange. As usual."

All the things Britt said yesterday worry me. She's probably overthinking my request to keep this a secret from Chelsea. It's not a big deal. Everything is casual and chill and . . . damn, this is really spiraling out of control, isn't it?

"Who knows? Maybe she's stressing over the wedding or something." It's *or something*. Definitely *or something*. The woman is not great at keeping secrets. I should've remembered that. Maybe if she could've, she wouldn't have had to make her dramatic exit from our lives, only to reenter *Adrian's* life six months later.

But she better fucking keep this one.

Chelsea groans. "Don't remind me about the wedding."

"Are you not looking forward to it?"

"Whatever, it'll be fine."

I desperately hope Adrian's not right about Chelsea wanting me there.

Oliver emerges from the bathroom, slowing to run his hand along the counter before settling back on the couch, not making eye contact with me.

"Want to do something this weekend?" I attempt to move this conversation along. "Are you free Saturday afternoon?" I love her, but I need to end this call and get back to that man over there.

"Yeah, sure. Oh, and next weekend, there's a field trip to Edinburgh."

"Sounds awesome. Can I come?"

"Mom." She sighs, but I can hear the smile on her face. "Coach David and his wife are chaperoning. Maybe Coach Oliver, too. I don't know. But I'm sure you can crash."

I search her voice for signs of the crush she has on Oliver. Did she sound different when she said his name?

"Maybe, sweetheart."

I glance over at Oliver, just in time to see him wave his phone at me and slip out the front door. My stomach drops and I lift my shoulders sharply, but a second later, my phone vibrates against my ear.

Chelsea ends the call and I quickly click through to the message.

OLIVER

Went to get a bottle of wine. Propping the door open for a minute. Be right back. x

Relief loosens my shoulders. I sigh deeply and let the quiet of the flat surround me.

The thing is, this fake relationship situation has taken on a life of its own. It became real the moment he pulled me into that nook in Melrose Abbey. I touch my lips as a visceral memory of him pressing me against the stone wall sends tingles across my skin. It feels like the type of memory that'll stay with me forever.

Or maybe it happened before then.

Maybe it was that first day, when he grabbed my hand to steady me on the soccer field. Maybe it started the second I approached him.

Whatever it is, it's getting to me. As good as it makes me feel to be around Oliver, I can't help feeling that I'm losing my footing. All those versions of myself are part of the foundation of my life. Chelsea. My job. Stella, Maddie, my mother, my great-aunt Evelyn. My house in New Jersey. Peanut Butter. What happens when something disturbs that foundation? Does the whole house crumble? Do I have to start over and rebuild?

What about my belief that true romantic love is fake?

I saw it with my parents. I experienced it with Adrian, and I can see it with Stella and her current boyfriend. For a second, it might seem like it's real, but then the truth comes out. It's not that people lie about who they are—I'm not that cynical. It's just that they don't understand themselves. I certainly don't.

Oliver lied to me about Lucas. Or did he? Was it a lie, or an omission bred by his insecurities? He definitely lied to Britt. This should be a deal breaker, but it feels different, somehow, and that's the thought that's messing with my head. It doesn't feel like he was trying to trick me. It was more like he was trying to protect himself. Can I blame him for that? I've always needed to protect myself, putting bars around my heart for years. And since the divorce, I've reinforced them with impenetrable meshing, vicious guard dogs, and an alligator-infested moat.

And then Oliver comes along.

He's like a wounded animal who needs to get through my defenses, as if I'm the only one who can save him. Is it reckless to cut a hole in the mesh for him? Maybe just enough that he can squeeze through?

My flat door creaks open and Oliver appears with a bottle of wine.

"Sorry to disappear." He approaches me and slides the bottle onto the counter. "I thought we could have a drink. I need one, anyway."

"Okay." I'm bursting with things to say, but they're things I would never, ever normally say to a man. They're things I've always kept bottled up.

But do I want to be that kind of person? Or do I want to be that next, better version of myself? I can't quite picture it yet. That new person is still submerged in the murky waters of the past few years. But I want to find her.

"Oliver."

He freezes with the corkscrew halfway into the bottle and meets my gaze. "Reese?"

"Please promise me that the next time something is eating you up inside, the next time there's some big secret you think you can't live with, you'll sit your cute ass down and talk to me about it." I fill my lungs with air.

I want to evolve.

Otherwise, the bars will get thicker, and no one will be able to see me through the layers of so-called protection I've built. I might starve in there all alone.

"Aye." Oliver nods slowly, dropping his hands from the wine bottle and stepping in front of me. He glides his hands around my waist and pulls me close to him, his hands sparking on my body.

"Or you can talk to anyone, of course. It doesn't have to be me," I hastily add. My words imply I'm going to be around for all those times when something is bothering him, when he needs to talk to someone. But I'm not, of course.

"I promise, Reese."

"You don't just abandon people. Not even when something shinier comes along. Someone younger, prettier, newer, whatever."

Now I'm definitely talking about my own situation, and it's so obvious that I cringe. "You fight for what's important."

How did I lose myself? And my marriage? Those bars had come up years before Britt fell for my husband. That Christmas Eve a few years ago? Adrian was already gone from our marriage. So was I, if I'm being honest. How can I stop myself from repeating those mistakes in the future?

Oliver's brow furrows. "Ah dinna ken how anyone could leave you, Reese. I wouldna be able to."

I let myself let him in. Warmth blooms in my chest, filling all the vacant cavities like thick, sweet molasses, a sugar high that pulses through my body. This feels real. This *is* real.

"Please don't hide important things from me," I whisper and run my hands slowly up his chest, feeling each ridge of muscle, then up around his neck.

"I willna," he promises and lowers his lips to mine for a brief kiss, then pauses. "So, you think I have a cute arse?"

I laugh and kiss him back, because what else could I possibly do right now? But there are questions brimming inside of me. What are we doing? Are we acting with each other, staying so close in our roles that we can't even tell the difference anymore? I just admitted to myself that this is real, not fake.

I don't want to ask him, because at this moment, I don't want to know. All I want is to enjoy having Oliver's arms around me and pretend the way he looks at me is genuine. I'll let my perfectly planned life fall apart just a little, even if, deep down, I know how dangerous it is to let him close to my heart.

20

OLIVER

Monday, 8 August
12 Days Before the Birthday Party
Tweed Park

What a weekend.

With a bounce in my step, I stride down the High Street toward Tweed Park, on the outskirts of town near where I drew by the river. Reese is waiting for me with a picnic lunch.

We spent all Saturday morning at her flat in bed, exploring each other's bodies—her memorizing the lines of my tattoos, me tracing the curves of her body. We eventually got up and went for lunch at the pub before she met with Chelsea. But she came back to my house later in the evening.

I stride past her flat and check my phone for a response to my text that I'm on the way. There are no new ones from when I left my house ten minutes ago, but I scan through the last few messages in the text chain, which continued the second we parted yesterday.

REESE

What were you like in high school?

ME

I was football. Only football. No other sports, no other friends, just the game. Worked out. Traveled. Trained. Repeat.

REESE

That's intense.

ME

Aye. You?

REESE

Small group of friends who I've lost touch with, aside from annual Christmas cards and the occasional reunion. I played field hockey but gave it up when my dad died.

The house isn't mine, but having her perch at my kitchen table, lounge on my couch, curl up next to me in bed . . . fuck. It's a bloody good feeling.

She makes me feel so real and connected. Grounded. Not like I'm floating through this world with no moorings to keep me from drifting off.

There was no talk of fake dating, her ex-husband, or ex-friend. Nothing about the part where this will end in two weeks.

My phone buzzes in my hand and I hesitate before answering the unknown number as I pass The Old Forge.

"Aye," I say.

"Is that Oliver Vass?" an English-accented voice asks.

"It is."

"This is Karla Smith, from Crenshaw Football Club. Do you have a minute to talk about your assistant coach application?"

I skid to a stop and step out of the middle of the sidewalk to lean against the front window of The Peebles Beans.

"Oh, aye, of course." I keep my voice calm and collected, even though my heart is beating fast and loud. It'd been quiet since I responded to her email with screening questions. I'd assumed they'd moved forward with someone else.

"Right, well, I wanted to call to say that we're very interested in talking to you further about the open coaching position."

I clench my hand in a fist, all my energy vibrating down my arm. "That's good news."

"We'd like to set up a video call for you this week with John, our head coach, and a few of the other staff members."

She lists a few dates and times and I agree to all. David will understand if I have to duck out of camp for an hour or two.

"Right then. There's just one more topic."

"No problem. What is it?"

"At Crenshaw FC, we're a very family-oriented club."

A perfect visual of the tagline from their website appears in my head: *We're Scotland's Upstanding, Ethical, Family-Oriented Football Club.*

"Aye." I scrunch my face and shut my eyes. Dammit. Here it comes.

"Naturally, we are very impressed with your career as a professional footballer. So we've no doubt you have the experience and expertise to get this job done." She pauses. "However, we need to ensure that all members of our staff will be held to the utmost ethics and moral standards. Please have a long think about how our ethics and values have been reflected in your life. I know John often asks about it in his interviews."

Fuck me.

All I've done my whole life is work my arse off to be the best footballer. Can they fault me for having a hard time coping with the wreckage of that focus in the year after I left football? Losing the plot of my life a wee bit?

Och. Maybe they can.

I get it. I fault myself. My teeth grind together.

"Ah. Well. I went through a tough time for a while after leaving

Winchester FC. But I've worked hard on myself over the past year, keeping in top shape and ensuring there are no more, uh, incidents." I cringe.

There's a pause.

"Hmm. Well, wonderful, I suppose. Don't worry too much about it. But I don't want you to be surprised by the question if it comes up."

I flash back to the worst of the incidents—the one that was plastered over all the tabloids. Wrecked, I'd gotten in a fight with some drunken Welsh rugby player at a club at two o'clock in the morning. I'd punched him in the nose, and there'd been a lot of blood. But he'd been mostly fine. Bloody hell, you'd have thought I'd murdered someone. That was a few hours after they'd photographed me with a scantily clad woman on my lap, a bottle of vodka in one of my hands, her thigh in the other.

Not my best night. Probably one of my worst. But what did Crenshaw FC expect me to do about that now?

"I will be in touch to confirm the day and time of the interview, and I'll send a link to the video call. Sound good to you, Oliver?"

I agree and we end the call.

How am I going to prove that they can trust me? What could I do to show her I'm not that same person I was two years ago?

I shove off the glass window of the coffee shop and continue on to the park. I'm excited to tell Reese, but there's something unsettled in my gut. I play back my conversation with Karla. What'd she say again? That she was worried about my family values? Well, shite. I'll have to figure out how to address that during the interview.

AT THE PARK, I spot Reese sitting on a bench, facing away from me toward a small pond. Her laugh rings melodically through the air, head tilting down to the phone cradled in her hand. I stop and take in the sight of her waiting for me, letting the anticipation of kissing her flow through my body.

"Stella, hush." Her voice drifts over. "It's just a fling, like you guys told me to have. Promise."

My throat suddenly tightens. I canna clearly hear the response from her sister on speakerphone, but Reese keeps talking.

"Fine, yes, I said crush before. But then I said fling." Reese laughs. "No, please, don't look him up online. I googled him and I regret it. I don't want your opinions on what you find there. Just believe me: this is nothing."

I take a step backward, blinking wildly. I can hardly swallow, air struggling to get through my throat into my lungs. I spin and put another twenty feet between me and the park bench, far enough so I can no longer hear Reese talking. My instinct is to sprint away from this place and hide from her words. The joyful anticipation of talking to her has vanished.

Reese saw the same things as Karla Smith. She's also worried about my reputation. My integrity. My worthiness.

I'll just leave. Text her that David needs me and we can meet up later today. Or later this week. Or just for Lucas's birthday party.

Or never again.

Her laugh rings out again and I inhale sharply, letting it out slow. But isn't this what we talked about? Not running at the first sign of trouble. Staying. I have to physically insist that my body not leave this park. That's what she told me on Friday. Dinna bolt when things get hard. I might as well practice this skill with Reese, even if she considers us *nothing. Me* nothing.

I turn back. Reese is still and quiet, staring out at the pond, and I assume the call with her sister is finished.

Maybe that snippet of conversation I heard wasna anything to panic about. I might be forgetting what is going on here. We're fake dating. We had sex a bunch of times. Fantastic, hot sex. And we told each other deep, dark secrets about who we really are. That's no big deal, right?

I groan and take a few steps toward her.

But her words—*it's just a fling* and *believe me: this is nothing*—continue to repeat in my ears.

It *is* just a fling. Two weeks from today, Reese flies back to the States with Chelsea, Adrian, and Britt, two days after Lucas's birthday party. One day after our fake breakup.

But she didna say it was *fake* to her sister. Some of the knots in my stomach loosen. Maybe there is hope.

Hope for what, though?

Reese looks over her shoulder and a beautiful smile crosses her face when she sees me standing there.

My hesitation melts in the warm light of her beaming face, and I stride toward her and slip onto the bench. This is complicated, sure, but I'm going to appreciate Reese while she's here, whether it's in this park in Peebles, kissing her in the dim corners of Melrose Abbey, or next weekend's trip to Edinburgh Castle with the team. I'm gonna let myself enjoy this *fling*.

"Hey." The corners of her eyes crinkle with an adorable smile.

I lean forward, connecting our lips and pressing into the kiss more intensely than I'd planned. She breathes out and leans into me, letting me wrap my tongue around hers.

"I missed you too," she murmurs, our lips still connected.

That's real.

Neither of us even looks around to see if anyone is watching.

21

REESE

Saturday, August 13
9 Days Before Departure
Edinburgh Castle

Edinburgh Castle towers high in the center of the city, set on top of the giant rock that made it a military stronghold starting in the Iron Age. Yeah, I googled it, obviously, and then I had to search for when the Iron Age happened, which apparently was 1200 BC to 550 BC. Crap, that's old!

As we made the climb up the cobblestone street leading to its entrance, I gave Oliver some highlights of the history of Edinburgh Castle. I think he liked it. Or maybe he just likes *me*, because he kept smiling and brushing up against my arm, secretly linking a finger with mine so no one else can see. By the time we get to the castle, my legs are aching, but the view is worth it. From the ancient castle, we take in the gorgeous gardens below and the main street through town, with rows of modern shops mixed in with old architecture.

The girls swirl around in front of the admission window as David and his wife, the official chaperones of the overnight trip, hand out tickets. Chelsea's in the middle of a group of girls, laughing and whispering.

And I'm standing with Oliver, Adrian, and Britt. They wormed their way into coming on the girls' field trip, just like we did, I guess. None of us are actually chaperones. We're all just tagging along, having a lovely adventure in Edinburgh together.

This whole situation is becoming more unhinged every day.

"Have you been enjoying your time in Scotland?" Oliver, who I'm currently sleeping with, asks Adrian, the father of my child.

"Yup, we are. Went up to see Loch Ness this week, then spent a few days in Glasgow." Adrian's eyes dart over to me, as if he's still trying to figure out how this all works. Should he be happy for me, annoyed by the situation, or completely ambivalent? Given the whole I-made-him-lie-by-omission-to-our-daughter thing, I'd guess he's leaning annoyed.

Britt slides over to me while Oliver gives Adrian travel tips for the remaining time we're in town.

"Hey. How was your week?" She stares into my face intently.

I've avoided meeting up with her since we got together for coffee ten days ago, when she inadvertently told me about Lucas. Her forehead is creased, and she sucks in her top lip. She's texted me a handful of times and I always respond quickly with surface-level answers, hoping it'll be enough to fend her off.

She's worried about me, but learning Oliver's secret only brought me and him closer. It strengthened our connection, made the sex more emotional, his touches more explosive.

"It was great. Thanks for asking."

She cringes at my too-bright response.

Something shifted in me over the vanilla lattes at The Peebles Beans. It was like that Christmas Eve, when I should have realized there was something going on between Adrian and Britt. I don't want to ignore this gut feeling that I screwed up, not by fake dating Oliver, but by agreeing to be friends with Britt.

She wants to be close with me again, but does she want me to be happy? I think she does, but maybe her worry has something else beneath it. Maybe she wants to have me in her close-knit group of people and it's driving her wild that I'm not letting it happen. She's lost that control best friends have over each other. I miss her, too . . . don't I? But what, exactly, do I miss? And is it even possible to recreate?

My body betrays me, and I step closer and whisper, "Everything is good with me and Oliver, if that's what you want to know."

In the background, Oliver is telling Adrian about Stirling, his hometown and a tourist destination, where the birthday party will be. And after it's over, we'll break up. And then I'll get on an airplane. Where has this month gone? A soft squeak escapes my constricted throat.

"Well, that's awesome. But just another week, right?" She lays her hand on my arm, squeezing gently, kindly, the way a friend would.

Dammit, but she looks deeply concerned, and I'm horrified to realize there's a stinging of tears in the back of my eyes.

I will not cry in front of this woman. Not about anything, especially not about a man. But I'm not sure that's what these tears are for. It's more complicated than that.

"Yup. Another week." I nod.

"Scotland is beautiful. I'm so glad we all came." She swallows visibly, her eyes glassy.

"You okay?"

Britt nods and attempts a smile. "I miss Jackson so much. I thought it was going to be fine to be apart for a month. I mean, I knew I'd miss him, but we have FaceTime, and he texts every day. But this has been really hard." She looks off toward the castle and the group of girls. "I would have only seen him for a weekend between camps, but at least that would have been something."

"I knew it'd be hard for you. A month is a long time. That's why I came. And stayed." I leave out the part about desperately needing a break from my life back home, where I'm constantly around Adrian and Britt. Because of them, I didn't get the reset I'd hoped for.

The girls trail after the tour guide ahead, while Coach David and his wife bring up the rear.

"You know me so well," Britt says, making my insides twist in response.

"I don't know about that."

She nods. "You do. And you're smart. You've always been more logical than I am. Reasonable."

"Mmm." I clench my jaw. That feels like a backhanded compliment. Was I being reasonable when I asked Adrian for a divorce? When I gave them my blessing? Agreed to be friends with her again?

Britt looks back at me. "Let's have coffee when we get back to New Jersey, okay? I just . . ."

She glances at the stone walkway, her pretty black eyelashes fluttering. I can feel another speech coming on, one about how she misses us being best friends, before she did what she did, before Adrian did what he did.

As soon as the group disappears up the winding stairs to the summit of the castle, Oliver appears next to me, sliding an arm around my shoulders, cutting in before Britt can finish her sentence, before I have to find a way to get out of this conversation.

He's saving me. Like he's supposed to. Touching me. Like I want him to.

I look up at Oliver. He's gotten me through my time here, not just as a buffer, but so much more. Three weeks ago, I thought the only thing I needed was protection from my ex and his fiancée. But now, I realize I've gotten myself into worse trouble.

My fake relationship has turned decidedly real. Maybe I need another kind of protection, but from myself and the growing thing in me, its smooth, beautiful, invasive vines burrowing into the crevices of my body. How could I have insisted to my sisters that this is just a fling? That it's nothing? It makes my stomach turn just thinking of the conversation I had with Stella in the park last week.

"Alright, Jersey?" Oliver's brow furrows.

"Yeah." I tilt my head up and he leans down to kiss me. Right in front of Adrian and Britt. But that's not even the point anymore.

I don't want to lose Oliver.

That's the unsettled feeling I've had all day. While we drove the hour to Edinburgh, skipping the bus ride with the girls, he told me all about his video interview with Crenshaw FC. It went great and they love him. I'm not surprised. He's amazing and any club would be lucky to have him. He's got talent, which is undisputed, but he's also got the patience and skills to coach. I've seen it myself.

I'm too scared to ask if that coaching job is what he really wants. A few weeks ago, I might have. Now I have more invested. Surely it's what he really wants. What do I expect? That he's going to choose me instead of the coaching job he knows he needs? There's no good endgame for us.

I have a life firmly rooted in New Jersey, like a thousand-year-old giant sequoia. Chelsea's got two more years of high school. I have a job, a life. Peanut Butter.

And Oliver's life is here—at least it will be—once he gets settled in a permanent job. Lucas is in Stirling, and Oliver wants nothing more than to be in his son's life, which is his whole point in having this fake relationship with me. He's got excellent job prospects coaching in Scotland. This is where he belongs.

He can't give it all up and come to New Jersey. And I can't stay here. A long-distance relationship would never work. It's hard enough having my sister that far away; a boyfriend is a no-go option. I refuse to put myself through that.

This . . . whatever I have with Oliver . . . is going to end in a week. And there's nothing I can do to stop it.

I SHOULD PAY MORE attention to the iconic Scottish heritage site we're touring, but all I see is Oliver. The waves of hair falling over his forehead, the comforting strength of his arms, the burning gaze he directs only at me.

Instead of exploring the many displays, we find quiet corners to kiss and touch each other. It's ballsy, considering my daughter and the other girls are wandering the castle. After soaking in the gorgeous view of Edinburgh and the gardens below, we head toward the exit, thinking we'll sneak out and grab lunch or a drink somewhere.

"Guys!" Britt calls us from behind.

"Wanna make a run for it?" Oliver whispers, his breath warm in my ear.

"I'm not a very fast runner."

"I am, hen. I can throw you over my shoulder."

I laugh, considering the offer, but turn anyway. Britt appears in front of us like an unwanted face-cream salesperson at the mall.

"Want to grab coffee somewhere? Adrian and I were about to leave, too."

Oliver waits for me to respond, squeezing his arm around my waist in solidarity.

"Sure," I say, even though my instinct is to say no. I take her in as she smiles widely at my agreement. I loved her once. That love is still there, somewhere, but now, it's mixed with so many other negative emotions, like pink and blue and green paint swirling together to make an ugly brown.

We all trek out of the castle grounds, down the steep cobblestone road, Britt and Adrian in front, us trailing. The two of them are whispering to each other. It doesn't look like sweet nothings. Perhaps my ex-husband has reached his limit on how much time he wants to spend with me? One can only hope.

I grab Oliver's hand and he entwines his fingers with mine, a perfect fit. There's a pub called The Bull and the Thistle in one of the alleyways, and Oliver glances down at me, eyebrows raised.

"Yes, please." A pint absolutely sounds like a better idea than coffee, given the circumstances.

"Let's duck in here," Oliver calls.

They nod and turn in. I was hoping it'd be too crowded for us all to sit together in a pub just a stone's throw from Edinburgh Castle, but alas, it's only eleven in the morning, and the tourists are still busy touring. There's a table for four next to the bar.

"Pints?" Oliver questions as we all get settled.

"I'll grab them." Adrian darts away.

Britt is smiling at us, a giant, wide grin, looking back and forth between our faces.

Oliver grins back and slides one of his hands on my thigh, rubbing up and down. Britt's eyes flit down at the movement. I stifle a squeak.

"So, Britt, what do you do back in the US?" Oliver asks.

She sighs with relief at one of her favorite conversation topics. "Oh, I run an app startup incubator. We do a lot of corporate trainings, specifically in video game format."

The worst thing about Britt is she's not only beautiful and kind—when she's not stealing husbands—but also super smart. She worked a normal corporate job for years, but after having Jackson and getting a prestigious MBA, she started a successful app incubator, running it out of her renovated garage, renamed The Idea Garage. She's a bit of a celebrity in our Jersey town.

Adrian returns to the table, sliding a pint to me and Britt before returning for the other two.

Oliver's eyebrows are raised, looking impressed at the pitch Britt is giving him. He runs his hands further up my thigh, dangerously high but still technically appropriate, and I turn in my hard wooden chair to stare at his profile.

His jawline is to die for, the kind that people draw in hot superhero sketches. His skin is smooth and clear, and his lips red and oh-so-capable. Wavy strands of hair hang on the sides of his face, and I have the urge to tuck them behind his ears, climb on his lap, and kiss his mouth.

"Reese?" Oliver's now looking at me, his mouth quirking on one side.

Uh-oh. "Sorry, what was the question?" I drag my eyes from Oliver's gorgeous face to the couple across the table from us, a much less impressive view.

Adrian's jaw is clenched, and he looks like he'd rather be anywhere in the world than where he is.

"I was just saying, I think you have some great business ideas that we could try to get a team for, right?" Britt smiles at me tentatively.

This again? Years ago—before all the drama—Britt and I had talked a few startup ideas related to digital graphic design. All of that got dropped, obviously.

"I'm pretty happy with my current job. They did let me come to Scotland for the summer, you know?"

"Oh, we could work that out, too. You'd be your own boss, mostly."

"Mmm." I stare at her, eyes growing wide as I picture Britt as my literal boss. Oliver squeezes my leg. I lay my hand on top of his and move it farther up. He lets out a quiet, amused grunt.

"How about you, Oliver? What are your plans after summer camp?" Adrian says, making it sound like Oliver is the one attending camp. My fake boyfriend doesn't flinch.

"I'm working that all out now." He keeps steady eye contact with Adrian. "I'm looking to coach professionally."

"Right. Here in Scotland?"

"Aye."

My heart twists at Oliver's confident response.

"Well. Good luck with that." Adrian's eyes flit toward me for a beat. "Britt's lucky she gets to be her own boss, but most of us don't have that privilege." Adrian glances down at his fiancée, a softer look on his face.

"It is pretty great." She flutters her eyelashes.

They're a beautiful couple. Perfect for each other, and they absolutely adore one another.

But there is no place for me in their relationship. What was I thinking? I can't be friends with her. Co-parents with Adrian, yes, absolutely. Casual acquaintances with Britt, sure. But this path we've been going down, coffee dates, trying to let myself open up to her again . . . it can't work. Why did I agree to that? And how can I possibly back out of it, after everything we've been through, after she lost her dad this spring? After I officially caved to her requests for friendship?

Maybe I just need more time, more space for everything to fade away. Maybe a few months—years?—will change how I feel.

I take their distraction with each other as an opportunity to whisper in Oliver's ear. "Hey, Picasso. Let's get out of here."

Adrian and Britt turn to look at us right away. I guess my whisper wasn't as subtle as I thought.

Oliver grins. "Well, this has been fun," he says to Adrian and Britt, draining his pint.

"So much fun." I nod enthusiastically and follow his lead, chugging my pint and getting it just below halfway. A bit dribbles down my chin and I wipe it with my sleeve, like the lady I am.

"Reese and I have a few things we're going to do in Edinburgh." Oliver pushes back his chair and stands, holding out a hand to me.

With a quick wave, I let Oliver lead me away from the bar and out the door into the Edinburgh streets.

It terrifies me to realize I'd follow this man anywhere.

"Thanks for rescuing me." I peer up at Oliver from under his arm, leaving The Bull and the Thistle at our backs.

"That's what I'm here for." He meets my gaze.

But I didn't just want to get away from Adrian and Britt back there. I want to be alone with Oliver. I wish I could climb into his head and see what he's thinking.

A week.

Deep down, I know I should pull away and protect myself more than I am, not let him sweep me up with his sweet words, vulnerable gazes reserved just for me, and hot-as-hell sex.

We walk down the curvy cobblestone street, the sound of bagpipes getting louder as we approach Waverley Train Station. The half pint warms my belly, and the sun is out, making the city glow and the people in it smile. But all I want to do is go back to the hotel room with Oliver.

We turn the corner and an older man in a kilt is blowing into a set of bagpipes, his cheeks as red as cherries, so red I'm afraid he'll pop a blood vessel in an eyeball. I grin and pull Oliver's hand to a stop.

"Do you have a kilt?" I ask after we move on from the

screeching sound. I immediately picture him in traditional Scottish gear.

"I do. It's in storage." He gives me a half grin and I prepare to say something dirty, but a woman's voice—with an incredulous ring to it—calls out from ahead of us.

"Oliver?"

We both look up at the source and halt in the middle of the sidewalk.

A tall, slender brunette towers in the middle of the sidewalk, six feet ahead of us. She's in ripped, wide-legged jeans, an effortlessly cute but casual cropped t-shirt, and is wearing a thin scarf around her neck and a small backpack over her shoulder. Impossibly trendy. Beautiful. And young. Light-blue eyes to match Oliver's, olive skin, and long dark hair parted in the middle.

It's the woman from my regretful Oliver Vass Google search. The one dressed in a sparkly, spaghetti-strapped black dress, cozying up next to a dashing Oliver in a fancy tux. The photo was taken at a movie premiere, the headline had announced. So she looks gorgeous in black tie *and* when super casual.

The woman's gazing at Oliver now, a mixed bag of emotions on her face. Her brow furrows, and she looks angry, but her jaw hangs open in surprise. The corners of her eyes *aren't* crinkling in a fond smile.

Not that this woman has one wrinkle or line marring her face. She's years away from spotting crow's feet. I run my hand through my hair after pausing first on my forehead, which is already sprouting well-earned cracks.

"Kendall, it's good to see you," Oliver says.

I turn away from the woman to see Oliver's reaction, but his face is a blank slate, betraying nothing. Kendall. The one who broke up with him when he got let go from Winchester FC. I swallow a lump in my throat and look back at the woman.

"Is it?" Her words have a bite to them.

He blinks at her. "Aye. It's been two years." His voice is soft and kind. Kendall glares at him and grunts, an ugly sound in contrast to her appearance.

"Feels like yesterday." She reaches up and smooths her hair.

Oliver stiffens next to me. Ouch.

"This is Reese," Oliver says after a beat's silence, not looking down at me.

I wait for him to say more, curious about how he'll define me, but he stops there, a hollow look on his face.

"Lovely to make your acquaintance." Kendall's pretty eyes narrow at me. I'm surprised she doesn't add something like: *you old hag*. Maybe I should save him from Kendall, the way he's been saving me.

"You too. We're just running to meet someone. Shall we, Oliver?" I slip my arm around his waist and tug on him, since he seems frozen to the spot.

He nods. "Take care, Kendall."

I pull him away and glance over my shoulder to make sure we put some distance between us and his ex, who is watching us depart.

"Wow. She hates you, huh."

"She's my ex, the one who dumped me as soon as I left football."

"I figured. Why does she hate you if she's the one that broke it off?"

He sighs and swallows audibly. "I wasna a good boyfriend. At the time, I resented her for breaking up with me like that, but I didna miss her. And I'm sure she didna miss me." Oliver's forehead crinkles.

"What's that face for?"

"She does seem like she hates me. I'm just . . . surprised."

"Maybe she *did* miss you."

I'd be pretty sad if I lost a man like Oliver. Which I will, in nine days. I used to think the problem was that we were pretending. It turns out, the real problem is that our lives are three thousand miles apart, separated by an ocean, and kept apart by kids who need us to be there for them.

Oliver grabs my hand and squeezes. Without even talking about it, we're heading in the hotel's direction, which is only two city blocks away.

"Kendall and I werena fake dating," he says after a block's worth of silence. "We were actually together. But never once did it feel as real as it does with you."

We stop at a busy road, waiting for the light to change so we can cross. I turn my body and pull him close. He wraps his arms over the top of mine and gazes into my eyes, his face as serious as I've ever seen it. My heart's thumping loudly in my chest and there's a lump in my throat.

"It's possible I'm pretending way less than I thought I would be." I tilt my head up to his, needing to feel his lips on mine. There are painful moments ahead of us, but for now, he's mine, so I don't want to waste any more time. Moving my hands up his chest and around his neck, I bring our mouths together, our bodies molding against each other.

"Let's go back to the room," he growls into my mouth.

***

OLIVER HAS me pressed up against the wall outside his hotel room, gently grinding his hips against mine as he fumbles in his pocket for the room key.

I'd paid for my own room, which was nonsensical considering there was no way we'd be spending the night apart, but I was too chicken to risk Chelsea or the girls seeing us go into a room together.

But right now, I don't care that we're in the hallway and anyone could walk by. I flick my tongue in Oliver's mouth and bury my hands in his hair, desire pooling in between my legs. I want him so much it hurts.

I'm not sure I'll ever get enough of Oliver Vass.

The door beeps. He pushes it open and drags me inside, his hand pressing hard on my ass so our hips don't lose contact.

I'd take him right now, against the wall of the hotel room. I would have done it in the hallway. Well, maybe not actually.

Oliver stops. "Let's take our time." He leans his forehead against mine, breathing heavy.

I moan and shove my hands under the bottom hem of his shirt, running them along his boxer line. "You want to go slow?" I whisper.

"Aye, Jersey. Slow." He grabs both my wrists in one of his hands and lifts them above my head, pressing them against the wall. After a long, lingering kiss that has me shaking, he buries his head in my neck, placing small kisses along my collarbone as he glides his other hand under my tank top and up my bare back.

Shivers run up and down my body.

"Oliver," I groan. His lips curl up against the base of my neck. I can't think, can't move, can't react. Oliver's my fantasy in physical form, plucked from my wildest dreams. Hot, ripped, sexy-as-hell with a growling Scottish accent—and all his attention on me.

I wish this were just sexual. Just lust. But there's so much more to it.

Oliver unhooks my bra and slides his hand around to my front, shoving my shirt up until my breasts are exposed, then pausing to pull my tank top over my head and slide my bra off my shoulders, finally releasing my wrists.

"You're so beautiful." He covers my mouth with his and wraps his tongue around mine, slowly exploring the inside of my mouth, as if we haven't been doing this nonstop for a week. His fingers rub my nipple, squeezing just hard enough to make me squirm, to make me breathe faster.

"Reese," he says against my lips, his hands sliding down around my waist.

"Mmm?" My breasts feel abandoned without his attention. I

bury my head in his neck, sucking on the bear's claws one by one, kissing them, licking them, breathing them in. I slide a hand down the ridges of his abdomen and over the bulge in the front of his pants. His breath gets faster.

"I . . ." He trails off, and I look up from my place on his neck.

"You okay?"

He nods. "Aye. More than okay." Something in his face tells me he wants to tell me more, but when he takes my hand off of his groin and yanks my jeans off my ass—along with my underwear— I'm too distracted to push for more.

Clothing is pooled around my ankles, and I step out of it, having to wiggle to get the damn skinny jeans all the way off. I swear under my breath, and Oliver chuckles.

"What? They're trendy. I think. At least they used to be. But fucking hard to get off."

"You're the height of fashion."

"Hey, are you making fun of my hoodie wardrobe?" I grab his hands and place them on my bare ass, needing him to touch me.

But he doesn't move forward. Instead, he steps back to look me up and down, licking his lips, his eyes burning for me.

"I'd never make fun of you." He runs a finger from my lips over my chin and down my neck, curving over my right breast, pausing on my nipple, then continuing down the center of my body until he gets to the top of my mound, burying his single finger into my wet core, gliding it back and forth, barely touching me, leaving me aching for a harder pressure. Damn, but this man knows what I like.

"Oliver," I moan.

"You're so wet for me, Jersey."

I pull him closer by his shoulders but he leaves a bit of distance between us, staring down at where his finger strokes me, adding another as the friction builds in my core. I squirm against his fingers.

"Fuck me, please." Yeah, that's me, begging for sex. What have I become? I don't hate it.

"Soon." He steps back from the wall and walks backward toward the bed, leading me with one hand on my ass, the other with two fingers pulsing inside me. He pushes me back onto the bed, my legs hanging off, then kneels in front of me, opening my legs to where his fingers are stroking me.

"Don't make me wait," I whisper.

"Open your legs," he growls, and I comply. "That's a good girl." He groans and I hear his zipper go down.

"Now, Oliver?" I'm desperate to feel him inside me. I need him. I need him now, because in nine days it'll be over. I want to remember every time, every kiss, every touch.

"Not yet."

Instead of entering me, he kisses the inside of my thighs, starting just above my knees. Right before he gets to my clit, he slides his fingers out and replaces them with his tongue, licking and sucking and massaging.

The edges of my vision start to blacken as waves of pleasure wait just around the next lick of his tongue. His fingers slide back in and he sucks me so hard, it pushes me over the edge. I scream out as the orgasm overtakes me. Oliver keeps his head buried between my legs until the waves of pleasure fade.

"Sweet baby Jesus," I whisper, unable to move.

He slides next to me on the bed, wiping his mouth on his arm and leaning on his side, his cock exposed and hard as a lead pipe against my thigh. Oliver grabs my hand and kisses each finger, his lips soft and gentle against my skin. I close my eyes and appreciate the moment. The peace. The anticipation. The . . . whatever else is brewing inside me.

"Reese." He switches to my other hand. "You are brilliant."

I turn my head and open my eyes. "*I* am? I think what you just did was pretty spectacular." It was more than spectacular, really. These past two weeks, I've had the best time of my life.

The best sex of my life, I mean.

He's so serious. I turn my still-naked body to his, pressing myself against him, his t-shirt still on, his hard dick against my belly. Warmth blooms inside my chest as we let the electric pulse of our feelings connect with each other, sparks flying. I bury my hand in his hair, needing another contact point between us.

Damn. This is too much. These feelings are too overwhelming. I refuse to name them, but they're there, whether I do or not.

I want to know more of what's going on behind those eyes. Is he realizing how incredible he is? How much he's worth, regardless of what anyone else has told him in his life? Is he seeing it reflected in my eyes?

I hope so. I hope he finds a life that makes him happy. I'm devastated to know I won't be a part of it.

How can I be?

23

OLIVER

Sunday, 14 August
6 Days Before the Birthday Party
Edinburgh Hotel

"I'm going to grab you a proper coffee," I say through the hotel bathroom door.

"The biggest one you can order!" she calls back. I bite back a raunchy retort and leave her singing an aimless tune.

I glance down at the text message I got a few minutes ago from Karla Smith at Crenshaw FC, asking me to call her when I have a free minute. The video interview went well last week. I talked to Karla, another one of the assistant coaches, and John, the head coach. We had a lively conversation about coaching styles and what I'd experienced as a player. Our interview felt cut short as he had to run to a training, but we connected on more than a surface level.

I'd been fashing about the personal questions, but there'd been no discussion about family values or probing around my previous bad behavior. I bet we just didna get to that part of the interview before running out of time.

After the call, I felt hopeful for the future. Maybe coaching would be fun. Coaching *is* fun. It's another version of football. I enjoy every day with the young lassies at camp. Maybe all my dread and hesitation have been for nothing, and this is what I'm supposed to be doing.

Then why didna I tell Reese I'm calling Karla?

I dash out of the hotel room, down the hallway and two flights of steps, shaking that thought out of my head. Once I'm outside in the quiet gray Edinburgh Sunday morning, I make the call. The city is quiet, but when Karla answers, I step down a side street lined with parked cars to avoid the occasional double-decker bus roaring in the background.

"Thanks so much for talking to me on a Sunday morning. I apologize for that." A keyboard clicks. "I'm trying to get things lined up for the week."

"It's nae bother." Getting things lined up sounds promising. I swallow and wait for her to continue.

"Well. It might be no surprise to you, but John was very impressed with your conversation the other day, and he'd like to schedule time to meet you in person this week for a final interview."

I grin and pump my hand in the air.

"I'm so glad to hear that," I say with a steady voice.

"How does Thursday look? I know you are working at a camp. Can you come up to Crenshaw-on-the-Sea first thing in the morning that day? It'd also be a chance for you to check out the town. It's a lovely little place, if you haven't been. Right by some truly breathtaking cliffs overlooking the ocean. Views made for postcards."

"Aye," I say without hesitation. I know David will support this, even if it means being gone for one of the last days of camp.

But as I agree, I realize that I'll be missing one of my final nights with Reese, as I'll need to drive up north the night before. She's leaving a few days after that. My insides twist and that feeling of dread snakes back into my core. Nae. I canna think about that now.

"Congratulations! I'll email you the details."

"So . . ." I sense she's about to end the call. "I guess there are no more concerns about, uh, how I'd fit in to the club? With the values and family-oriented foundation?" I sound like a confused twat. I dinna wanna directly ask the question: *Do they care about my drunken antics and womanizing from that short time of my life, which is captured all over the internet?*

She pauses for a beat, and the silence is as heavy as the rock Edinburgh Castle rests on.

I want this job, and I'm afraid I'm not worthy of it. *That's* what the feeling of dread is telling me. Reese is amazing, but she's distracted me from my goals this summer. It's been a braw distraction, but one that's going to end, and I'd best keep that in mind over the next week.

"Everyone was very impressed with you. But we have two other candidates coming in person this week. The team will take everything into consideration after they've talked to all three of you. Fit is very important to us."

Fuck me. I sigh, then realize she'll have heard that over the phone. After clearing my throat, I give another sales pitch.

"I'm rebuilding my life. It's taken a few years after leaving Winchester FC, but now all that's important to me is my son"—I swallow, thinking of how I'd kept him from Reese—"and coaching."

"Of course," she murmurs in agreement.

"And I have a wonderful, er, wholesome girlfriend now." I cringe as soon as the words are out of my mouth. Wholesome? I'm a wanker. That word should've stayed locked away in my head. What am I doing, telling her about Reese? But maybe Karla and John and all of Crenshaw FC *do* care about my personal life, and maybe more details will help them understand I could be who they need in a coach and a role model.

"Oh?"

"Aye. Her name is Reese. She's coming with me to my son's tenth birthday party next weekend in Stirling."

I shove my free hand in the pocket of my athletic shorts and squeeze my eyes shut. *Fucking oversharing.*

"Oh, lovely," Karla says. I canna read her tone.

"She's American and has a teenage daughter. She's perfectly normal. Nothing like anyone else I've been with before."

What I don't say is how beautiful she is. How her skin feels beneath my hands. How she treats me. Like I'm more than just a footballer. Like I'm a complete human being. In a few short weeks, she's made me start to feel whole again.

Karla's quiet.

And the woman who has done all that is leaving in a week. I run my hand through my hair, pulling too hard. I haven't told Reese any of these things. But what's the point? This was always going to be temporary. A fake arrangement.

Well, it's no longer fake, but it's definitely still temporary.

"Good for you, Oliver. That transition can be hard for a lot of footballers."

So Karla *does* know how I behaved. She has seen the pictures. A quick online search brings them up straightaway. Googling me would've been the logical thing to do.

"I'll send off a picture of Reese, Lucas, and myself at his birthday party." It's a brilliant but terrifying idea to send Karla a picture of the three of us. I have plenty of selfies of me and Reese, but no recent pictures of me with Lucas, let alone me, Reese, and Lucas, as they've never even met.

Reese will understand what I need to do to establish my new life. For Lucas. Or, I'll just not tell her this bit. I have to prioritize getting this job over everything else.

"No pressure to do something like that, Oliver." Karla's voice softens. "Just be yourself, and that will be perfect. I know John is eager to get someone on board, so he wants to decide within a week."

It doesna sit well in my belly to use Reese like this, even though this whole arrangement has been about using each other to get what we needed this summer. But still, it's like running into Kendall yesterday: a reminder of a life in which I used people, and they used me. I thought Kendall didna care, that losing me was no big deal. But seeing her yesterday? I'm no longer sure that's true. She seemed more upset than I would've thought.

Debris from my past swirls around my insides like a tiny tornado. Somewhere in there is how I feel about Reese, a crackling power source yanked up from the earth and thrown in the air. But I'm feart to jump in the middle of that chaos and grab it. I'd definitely get hurt if I tried to put a label on how I feel.

Not when she's going to return to her life in New Jersey, and I'm going to start a new life here.

Long distance canna work. There's absolutely no ending that has us living on the same continent at any point in the future, so there's no point in trying to make a relationship work, even a long-distance one.

Not that we've ever discussed that as a possibility. And we never will.

My focus is on me and Lucas. My new life in Scotland. If I can get this job, if I can be in Lucas's life . . . that's the new foundation I need. I wish Reese could be a part of it. But it's not possible. She'll leave and I'll have to face the world alone again.

"It's no problem. I'll send you a photo on Saturday, next weekend. It'll be after my final interview, but hopefully not too late."

Karla ends the call, and I open my eyes to a couple strolling along the street, holding hands and murmuring to each other, in their own little world.

The coffee shop I have in mind is two blocks away in the direction of the towering castle. I stride in that direction, building a fortified wall around my heart, keeping out the feelings of regret trying to get inside.

None of this is settling in my mind, and ah dinna ken why. I'm getting exactly what I need. I should focus on what's ahead of me. Not Reese.

Then why do I want to forget the coffee and go for a punishing run? Why do I want to run back to Ireland and hunker down in Ian's tattoo parlor?

I shake my head. No, this doesna feel right.

24

OLIVER

Tuesday, 16 August
4 Days Before the Birthday Party
Oliver's House

Cat stands on my front porch, her red curls piled in a bun on her head, prominent freckles leading a messy parade from the bridge of her nose to her cheeks, her lips pressed in a tight line. When the knock sounded on the door, I'd assumed it was Reese, and I was about to remind her to just walk in.

I wasna prepared to greet my son's mum instead.

Seeing Cat's face brings up so many emotions, with regret for how things ended with her long ago always prominent. I fled Stirling after breaking up with her a decade ago, and a month later, when she called to tell me she was pregnant, I became an absentee father as well as a wanker ex-boyfriend.

"Cat. Hallo. What are you doing here?"

"Hi, Oliver." Her voice is confident. She's beautiful, even more so than when I left her at twenty-two. Cat easily stepped into motherhood, at least that's what it looked like from my point of view. She got a job in our hometown in retail, eventually moved

196

out of her parents' house with Lucas, and all four grandparents have helped raise him. She's given Lucas a good life so far, with only financial help from me.

But what is she doing at my doorstep in Peebles on a Tuesday evening, when I'm gonna see her in Stirling on Saturday?

"Can I come in?"

I nod and move aside. "Of course."

She steps into the house, and I let the front door swing shut.

It's been eighteen months since I last saw her. Eighteen months since I showed up at her house with just an hour's notice, hungover and with my life in shambles. That day will stand out in my memory forever, shrouded in shame. I was rude to her boyfriend and angry that my son knew him better than he'd ever known me. And then she kicked me out and told me not to come back.

"Are you still coming to Lucas's party this weekend?" She crosses her arms.

"Aye, of course."

"Well . . ." Cat sighs deeply. "I just wanted to double check. I havena told him yet. I dinna want him to get his hopes up." She tilts her chin in the air.

"Ouch." I flinch.

"Your parents will be there. Grant, too. A bunch of other people. Will you be able to handle that?"

She's got no faith in me. I suppose I deserve none. I've always prioritized football over Lucas. And I bet when I left the game two years ago, she thought I'd give him more time. Make more space in my brain and heart for them.

I failed that test.

Her jaw clenches and I take a second before responding. She drove an hour and a half to screen me in person for this party.

"Cat . . ."

She sucks in her lips and crinkles her forehead. She's nervous.

Anxious that I'm going to let our son down once again. A giant lump forms in my throat.

"Are you going to be there or not, Oliver?"

"Aye, yes. I promise. I'm coming." Ah dinna ken how to reassure her that this time—unlike every other time I've flitted in and out of their lives—I'm committed. "I'm starting a new life. Yeh ken? And I want to make sure Lucas is in it. Or, at least, I'm in it for Lucas."

She examines my face, eyes narrowed, deciding whether or not to believe me.

"Grant and I are engaged now. He was there the last time you came by. He's always there." She pauses and lets me remember, once again, that disastrous last visit.

"Congratulations, Cat." I swallow. I'm happy for her. She deserves someone dependable. For her and for Lucas. But it's still like a punch in my gut that there's already a father figure in Lucas's life. Someone who's been around and will always be around.

Thank fuck Reese will be with me on Saturday. Between seeing Cat and Grant as Lucas's happy little family and facing my distant, cold parents . . . But I think I can stand anything with Reese by my side.

"Grant moved in with us last year. Lucas loves him." She uncrosses her arms and touches her stomach. "And I'm pregnant."

"Wow," I say. "Congrats, again."

"Why *wow?*" Her eyes narrow. "I'm thirty-two, in a loving relationship with a man who has a good job. I love him, and he loves me and Lucas, and this baby."

"Cat . . ." Fuck, I'm screwing this up before I even get to the party.

"And if you are going to be anything but lovely to Grant and everyone there, you are not invited. *Yeh ken?* We have a good thing going, and I dinna need you messing with Lucas just when we're all truly happy."

There are tears in Cat's eyes, and I struggle to decide what to say to her. I can only imagine how happy the four of them will be. I dinna want to mess that up. For an instant, I'm tempted to bolt. To tell her I, too, dinna want to risk messing things up for Lucas.

Then I remember Reese, and the thought of her brings me strength. She told me I could be a father to Lucas. That I deserved to get the chance. Maybe she's right.

"I have no intention of causing any kind of chaos for you or Lucas. I just want a chance to be in his life."

Her face softens and she blinks. It occurs to me that Cat maybe doesna want me to fuck up, either. That she doesna want me to fail as a father or as a person.

"Sorry for jumping down your throat." Her shoulders lower and she rolls her neck, as if she'd been tense.

Maybe if I'd taken the time to get to know her over the past decade, we could've been friends.

"No worries. I understand why you did." I attempt to relax my face. It's not surprising we dinna trust each other. "Actually, I'd like to bring my, uh, girlfriend, to the party, if that's okay."

"Your girlfriend?" Cat tilts her head, and the softness morphs to suspicion.

"Aye." I gesture through the family room to the kitchen. "Wanna have a cuppa?"

Cat glances at the door, then at my kitchen table before nodding.

I lead the way and she slides into a cushioned chair while I put the kettle on.

"Tell me more about her."

It's an obvious question Cat would ask, but the answer—the American mum of one of the campers—doesna exactly inspire confidence. I dodge the inquiry.

"It's hard to explain what it is with Reese, but there's something special between us." I didna expect to have a close one-to-one conversation with my son's mum about my relationship with Reese, but here we are.

"Hmm." She's examining my face, not quite buying my story, but also not telling me to sod off.

"And I have an interview with Crenshaw FC on Thursday for an assistant coach position." I pour hot water into her mug over a Scottish breakfast tea bag and slide it over.

"Wow." Cat raises her eyebrows and accepts the steaming beverage. "I didna realize you wanted to coach."

"What else would I do, right?"

She nods. "Aye, that's true."

Reese thinks I can do more. She balked at the assumption that I'm defined by football.

"I have no other skills."

"Mmm." The sound is neither an agreeing nor disagreeing one. Yet Cat must agree that I have no other prospects. My heart lurches. I wonder what she says to Lucas about me. If anything.

"How do you take it?" I pause by my refrigerator. I dinna know how my son's mum takes her tea, and that seems like the perfect manifestation of me never being around.

"Cream and sugar."

I nod and bring them over to the table.

We sip our hot tea in silence for a moment, staring at each other. She's assessing me—judging me—assuming I'm gonna fuck it all up. She's probably right, somehow, no matter what Reese says.

"Well. And what about this girl? Where'd you find her? Some football groupie? How old is she?"

I flinch. For her to even ask how old my girlfriend is says something about my past.

"She's thirty-seven."

Cat's eyebrows shoot up. "A wee bit old for you, nae?"

"Only five years older. I'd hardly call that a major age gap."

"Aye, ah ken you didna mind going the other way. What was the last one called? She was always in your lap at some event or the other. Or was she different from the one that got you in the tabloids?"

I bite my tongue. There's nothing I can say to defend my past choices. And maybe my current decisions aren't great either, as I'm talking to my ex-girlfriend about my current (fake) girlfriend, who I have a breakup scheduled with for this Sunday. I'm reminded that I need to be focusing on my future, which doesna involve Reese, and I should keep that in mind for these last few days. To protect myself.

I open my mouth to say something, but words fail me. Instead, I reach my hand over and cover one of hers.

"I'm sorry, Cat. For being so shite. But I'm starting anew. I'm going to be different from now on."

She takes her other hand and lays it over mine, a small, sad smile crossing her face.

"I hope so. It would mean the world to Lucas. And to me."

The look on her face tells me I'm doing the right things. Cat doesna hate me. I willna screw things up with Lucas. I have a future, and for the first time in years, it doesna feel bleak. If I just repeat those words to myself, maybe they'll come true.

A second too late, I realize my front door is open again and Reese is standing in the entrance watching us, a distressed look on her face.

25

REESE

It takes a second for me to figure out what I'm looking at. Oliver is holding hands with another woman at his kitchen table, looking warmly at her pretty, freckled face.

My jaw drops, and I can't even stutter out a greeting.

What the hell?

He's got someone else. Someone he's known for much longer than a few weeks, if I had to guess. Someone younger, prettier, probably funnier, and without all the baggage I drag around with me.

The room sways. It's the same feeling I experienced that first day on the soccer field, with a dark edge around my vision threatening to make me black out.

I should've known. I shouldn't have let myself get so attached. Not when this would never last. Not when it was all fake, anyway.

Oliver stands, pulling away from the woman's hand, not with a yank, but a gentle tug.

"Reese, alright?" The soft look he had for her falls off, and he's replaced it with intense concern etched in the crevices of a face I know so well.

"Mmm-hmm." I bite my tongue, hard, and wait while the

blood rushes back to my brain and my vision clears. I study his face. Why doesn't he look guilty that I caught him with another woman? Maybe it's not a girlfriend. A sister who he never mentioned? A close friend he'd not told me about? But I know about all his close friends. He's got Patrick, David, Ian. That's it. No sister.

But he's already not told me about someone important to him. The most important someone.

I hate the doubt I'm feeling. Hate that he might still not be telling me everything I should know. Because I want to know him, all of him. But seeing this woman sitting at his table so casually makes me realize I might not ever really get to do that. For so many reasons.

"Och. Hey." Oliver reaches out his hand, realization settling on his face. "Reese. Come here."

When I hesitate, his face falls, and he presses his lips together, glancing at the woman at his table.

"I thought I was supposed to come over?"

"You were. You are." He patiently holds his hand out to me, and there's something in his eyes begging me to put my hand in his, to trust him.

I let myself look at her. She's examining me with wide, curious eyes, her gaze pausing on my beat-up sneakers with a quirk of a smile before returning to my face, her eyes flitting to the messy bun on top of my head that matches hers. She's wearing minimal makeup, her gorgeous red curls accentuating her green eyes without the help of heavy eyeliner, and she's wearing jeans and a loose sleeveless shirt in a matching green.

Done with her inspection—as am I—and clearly unbothered by my arrival, she raises her eyebrows at Oliver.

"Am I interrupting date night?" she says to him.

Oliver rolls his eyes without turning to her and steps toward me. Is this where I find out the next big secret? Where it's confirmed that everything is fake, love isn't real, etcetera?

Not that anyone's talking about love. *Calm the fuck down.*

I take his hand and he releases an audible sigh.

"Reese. This is Lucas's mum, Cat. Cat, this is Reese, my girlfriend."

"Hi," I say with a relieved half laugh.

Of course. Lucas's mom.

So yeah, another woman, but not the way I'd thought. I'm not sure what she's doing here, but my jaw unclenches and the vice that was wrapped around my insides loosens.

Oliver pulls me close and wraps an arm around my waist, planting a kiss on my forehead, letting his warm lips linger. My eyes shut briefly. Relief courses through me, making my knees wobbly.

He called me his girlfriend so easily, without a second of hesitation. Sweet baby Jesus, but I could be his girlfriend. I *am* his girlfriend. The idea brings me a moment of joy before I remember the situation we're in and where I'll be a week from today. Home, in New Jersey.

I do not want to lose this man.

"Nice to meet you," I say through my jumbled thoughts.

"And you." Her voice is hard to read, but she doesn't have the hostility Kendall did last weekend. "I should go," she says to Oliver, standing. "And you have plans, apparently."

"Thanks for stopping by."

"I'll see you Saturday." Cat walks past me toward the door and Oliver releases me from his embrace and follows her onto the front porch.

"Not your usual type." Cat's voice drifts in.

"Is that such a bad thing?"

The sound fades as Oliver walks her to the driveway. How did I not notice an extra car parked out front? I was so intent on getting inside to Oliver, I must have skimmed over it.

"Well, shit." My voice rings out in his empty house. I slide into the chair where Cat was just sitting, staring at her half-empty mug of tea.

Five minutes later, Oliver walks back through the door.

"I'm so sorry you walked into that without warning." He strides over and kneels in front of me, pushing between my legs and looking up into my eyes.

"S'okay."

He stares intently at me, running a hand along my jawline and into my hair. A gorgeous man on his knees between my legs, asking for forgiveness for something he didn't do wrong. I could get used to this.

"Come here." He stands and pulls me up and against him until our foreheads are touching. "You looked like you were freaking out."

"Sorry. Yeah, maybe I was. Just for a second." I was absolutely panicking. Only now my heart rate's stabilized. "Why'd she come here?"

"To check up on me." He kisses me. "To make sure I'm gonna behave on Saturday. And to tell me she's engaged and pregnant."

"What? Wow." I pull back and search his face.

"That's what I said." He smiles, but it doesn't go past his mouth.

"Are you okay? That sounds like a lot to take in."

He scrunches his nose and looks away, dropping his hands from me. "I'm happy for her. Her, uh, fiancé has been around a while. So it's not that. It's just . . . they have no faith in me."

I bite back that I had my own doubts when I first saw him and Cat together. That I thought this was all over already, and he had someone else.

"*They* shouldn't underestimate you—Cat, your parents . . . Lucas." I grab his hands and bring them back to my waist.

"The only way I could convince her I'll not be a hot mess was to tell her I have an interview this week and that I'm bringing you to the party. That I'm not just fucking around."

"Oh, Oliver." I run my hands up his chest. "I'm sorry she's doubting you."

"And I'm sorry I keep having to throw you out there like some pawn in a game of chess." Now he looks guilty.

"That's what I'm here for." My voice is smooth, but my breath hitches. I frown and look deep into his light eyes. "They need to give you a chance to prove how much you've changed."

I didn't know him before, but once again, anger pools in my belly. These people are waiting for him to disappoint them.

"Maybe they're right." He visibly swallows and covers his face, taking a step back from me. "Cat's fiancé is already a good father to Lucas. What can I really add? Why would Lucas even wanna know me?"

"Look at me." I close the distance between us and pull his hands away from his eyes. "You are an amazing man. You are his father. Lucas deserves to know you. And you deserve to know him."

We stare at each other for a full minute before he pulls me into a full-body hug. My body tingles against his. I start to think I could exist in his brawny arms forever.

I'm too invested in this. I know it. I want nothing more than to help him make a good impression at this party. I don't know what I'll do come Sunday when we break up, or Monday when I get on the plane.

It'll be over, and I'd do well to keep reminding myself of that.

26

OLIVER

Saturday, 20 August
The Day of the Birthday Party
Cat's House, Stirling

Reese hands me my phone as we sit in the parked car a few houses down from Cat's.

"It's gorgeous," she says. "When are you going to get it done?"

I glance down at the screen. It's the drawing of the boy I sketched on the banks of the River Tweed a few weeks ago, right when camp started in Peebles, before things got intense with Reese. I've worked on it since, defining the boy more, fading the background, making it something that could be inked onto my body. I'm thinking either my arm or my calf.

"Ah dinna ken. I don't even know where I'm gonna be next week. I'll wait to see if I get the job before scheduling an appointment."

Reese flinches. I'm not looking directly at her, but I can see it out of the corner of my eye. I can feel it. This is all ending. Last night was the final family dinner at Bella Italia, where it all started. David gave out team awards, one for every girl, and there was a lot of celebration and tearful goodbyes. I sat with David, and Reese was with some other parents, across the room from Adrian and Britt. Both of us separately snuck out at the earliest appropriate time to meet up at my house, and we've spent all of today together since Chelsea is on a day trip with her father and Britt.

And the day after tomorrow? They all get on a plane.

I reach out and grab her hand, but I canna say the words. I canna say what I'm feeling. That I'll miss her. That I need her. That I'm hers. There's more, but it's too much to even think. I examine her hands, her long, slender fingers, memorizing every detail, letting my eyes rest on the smattering of freckles on the top of her right hand, shaped like a heart. I pull up her hand to kiss it, letting my lips linger on her skin, then lean over and kiss her soft, familiar mouth.

There's no point in talking about it. I think we both agree on that. I need to harden myself for what's coming and make sure my priorities are in the right place. I need to pull away, but how can I do that, when I'm literally kissing my dream woman? When she just made that sweet, almost inaudible moan that she often does when our lips are locked? We separate and our foreheads rest together, more intimate than when we're completely naked.

Shite. She's not my dream. My *dream* is to be a good father to Lucas, and I'd best stay focused on that.

"Ready for this?" she murmurs.

"Nae." I sit up straight and squeeze her hand. "But let's go in anyway."

Reese and I walk hand-in-hand up the front pathway to Cat's small, tidy home. This time, it'll be better. *I'll* be better. Ah ken it, because I'm not alone, not physically, not mentally, not emotionally. Whenever the doubts creep into my brain—the doubts that say Lucas is better off without me—Reese is there to squeeze my hand or touch my back or tell me I'm worthy.

It's okay that Cat doesna fully believe me. Yet. But she will. It doesna matter that my parents canna stand me. They're not the important ones.

I raise my hand to knock on the door but freeze in place, overwhelmed.

"Hey." Reese runs her hand up my other arm. I turn to her and her brow furrows, eyes trained on me. "This is what you've been working toward. This is it. I'm here, okay? And so are you."

"Maybe I shouldna be." I glance back at the car and lower my hand. Maybe it'd be better for everyone if we get back in and drive away. But I dinna say it out loud, because if I do, she'll just reassure me, convince me it'll be okay. She's too good for me.

"Oliver." Reese touches my face, forcing me to turn to her. "You just have to show up sometimes, remember? Even if it's weird . . . Even if it doesn't go exactly as you picture it should . . . Just being here is the exact right next step. That's what Lucas needs you to do. Be here. Starting today. Starting right now."

She's in my head. How does this woman know me so well, already?

"But then what?" I'm frozen in place, mesmerized by her words, terrified of what awaits on the other side of that door. My legs tense up, as if I'm about to start a run, adrenaline flowing, body ready to flee.

"You figure out the rest later." She drops her hands from my face and throws them in the air. "I don't know. Who does? If you are trying to completely figure out how to be a parent, that's too much all at once. No one knows that shit. You live through it one day at a time." She pauses, examining me. "Okay?"

I swallow the lump that's sprung up in my throat. "Where did you even come from?" My voice is raspy. Without Reese, I would've bailed and continued to disappoint myself, Lucas, and Cat. But now, even though I might still disappoint a lot of people, I know I'm doing the right thing.

"I told you, New Jersey."

I laugh. "Let's go in."

CAT ANSWERS the door and waves us in, nodding to me and checking Reese out with an open smile, acting much friendlier than she did on Tuesday.

"Good to see you again," Cat says to Reese.

"Thanks for letting me tag along with Oliver." Reese smiles back and then looks around. "You have a lovely home. And I just adore the pink flowers out front. And the thistle! I didn't know people grew it in their gardens."

"Oh, that? Thank you. I have little free time, but I do love to spend it in my wee garden."

I hadna even noticed flowers.

"It's delightful. All the different colors, I love it. And I hear you're expecting? Congratulations. Oliver told me after you left on Tuesday."

Cat blushes and touches her belly. She's wearing a loose-fitting, green-patterned dress, but there's a hint of a bump when she presses the fabric against her stomach. It wasna noticeable the other day.

I look back and forth between these two women grinning at each other and realize that Reese is charming the shite out of Cat. Something I havena ever been able to accomplish.

"Thank you. Grant and I are thrilled."

"Nothing is better than a baby. My daughter is sixteen, but I haven't forgotten that feeling. Let me know if you need a baby holder."

Cat laughs, a dreamy look in her eyes and a rosy blush on her cheeks.

Reese is a miracle worker. She pulls me close to her side.

"Well, thank you for bringing Oliver," Cat says.

"I'm right here, you know." I wave my free hand.

She ignores me. "Lucas will be . . . happy." She turns, finally acknowledging my presence. "Your parents are in the backyard—

just a warning. I told them you're coming, and they seemed, well, not super impressed."

"They've never been super impressed with me, so that's not surprising." My stomach turns, but before panicking, I try gripping Reese's hand tighter. It immediately grounds me.

"Aye. Well, dinna let them push you around. My parents are coming late, but Lucas is in the back with some of his friends. I'm gonna run to check on the food. Make yourself at home."

With that, Cat disappears into the kitchen, where a group of people I dinna recognize are lingering and laughing. That whole interaction with her was worlds better than anything that's happened in the past ten years. It's almost like this time she's on my side, rooting for me to not screw up, instead of expecting me to.

Och. I am not looking forward to the look Cat will give me when I tell her Reese and I broke up.

"First step: talk to your kid's mother. Done," Reese whispers in my ear.

"Aye. The rest will be more difficult."

"I bet Lucas will be thrilled. Let's go find him, shall we?" She pulls at my hand, but I stay solid and reach for her other one.

"You look bonnie today," I murmur, trailing my gaze from her eyes to the v-shaped neckline of her long blue dress that shows just a hint of the swell of her breasts. Kids' party appropriate cleavage. The fabric gathers in a textured waistline, accentuating her curves, making me wish we were back in my bed and I could strip it off her.

Now it's her turn to blush as I push back a chunk of her curled dark hair. She's got on more makeup than usual, but I could drown in her gray eyes, with or without the dark eyeliner.

"You're procrastinating." But she doesna push me to walk away.

What's she thinking? I wish I could be in her head. I wish I could take some of her strength and make it a part of me. I wish I could make *her* a part of me.

"Lucas out back?" A man's voice drifts from the kitchen, grabbing my attention.

"Aye, and I'm heading there now. I can take the water bottle to him," Cat says.

"Let's go." I can do this. I can go talk to my son. I lead Reese through the living room and into the kitchen, dodging curious looks and ignoring the way the conversation ceases when we walk through. Out through the back door where Cat just disappeared, a group of kids are kicking a football around.

Because of course they are.

Reese slides her arm through mine. "Which one is he?"

My eyes settle on my ten-year-old son. Lucas is tall—taller than his friends, taller than I thought he'd be—but what do I ken about ten-year-olds? He's got Cat's bright-red hair, but nae a freckle on his pale skin. He's skinny and dribbling with impressive footwork around his friends, who are desperately trying to steal the ball from him three-on-one.

I swallow and soak it in. Watching my son play football with his friends in the backyard of this suburban home, in the same town I grew up in . . . it hits me. This coulda been my home. My life.

Lucas looks up and someone takes the ball from him while he's distracted. His eyes meet mine and his whole face lights up.

"Da!" Without hesitation, he stops playing and runs over to me.

My heart squeezes and I inhale sharply through my nose. I wasna sure if he'd scoff at me, blow me off, or be bored at my presence. But Lucas hugs me as soon as he reaches me. I pull him close. He smells like a sweaty kid, and I breathe it in. He's all bones and wiry muscles. I bite the side of my cheek when a lump forms in my throat. How have I been missing this for the last eighteen months?

"I canna believe you're here." Lucas, with a face dominated by a huge grin with missing teeth, steps back and looks at me, then over his shoulder at his friends, who are whispering and pointing.

"Happy birthday, Lucas," I say. "You looked good out there. You play a lot?"

"Really? Yeah, I want to be a professional footballer, just like you. But Ma makes me do other things, too. Like study. And art. I love painting, and Ma takes me to art classes."

"Your ma's smart." My voice shakes. I didn't know he loved painting. I'm so thankful for Cat. She obviously doesna make him hide it. In fact, she seems to encourage it. "You should keep that up. Dinna make football your whole life."

Fuck, who am I?

But I know. I'm someone who wished they had something besides football in their lives as a kid. Hobbies, activities, friends, anything. Cat's making sure Lucas has that. He's also an artist.

My son inherited more than one of my talents.

"You did that, though, didna you?" he asks, his face curious and smooth, youth glowing as bright as the lights at Wembley.

"Aye. You're right. But it's good to be able to do more than one thing." I want to tell him I draw, and I decide that I will do just that, one day. Not today. But Lucas and I will talk art, I swear it to myself.

"Yeah, I guess."

There's movement in the far backyard by the grill that catches my eye. My parents. My insides twist into instant knots.

Reese doesna see them, she doesna even know who they are. Instead, she touches my arm and gestures to her bag with Lucas's present inside.

I nod. "Hey, Lucas, this is Reese." Lucas gives her a quick glance and says hi as she reaches into her bag and presents the wrapped package.

"Happy birthday, Lucas," she says.

He grabs it from her hands and rips open the paper.

"This is pure barry!" He flips through the stack of three

video games and stops at the World Cup one. We'd checked with Cat about what game system he has. "I have to go show my mates!"

He dashes off to the crowd of boys, who huddle around him.

"Pure barry?" Reese looks at me with wide eyes. "Even after a month, I still feel like you're all speaking a different language."

I chuckle. "Means brilliant."

"Right. Well done, then."

"Oliver?" Ma's voice tentatively calls out from behind me.

Oh, no.

I turn at her voice, both familiar and foreign, and reach back down for Reese. Ma glances at the movement but shows no reaction—not a grimace nor a grin. My father trails behind her.

"Hallo, Ma. Da." I make no move to hug or kiss them. Reese emits a small sound next to me. She's about to see my dysfunctional family close up.

"Your hair is so long," Ma says, lifting a hand as if considering reaching up to touch my curls, but she changes her mind and lets her hand return to limply hang by her side. Her hair is as dark as it was when I was a kid, except for the roots, where a bit of white is sneaking through. There are also more lines etched in her face than when I last saw her.

"Son. Hello." My father nods his head at me, expressionless. He looks so much older. *His* hair is completely white, and he's got a frail aura around him. I feel like I could accidentally knock him over with a gentle tap on the shoulder.

"It's been a long time," I say.

"We talked at Christmas," Ma states. "What happened in Ireland?"

I blink rapidly at her. Reese breathes in sharply.

"Nothing happened. I'm just . . . back now."

"Reese," Cat calls from the door to the kitchen. "Can you come here?" Cat's eyes widen right after Reese turns, revealing my parents standing with us. Cat mouths an apology.

"Go ahead," I say to Reese, detaching our hands. This is my battle. My parents.

She walks away with a worried glance over her shoulder, and I'm alone with them, something that shouldna fill me with dread, but it does. We're silent, frozen in place, like the hobgoblin statues at Melrose Abbey.

"Right. I'm gonna get a drink." Da wanders away to the drink cooler. He's not even interested enough to stick around for the awkwardness.

"Oliver." Ma steps forward and glances around, as if checking for eavesdroppers. "I wanted to tell you that Lucas is happy. He really is. He *adores* Grant." She emphasizes the word adores, as if I wouldna get the hint otherwise. "That man is like a father to him." She nods her head toward my son, who is now standing next to his future stepfather, showing him the video games and chatting excitedly.

But Lucas points to me and waves when we make eye contact. I look away before Grant can follow his gaze.

"That's wonderful news," I murmur, but I desperately want this conversation to be over. I canna handle much more.

"I love you so much. I want you to be happy, somehow, finally. But I dinna want things to go wrong for Lucas. And I'm afraid . . . well . . ."

"That I'll fuck it up?"

"He *practically* calls him da."

It's like a dagger in my heart. "Lucas calls Grant da?" I sway on my feet. No. Cat wouldna allow it. Would she?

"Well, not exactly." Ma waves her hands in the air, as if she's swatting away a fly. "But I bet Grant told him he could if he wanted to. Or he would, anyway, if Cat would let him."

The fuck, Ma? Now she's just making shite up.

"You could've been a father to Lucas." Her voice is soft, sympathetic, but judgmental. "But you've not been here."

Rage surges through my veins and I clench my fists at my side.

"Ah ken I've not been there for Lucas. But I'm changing that now. I—"

I stop, because I dinna need to explain myself to Ma. She wouldn't listen anyway. Even now, she's got her lips pressed together and is moving her head slightly back and forth in disapproval.

"It's been two years since you left football. And what have you done? Nothing, right? You need to figure out your own life before you mess with our Lucas."

"I'm working on it." I clench my fists by my side.

Should I say more? Or walk away now? Ah, fuck it.

"I was only football for my whole life because that's all you and Da told me I could be. So I'm not just going to wake up the next day and have it all figured out."

Reese has helped me to see that what my parents told me is not true. The anger grows like a rolling snowball inside me, gathering speed and size, an avalanche careening down a mountain.

"Oh, Oliver, why would you have thought that? That's your own misconception." Ma shakes her head at me, her face pitying. "*You* chose football, not us. Dinna you see that? We would've been happy with whatever you ended up doing."

I shrink in front of her, morphing into the wee ten-year-old boy who didn't make the team and was punished with the silent treatment. She's gaslighting me, even if she doesna realize it. And I dinna have to stand here and take it.

"I have to go find Reese. Good seeing you, Ma." I stride back to the house, only to stop when Reese appears at the back door, smiling widely at me, two bottles of water in her hands.

Her face falls. "So sorry I left you alone. Are you okay?" She closes the gap between us until we're standing centimeters apart. "What did she say to you? I knew I shouldn't have gone inside. Cat felt terrible. She didn't see them standing with us."

Reese hands me a water and touches my arm, stroking gently with her thumb.

I glance back at Ma, who is watching Lucas and his friends, seeming to have forgotten all about me in the ten seconds since I walked away. I'm that unimportant to her.

"They're awful, as always." My teeth ache from clenching my jaw, so I make an effort to open my mouth.

"Hey. Don't let her chase you away from your son."

I turn back to my fake girlfriend and kiss her on the forehead, breathing in the coconut scent of her hair and knowing how lucky I am. I squeeze my eyes shut and try to untangle my heart from hers. It needs to be done.

"Did you tell her about the job?"

"Nae. None of her business."

The interview in Crenshaw-on-the-Sea last week went really well. John didna seem worried at all about my past transgressions. I told him how I'm starting a new life in Scotland, how excited I am to coach, that I'm a different person now. He'd only nodded. All I need now is to seal the deal with a photo of me, Reese, and Lucas.

When Lucas trots back over, I ask someone standing nearby to snap some pictures of the three of us. Reese leans into me and wraps her arm around my waist, reaching for Lucas over my back.

The pictures are everything. I flip through them, staring down, soaking in everything that they could mean. What the future could be with Reese.

But it willna be.

No matter how good she's been with me tonight, no matter that she charmed the pants off of Cat and has been there for me over the past month, letting myself fall for her is the worst possible outcome. She canna leave me here with a broken heart.

Good thing I've not let it go that far.

But the thought rings false in my head. I push it away. It's just too good with her right now.

"So sweet. Look at his face, staring at you in this one." Reese leans on my arm, gazing at the picture. Lucas is looking up at me in the first one, and even I can see the adoration in his gaze.

I'm gonna be there for him from now on. Whatever that looks like, whatever he and Cat will let happen. I'm gonna be his Da. Then I have the weirdest thought. It's that I wish Chelsea were in the picture, too. That we could imagine ourselves a little family. As soon as the thought pops up, I squash it. It's not worth even considering.

"Send it to me?" Reese murmurs.

But I bet she can picture it, too.

27

___

REESE

"I have to use the restroom. I'll be right back." I squeeze Oliver's hand and book it to the house.

I'm not normally an impulsive person, but I can't let this chance go by. I pause only for a second at the back door to Cat's house, glancing over my shoulder to see Oliver kicking a soccer ball to Lucas. After the initial drama with his parents, everything's gone perfectly at the party.

I dash through the kitchen, hoping Cat doesn't look over from the conversation she's having as I slip past the bathroom and out the front door, where Oliver's parents departed just a second ago.

"Hey!" I call to them after pulling the door shut behind me. I don't want anyone witnessing what I'm about to do, especially Oliver, or Cat, who's right inside. Adrenaline courses through my body, and my neck and shoulders feel rock-hard with tension.

What, exactly, *am* I about to do?

Oliver's mother and father stop at the sound of my voice, just a few feet down the sidewalk from Cat's front walkway. His ma clutches the strap of her purse, her lips hardening into a straight line. Her husband pulls out his mobile phone and stares down.

I trot down the steps, ignoring Cat's glorious patch of thistle. My stomach twists and I swallow a lump in my throat.

"Well, hallo," his ma says, a thick Scottish accent so much like Oliver's.

Oh, I think I might vomit. I stride toward them and try to look as confident as possible despite my turbulent insides. When I halt a few feet away, they wait for me to say something, looking uninterested at best. Or his ma does, at least. His da hasn't looked up from his phone. I harvest inspiration from the anger and indignation I felt when they completely disregarded their own son in Cat's backyard. I didn't hear what they said to him, but I got the gist from Oliver.

"You could be supportive of him, you know." I'm thrilled at the sharp edge to my voice. I sound pissed. I *am* pissed.

Her forehead crinkles. "Of course we're supportive of Lucas."

"Of Oliver. Your son."

She doesn't quite roll her eyes, but it's close enough. She knew who I meant.

"He's trying to do the right thing. He's trying to be a part of Lucas's life. And he could use the love and support of his parents."

"Child, you have no idea. When did you even meet Oliver? You're new, aren't you? Yeh dinna ken him."

I blink back surprise. Sure, I just met him, but I know him. I do.

"When I met him has nothing to do with this."

She nods knowingly. "He's no built to be a father. He knows that, which is why he's stayed away all these years. It's for the best, trust me. Besides, Lucas has Grant."

"Oliver is Lucas's father. It's awesome that he has Grant, but a boy still needs his dad. You made him feel like the only thing he could be in life is a soccer player. You put that idea in his head."

Somewhere inside me a connection is made. Chelsea needs her father, and he's been there for her. But maybe she doesn't need her father and mother to be best friends. I shake my head and focus on Oliver's parents.

"It's football, not soccer," Oliver's father says, not bothering to look up. Is he playing a game? Scrolling Facebook? I want to kick him in the shin.

"Whatever. He's so much more than that. And now he's trying to figure that out. But you're his parents, who are supposed to love him no matter what. Only you've not shown that at all. Get over the mistakes he's made in the past and support him in what he's trying to do with his life now. Don't just blow him off. Be a mother. Be a father. That's what *he's* trying to do."

I clench my teeth. His ma's jaw drops open with a look of surprise, and his da actually looks up from his phone. I wait for them to defend themselves, argue back, agree with me, something, but instead, she lets out a big sigh and glances at her husband, their expressions flat.

The tension disappears from my shoulders and my heartbeat slows. I guess I did what I meant to do, which was defend Oliver, like some badly trained knight in borrowed armor. Now all I want to do is get out of here.

"Well, it was nice to meet you." I spin around and jog back to the house. Somehow, the door's open a crack, so I slip back in and click it shut behind me.

We drive the hour and a half back to Peebles in mostly silence. It's late and dark outside. After Oliver's parents left, we'd stayed longer than planned. Oliver played a heated game of sharks and minnows with Lucas and his friends, then went inside and cracked open the new video games. Cat's parents showed up, and I'd chatted with them, Cat, and Grant. He'd been a delightful guy. Everyone was more relaxed without Oliver's parents around.

Lucas is lucky to have so many people in his life who love him.

Oliver's childhood must've been so lonely. I can't believe his parents didn't even hug him today. Not so much as a squeeze on his arm or a trace of affection.

No wonder he's so scared of getting it wrong with Lucas. Is that why he hid him from me to begin with?

My parents' marriage was far from perfect, but I never doubted they loved us. And Mom's thanked me a hundred times for stepping up to help with Stella and Maddie after Dad died. We always say I love you. All of us. We take care of each other. Okay, maybe I do a bit more of the caretaking than the others, but there's so much spoken love in our family.

I shift and watch Oliver as he drives, resting my head against the seat.

I could see being friends with Cat. She cares about Oliver. If she can just keep her heart and mind open to him, maybe he'd have someone on his side. But Oliver will have to communicate with her, and she'll have to trust him, and there's so many ways they could mess it up.

I wish I could be here to help.

I reach over and slide my hand on Oliver's thigh.

"Lucas is a sweet kid."

"Aye." He keeps watching the road. I can't read him.

"You did great with him."

"Maybe." A small smile peeks through his cloudy expression.

"And I don't think it's too late. I think he's ready to have you in his life, no matter what your parents say. He was elated when you played soccer with him and his friends. It was beautiful."

I took a few pictures of the two of them playing together. I'll have to send them to him later.

Oliver navigates a roundabout into the Peebles town center. I look away from his profile and trail the familiar storefronts and landmarks.

I don't want to think about tomorrow. Or the next day. But at least we have tonight.

The car pulls to a stop in front of the fish and chips shop and Oliver turns his body to mine. He opens his mouth, then closes it.

I bite my lip and wait for him to speak. Surprising tears spring up in my eyes and I will them to stay put.

Instead of speaking, he clenches his jaw.

"Shite." Oliver breaks eye contact with me and grabs his phone from the cup holder. "I need to send something to the Crenshaw FC human resources woman real quick."

"Okay." I blink, a bit jarred by the transition. He clicks through to his photos and up pops the one of us with Lucas. Maybe he's texting it to me before he forgets.

But then he taps a few buttons and a blank email pops up. Catching me watching the screen, his eyes grow wide for a second and he freezes.

"Are you sending her a picture that was taken tonight?" I'm so confused. An unpleasant twist of suspicion worms its way into my belly.

His face contorts. "Bad timing. I should've waited."

"Waited for what?"

Oliver sighs. "Aye. I was sending her the picture from tonight."

"But, why would you do that?" I know I sound accusatory. But the twist in my belly unravels and grows longer, burrowing into the nooks and crannies of my body like an ugly weed, seeding doubt and more questions.

He rubs his hand roughly over his face and when he stills, he looks calm and resolute. What's he doing?

Oh. Shit. He's pushing me away.

"The interviews have gone great." Oliver had a glowing smile on his face when he showed up at my flat on Thursday night, fresh from his trip to Crenshaw-on-the-Sea.

"Yeah, I know."

"But they're worried about me fitting in. They're a family-oriented club, aye? So a picture of the three of us would help prove

I am family oriented. That I'm trying to be a father. That I have a . . ."

"Girlfriend like me?" My body ices over and everything becomes clear. I mean, it should've been clear before. It *was* clear. We literally talked about this being a fake relationship and exactly what we'd both get out of it.

He hesitates, then nods.

He was going to get a date to his son's birthday party with a woman who was completely unlike the ones he used to be with. A good influence. *Wholesome.* That awful word he used when he asked me to come to this party to begin with. I'm not his type. I knew that. I never was.

Boring. Uninteresting. Not young and hot. Can I really blame him if he decided to extend that boring, uninteresting, *wholesome* girlfriend story to his job search as well?

"Damn," I whisper and lean back against the seat of the car, ripping my hand back from his leg like it turned too hot to touch.

Yeah, I can definitely blame him. I know it's not fair. I'm over-reacting. I breathe deeply.

"Reese." His voice is firm now, so unlike what I'm used to hearing from him. He delivers the final painful blow. "This was always going to end."

I breathe in sharply, his words a kick to my gut. I turn to study his face, and an undercurrent of emotion rolls across his features. He's biting his tongue on the inside of his mouth. He keeps looking down at my lips.

"I know that," I whisper. "Are you picking a fight with me? Trying to make it easier to say goodbye?"

"Nae, ah dinna mean to. I'm sorry." His voice softens. "That came out so harsh."

But he doesn't take the words back. He's right. It was a fake relationship from the start. And even though we both got a bit carried away, that's all it is now. Maybe he's not picking a fight so much as finishing what we started.

"We . . . helped each other this past month. It was a good time doing it though, aye?" His voice ends up even softer, but the words are cutting. Shallow. They hurt.

I know this was more than a good time. Or was it? It's my fault for thinking there was something more. For letting myself . . . no, no. I didn't let myself do anything.

This—what happened over the past month—is literally what I know about love. That it's not real. So why does it feel so awful? Why do I feel worse than when I got here for my reset month?

"Och. Reese."

Our eyes are linked together, like a skeleton key stuck in an old lock.

"What?" I hate the lump in my throat and how my voice shakes.

"This has been a remarkable summer with you."

I wait for more, but that's all he gives me.

"I guess I thought the rules had changed." I squirm in my seat, wanting to leap out of the car and away from him, even though that's what I told him not to do. I'd told him to stay and fight for the people he cares about. Only maybe that's not me. Maybe it's okay to run away from him, my fake boyfriend. "But you sending a picture of us to human resources feels really . . . cold."

It hasn't felt like he's my fake boyfriend for a long time. In fact, this afternoon at Lucas's party, it felt like we were family.

"That isn't fair, Reese." His face crumples and he runs his hand along his neck and down his arm, over his ink.

He's right, but I'm glad he looks pained. Maybe it was my responsibility to protect my heart. But I thought we were in this together. With what end, though? What did I think was going to happen? Damn. I let this get way out of hand.

"I know." Nothing about this is fair. I can't stop my time here from ending. I can't help that I have a job and a life on another continent.

I've got to get out of the car and away from Oliver. I only have thirty-six more hours in Scotland. Maybe I can ground myself before I fly back to New Jersey with Chelsea, Adrian, and Britt. I have to get ready to face my real life. But I can't do it if Oliver is in my bed. I can't look at his face and understand what is real and what is not.

"Jersey." His voice is sweet. "Can we go in and talk?" He nods his head to the door to my flat. Now his forehead is crumpled and his glassy eyes show real regret. He reaches for my hand.

I shake my head. "No." I press my lips together and pull away, wanting to lean over for one more kiss. He would kiss me. He'd come inside and we could have one last night together.

But it's over. More will just make it harder.

"Please?"

"Goodbye, Oliver."

And with that, I get out of the car, ignoring his protests, and attempt to unlock the door to my flat, my hand shaking too much to get it on the first try.

"Reese, come on." He's behind me, his presence filling all my senses.

I freeze for a second. It would be so easy to say yes. To turn around and let him into my flat, into my heart for one last night.

No. Now is the end. Not tomorrow. Tonight. This exact moment.

The key turns in the lock.

I push the door open and disappear into the building, leaving Oliver on the street by himself.

28

OLIVER

Sunday, 21 August
Fake Breakup Day
Oliver's House

I'm an absolute bawbag. No matter what I do, I canna get the look on Reese's face from last night out of my head. I hurt her. Why the fuck did I do that?

But I know why: because I'm feart. I'd rather have her pissed off at me than have us clinging to each other like we're meant to be, or some shite like that.

I hate myself for it.

At noon, while I'm stretching to go out for a run, my phone buzzes with a text and I pounce on it like a starved feline on a bacon-wrapped rodent.

> **KARLA**
>
> Lovely photograph. Expect good news later today.

My eyes widen. For just a second, I forget, and instinctively click over to my desolate text chain with Reese. But after weeks of

227

texting fifty times a day, our text chain is dead. No more questions and answers, gentle teasing, warmth radiating through words on a phone screen.

Fuuuuuck.

I stretch my hamstrings one at a time. I should be pumping my fists into the air, celebrating. I'm gonna get the job. I scored a coaching gig two years after leaving professional football. Sure, it's an assistant coach job, basically entry level, but it's a start. The start of my new life.

Instead, I feel a cold, bitter acceptance. Victory, but not joy.

This is who I am. A footballer. Not an artist. Not a boyfriend.

But I'm gonna be a da to Lucas. That's all that's important now.

And all the shite that happened between me and Reese, from that first conversation on the football field to the painful ending last night? Just filler. Not real. We were fake dating, for fuck's sake. Pretending to be together. Pretending with benefits.

The sex? Aye, it was out of this world. The best I've ever had. But that's only because I was celibate for a year in Ireland. I've dated way hotter women than Reese. She's a thirty-seven-year-old suburban football mum. Sure, her body is incredible, her smooth curves like a powerful magnet to my hands, and those serious gray eyes a live wire to my own.

I can find a new girlfriend. Or not. I dinna give a fuck.

I race out of my front door and turn away from town into the light rain, jogging at a fast pace, hoping the burning in my thighs will distract me from thinking of Reese.

She used me, just like I used her. We agreed to it. We talked terms and conditions. There were no illusions as to what this was. And I had to work a lot harder than she did to fulfill my end of the deal. All that time with Adrian and Britt. They were fucking awful. Awful to Reese. We did an excellent job of deceiving them, plus we kept it between the four of us.

The problem is, I think I also deceived myself.

I run faster around the curve with the blind spot, along the fence where a lone sheep stares at me. After over a month in Peebles, these roads and curves and sheep are so familiar to me, it almost feels like home.

It's not. Even if I'd made a wee life here. A *temporary* life.

But why do I feel so damn awful about how things ended last night? Why was it so hard for her to accept that I sent that picture to Crenshaw FC? What's the fucking problem?

My fists clench and I push myself faster. A lorry drives by and swerves into the other lane, and I dash down a gravel path along a pasture, slowing to a jog and leaving the road behind me. I keep going until the pasture ends and a small forest of trees stands ahead. I lean against one of the towering oaks and close my eyes, letting the soft breeze cool my sweaty skin, the leaves gently rustling above me, a cow mooing in the distance.

"Fuck."

I've betrayed her.

That's what's wrong here. That's the fucking problem. As soon as I think it, ah ken it's true. How did I betray her? The picture. And I did it on purpose. I knew she would see it, I knew it would upset her, and I knew it would make it easier—if that's what this is—to make a break from her.

But I'm thinking it feels just as bad. Or worse. Probably for her as well.

My eyes fly open.

Today's our fake breakup day. Even though she ended things last night, she originally wanted to make it more public, creating an easy-to-believe story for Adrian and Britt. We hadna even planned the details yet. Neither of us had wanted to talk about it. But here I am, reneging on the last thing I promised her I'd do.

I grab my phone from my pocket and click through to our silent text chain and type quickly.

ME

> I'm so sorry about last night. Is the fake breakup today still on? Do you need me?

I press send before I can overthink it, but staring down at the message, it looks too flippant, too casual, too light.

ME

> I can come today. I mean it. I'm sorry.

There's no response for a full minute, and I hang my head and walk back up the gravel path toward the main road, about to give up, when the phone vibrates in my hand.

REESE

> It's okay. I'm at The Peebles Beans with Adrian and Britt. It's too late.

"Nae." I speed up to a jog, then a full-on run, tearing back down the winding road toward town, running past my house with the yellow shutters, and slowing when I get to the High Street to catch my breath.

I pull my shirt up and wipe the sweat dripping from my face. I'm going to walk into the coffee shop and do what, exactly, as this sweaty disaster?

But fuck it. I said I would help her, and I have to at least fulfill my role as her fake boyfriend.

I duck into The Peebles Beans and look around. People out for their Sunday cup of coffee fill the place: a family with a toddler throwing bits of muffin on the floor, an older couple sipping steaming mugs by the window, a long line at the register, and to the side, Reese is at a rectangular table with her ex-husband and ex-best friend. There's an empty chair beside her.

She looks miserable.

Adrian and Britt sit on one side of the table, chairs pulled close together, Britt perched close to him, not touching, but close enough they might as well be. And even from a side view, I can tell they're both looking at Reese with the look she hates the most —pity.

Now that I'm here, I'm not sure how to not make this worse. What should I even say?

ME
I'm here.

She glances down at her phone and then sharply looks up and around, meeting my eyes. For a second, her face opens up and I see relief and a flash of a smile. But then she remembers, and a shadow passes over her expression. She stands and walks my way without a word to Adrian and Britt, who trail her movement with wide eyes.

I dinna give them more than a quick glance, because I want to appreciate the sight of Reese. In contrast to yesterday, when she wore the long blue dress, today she's wearing a hoodie that says Rutgers and jeans, her hair laying straight on her shoulders. She's even more beautiful today. I imagine spending the day cuddling next to her on the couch, watching movies or reading a book or just talking. When she stops in front of me, arms crossed across her chest, I'm left practically speechless.

"What are you doing here?" she says, a forced frown on her face. She looks me up and down, noting the sweat glistening on my forehead. "Were you out for a run?"

"Aye." Maybe I should have gone home to change first. "But then I remembered it's our fake breakup day, and I didna want to make you do it alone."

"How considerate." She almost, but not quite, cracks a smile, but instead presses her lips together and glances back at the table where Britt is whispering into Adrian's ear, her hand now on his thigh.

"Sorry I'm late." I want to apologize for so much more than my arrival time.

Reese shrugs. "It's done. They already think we broke up

because of the distance. Of course, they assume you dumped me." Her arms wrap tighter around her chest, a protective move. Protecting herself from me.

The air disappears from my lungs like a football to the gut. I want to tell her I'd never dump her. If I could hold on to her, I would. I'd never let her go.

But the look on Reese's face shows she hasna figured that out. It's for the better. Her eyes flick down to my lips and she sighs, her shoulders raising up and down slowly.

I'd only fuck things up more if I stuck around in her life. If I even could. Which I canna.

"Listen." I step closer to her so we're within kissing distance. I canna tell her how I really feel—not that I understand that myself —but I can give her a version of it. "If we'd actually been together for real, I'd never have broken up with you." I reach for her. She unfolds her arms and places her cool hands in mine. I'm sticky and gross, but she doesna flinch at my clammy grip. She's staring at me like I'm the only person in the world. Sparks jump between our eyes, and I want to wrap my arms around her.

In no universe can I imagine ending things with this woman, if it were up to me. Which it's not.

Reese swallows, her eyes wide, like an entire planet could fit in there. An entire universe. My universe. "Too bad we weren't actually together."

Can she see directly into my soul? She might. If so, she'll understand me better than I do myself. Because right now, ah ken nothing.

"Too bad." I move my thumbs along her hands. "Jersey. Let's kiss one last time. You can tell them I came to ask you to take me back." I'm whispering. "That I'm begging you to forgive me for any way I hurt you. And you tell me no. Your life is across the ocean. Mine is here. There's no way it'll work."

The room fades around us.

"No way it would work," she parrots back to me in a wispy voice.

"And I tell you how the past month has been the happiest of my life, knowing I would get to hold you in my arms and kiss you and tell you everything that came into my head."

"The happiest, Picasso?" Reese tilts her head up to mine and I release one of her hands so I can bury it in her hair.

"The happiest." I lean down and kiss her, sliding my other hand on her waist to pull her closer to me, only feeling bad for a second that I'm sweaty. Our lips linger against each other and it feels every bit the goodbye kiss, the mirror image of the first time our lips touched at Melrose Abbey, tucked in the stone nook, the sun shining above our heads at the start of this adventure.

It was always going to end.

I lean back and touch our foreheads together. "Goodbye, Reese." Finding it hard to break contact, I hesitate, waiting for her to say something to stop me, for me to say something that changes everything, for one of us to fight to find a way to be together.

But there's nothing. Both of us stay silent, and after a few seconds, I turn and slip out of the pub. I don't—can't—look back.

29

REESE

My lips feel naked without his mouth pressed against them, reminding me of a nightmare I once had where I forgot to put on pants before a big presentation, back when everything was in person. I bite the inside of my cheek to keep tears from forming. I won't cry over Oliver Vass today, and I will definitely not cry over him in front of Adrian and Britt, still seated at the table behind me.

Okay, maybe I cried last night on a video call with my sisters, then regretted it and forced myself to pretend that I wasn't that upset. They definitely didn't buy it. I cut the call short and laid in my bed alone, staring at the ceiling, wondering how I got to this place. Physically, in Scotland. Emotionally, wherever the hell I am with Oliver.

Everything's spiraled out of control this month, and it's all Adrian and Britt's fault. If they hadn't shown up, I would never have nearly passed out in front of Oliver, he wouldn't have grabbed my hand, I wouldn't have whispered in his ear, we wouldn't have bonded at the pub, and he wouldn't have had the unhinged idea to fake date.

Adrian and Britt. I clench my hands at my sides and squeeze the muscles in my abdomen, tension building up to something.

When I came to Scotland, I thought I just needed a few weeks to reset my life in a gorgeous Scottish village. I thought I could still be friends with Britt and maybe rebuild what we once had. But something's shifted inside me and I don't know that I can push it back where it was.

I don't even know I want to.

I'm frozen in place, my back still to them, but I know their eyes are on me. Judging. Pitying. Britt's waiting for me to fall apart so she can swoop in and be there for me, like I was for her after her painful divorce. Her heart's in the right place. But does that even matter?

Anger swirls in my stomach, the tension exploding into rage. This would have been better at the pub with alcohol instead of coffee. Caffeine's not enough for me.

I know she's not spiteful or manipulative, but what if she's secretly happy about this breakup? Maybe she's sensed that I'm pulling away from her—from them—and she's freaking out that I'll change my mind about rebuilding our friendship.

"Everything okay?" Britt says when I return to the table, her voice a soft murmur, genuine concern etched in her face.

I want to scream, something wild and freeing. I don't know how she does it, sitting next to my ex-husband, thinking we can actually be friends. There's no way. *What was I thinking?*

"It's fine." I shrug and clear my face, hoping to portray the ultimate nonchalance. "He was just saying goodbye." I flick my eyes to my ex-husband, whose brow is furrowed. "It was a summer fling. It meant nothing, really, just a bit of fun during my month in Scotland."

I silently moan, the lies coming out of my mouth threatening to betray me—the same lies I told Stella earlier this month. The same lies I've been telling myself.

Britt looks at Adrian and bites her lip.

"Okay. Well, I hope you're not upset, but I have to tell you something."

My stomach twists.

"Chelsea knows about your, uh, fling with Oliver."

"What?" My face contorts and my stomach clenches so suddenly that I might throw up. "How does she know?"

But I know how. Britt told her. I can see it in the guilty lines around her eyes, the way her mouth turns down, her lower lip jutting out.

Adrian sighs like we are exhausting him, and even though I want to punch him in the face, I wonder if he's sick of this charade of friendship as well.

My former best friend breathes in sharply. "I'm sorry, Ree. It came up when we were with her yesterday. We were talking about day trips . . . and got to talking about Melrose Abbey . . . Well, Adrian didn't want to lie to her again, so it all came out."

I press my lips together so hard that it causes a pulse of pain.

"We didn't want her to find out some other way." She glances at Adrian, who looks away from me.

"Some other way? What other way besides you?"

Britt and her over-the-top obsession with being honest with those around her. She thinks she's doing the right thing all the time, but instead she's like a beautiful bull in a china shop filled with teacups of people's feelings.

Adrian says the words that I'm sure came right from Britt. "We thought she might know, anyway. She's pretty observant. And she was upset when Britt talked to her about it." Adrian looks at me the way a father might look at his teenage daughter—lecturing but not really believing his own words.

Chelsea was upset? Shit. All of the time I spent worrying about her finding out . . . All of the reassurances Oliver gave me that she wouldn't . . . They're all gone, like the breath from my lungs. I let it all sink in.

My daughter is going to hate me. I had an ill-fated fling with her soccer coach. Her crush. What kind of mother am I? Damn! She'll be so embarrassed. She's going to think I'm the worst, most irresponsible mom ever.

At least she doesn't know it was fake. That would be worse.

"You didn't need to tell her." I focus my most withering glare on Adrian. "If you were so concerned about her knowing, you should have talked to me first. I should've been the one to make that decision. You had no right."

"We're so sorry." Britt tilts her head toward Adrian. He touches her back, a supportive gesture to let her know he's on her side, that they're a team.

The shift in teams still hurts. Two against one. Them against me.

Horrible, hot words brew in my mind, and I hold them back, as usual, biting my tongue until they cool down. I never say what I'm thinking around them, because *that* would get ugly fast, just like it did when I first found out they were together.

My face burns and I clench my hands under the table.

"Why'd you guys have to come to Scotland?" I whisper. They ruined my entire summer. I wish I could tell them to fuck off. I wish there were no repercussions to doing something like that. I wish I didn't have to care about co-parenting, or being the best example to Chelsea, or having any kind of relationship with these people.

I bite my tongue again, this time hard enough that it hurts. I can't be friends with Britt. Best friend coffees? Never again. I want to tell her that right now, that this toxic relationship between us is officially over. We'll never be one big happy family again. I tried. I used to love her. I used to love *us*. But it's too much, too soon, and probably too impossible.

Instead, I stop myself and let that last question linger in the air between us.

Britt squeaks. "Oh, Reese. We didn't know you were coming . . ." Now *she* looks like she's going to cry.

It's never her fault, is it? She's always done the right thing, even though she ended up engaged to Adrian. She's a good person. But that doesn't mean I have to be friends with her.

"I'm going now." My voice is flat. Dead. Completely emotionless.

I shove back the chair with a loud scraping against the floor, grab my bag, and stride out of the cafe, ignoring Britt's weak call to me. It's all too much to process.

The rain has stopped but the clouds are dreary and gray, Scotland's farewell to me, I suppose. Instead of pivoting into my flat at the fish and chips shop, I keep walking. I stride right by Oliver's house without even turning my head. My feelings for him are way too complicated. I'll put a pin in them for another time—hopefully never—because there's no point in dealing with that kind of pain.

I'll never see Oliver again.

A little moan comes out of my throat as I leave his house behind and pass the soccer fields. I can't worry about him. The only important thing is my daughter and what she's thinking right now.

I tap out a text as I approach the brick building behind the hotel where the girls are staying.

ME

Chelsea, do you have a minute? I'm outside your building.

There's nothing for a full thirty seconds. I was such an awful role model for her this summer, when my intentions were the exact opposite.

CHELSEA

Sure. I'm just packing. Coming down now.

A minute later, Chelsea trots out of the entrance and abruptly stops a few feet away when she sees my face.

"You okay, Mom?"

Chelsea doesn't seem mad. She can never hide her negative emotions, and when it looks like she's *trying* to hide something, that's when I know she's the most upset. But her face is smooth and unconcerned, her arms hanging by her side, one hand clutching her phone.

"I'm fine, sweetheart." My insides squeeze in disagreement, but I ignore them and keep talking, entwining my hands together. "I just had lunch with your father and Britt. I know she told you about . . . about me and your coach." I flinch. It sounds so much worse than if I'd just called him Oliver.

Chelsea raises her eyebrows and quirks her mouth into an amused grin that fully reaches her eyes.

What's that about? I have to keep talking. Maybe it's a spiteful grin. A mean one. Like she's angry at her skanky mother. But that's not really Chelsea's style, is it?

"It was inappropriate of me to get involved with him. I'm so sorry if this embarrassed you or made you feel uncomfortable." I twist my hands. So many poor decisions I can't take back.

But would I *want* to take back the decision to fake date Oliver?

"Mom."

I close my eyes. "I should be setting a better example for you."

Chelsea slides her smooth hands over mine. "Mom. Open your eyes."

I comply, and her unlined face and dark gray eyes, ones that mirror mine, are staring at me with compassion and kindness.

"Chelsea . . ."

"I'm not mad. I'm . . . actually impressed." Chelsea raises her eyebrows. "Coach Oliver is hot. Super broody and, like, untouchable. Most of the girls have crushes on him. Luckily, I'm not one of those girls, because that would be hella awkward."

I burst out laughing and fireworks of happiness explode through my layers of angst. "Seriously?"

"Seriously. He was—is—an amazing footballer, but he's super old. Not my type."

I laugh. "Well, that's a relief." Relief is an understatement. The tension melts from my body, leaving me weak. "And now we're calling it football?"

"Of course. That's what it is, right?" She grins at me. "Are you happy with him?"

I shake my head. "I was, but we're leaving tomorrow, so we agreed to end things."

"Oh, Mom, I'm so sorry." Chelsea throws her arms around mine and pulls me in.

"Who's the grown-up here, anyway?" I whisper in her sweet-smelling hair.

"You are." She leans back and looks at me. "You always are. Even now. Mom, you deserve to be happy. I was upset when Britt told me about you and Oliver because it pissed me off that she's the one who told me."

"Oh . . ."

"*Not* pissed at you. I can kind of see why you didn't tell me. But it wasn't her place. She's always stepping out of her lane, and sometimes I kinda hate her for it."

A cackle escapes my throat before I can rein it in. I love this girl beyond words.

"But she's going to be your stepmother, so it'd be best if you didn't hate her."

"Ugh. Don't remind me." She drops her hands from my arms. "But, Mom? It'd be okay if you told her to fuck off every once in a while, you know."

"Chelsea. Language."

She rolls her eyes. "I'm just saying. Don't let her bully you into being friends again. Things happened just as you remember, and if she tries to convince you otherwise, that's called gaslighting. I was there too. I saw it all happen. It wasn't right."

I freeze and let Chelsea's words wash over me. I stopped myself from telling off Adrian and Britt just now. It's always up to me to behave, to pretend it's okay, to be the accommodating co-parent, the willing friend.

But maybe Chelsea's right. Maybe I shouldn't hold back as much.

"I'll let you get back to packing. I've got to get my stuff together, too." I pull her into a hug. "Love you so much."

"You too, Mom."

I head back to my flat, my brain a jumbled mess of thoughts, my heart already on the airplane.

OLIVER

Monday, 22 August
The Day Reese Leaves
Oliver's House

I canna believe it. After all the worry about my reputation and lack of coaching experience, Karla sent through an offer email late last night. I sit on my bed and read it again.

From: Karla Smith
Subject: Job Offer for Assistant Coach Position, Crenshaw FC

Hello Oliver,

We are so excited to offer you the position of Assistant Coach at Crenshaw FC. You are a perfect fit, with your impressive professional football experience, your passion for coaching, and your commitment to our family-oriented club.

Expect an official offer letter tomorrow. I'll ring you in the morning to touch base.

Kind regards,
Karla

The phone sounds in my hand, and it's Karla.

"Good morning," I say.

"Hello there, Oliver! I just sent through the offer letter email."

"Wonderful, thank you." I tap back to my email, close yester-day's message from Karla, and return to my inbox. There it is—the official offer from Crenshaw FC.

"Have a look and let me know if you have any questions."

At a quick glance, it looks perfect. The salary is acceptable. The job is as I thought. This whole situation is exactly what I wanted. Ah dinna ken how I pulled this off. Maybe the picture pushed them over the edge . . . or maybe Reese gave me the confidence to go after what I want.

"So I guess John was happy with my answers to his questions about my past?"

Karla is silent on the line for a beat. "There was never a question about your past, Oliver."

"But I thought when you said family-oriented, you were hinting at . . ." I trail off, confused, not wanting to give her a reason to rescind the job offer.

"Oh, Oliver, no. That's just the speech we give to all job applicants who apply to become part of the Crenshaw family. We understand everyone has a rough go of it sometimes. What we care about is who you are today and what you can contribute to the club."

She ends the call a minute later and I sit on my bed, dumbfounded. They never cared about my terrible behavior after I left Winchester FC? So there was no reason for me to tell her about Reese and send that picture?

I play back some of the conversations I had with Karla and John. I guess they never asked specifically about the nonsense in the tabloids, the pictures, the rumors, anything like that.

It was all in my head.

My own insecurities. And I manifested that into reality and burdened my relationship with Reese. Regret grips me, but it's too late. She's already at the airport.

Not that it matters. We still live on different continents.

It's truly over.

They want me to start next week, and I start pulling clothes out of drawers in preparation to leave Peebles. What's the point of staying here for another week and walking past Reese's empty flat every day?

My phone buzzes again and I jump. I've checked my messages a hundred times since we parted at The Peebles Beans yesterday. But we already said goodbye.

There's no message from Reese, but a new one from David. I rake my hand over my face.

What else would I say to Reese? Goodbye, again? Goodbye, but harder? Another long, lingering kiss? There's nothing else to say. Nothing else to do.

I open David's text.

> **DAVID**
>
> I knew you could do it, lad. You're a gifted coach and will do great things with Crenshaw FC. One day, I'll steal you away from them.

After typing back a quick thank you, I collapse back onto the bed, phone gripped in my hand. The space next to me is vacant—space Reese took up just a few days ago. Turning my head, I can see the ghost of her gazing at me, her bare shoulders angled toward my body, the curve of her waist and her hips . . . how my hand fit perfectly in that spot.

She took up more than the space of her body. She lived rent-free in my head. *Lives.*

I miss her already.

I roll up slowly in an extended abdominal crunch and head to the kitchen to make tea. As the kettle's heating, my phone buzzes again and I look at it, desperate hope shooting through me like a star in the night sky.

But it's not her. Again.

"Fuck." I need to get a grip.

CAT

How are you? How is Reese? She was lovely.
I'm glad you brought her on Saturday.

Besides the initial shocker that Cat is sending me a casual, chatty text, I absorb that, *of course,* it's about Reese. I finally get Cat's approval on something, and that thing is already gone.

I groan and tilt my head back, looking for strength in my kitchen's ceiling.

CAT

Lucas loved having you at the party. You did
great with him. I hope you were serious about
starting over. Being his da for real.

I havena gotten such engagement from Cat on my personal life since we were together over a decade ago. It feels like she's always hated all my life decisions. I'm used to being a constant disappointment.

But these days, she seems to care.

Too bad I've fucked this up already. But it was planned. I didna do anything wrong. It was always destined to be this way: me, alone, at the end of the summer.

Right?

Och. Then why does it feel so wrong? Why does it feel like I messed up?

Teeth clenched, I tap out a response. Might as well rip the damn plaster right off and go back to disappointing Cat.

ME

Reese and I split since she's heading back to America. Today.

I pause and wait before continuing to type.

ME

But the good news is I got the coaching job. I'm heading to Crenshaw-on-the-Sea later this week. I'm gonna be around for Lucas.

My phone vibrates and Cat's name dances on my screen as an incoming call. This was important enough for her to call? I'm not sure the woman has *ever* called me.

"Hallo." I put her on speaker and lay the phone on the counter.

"Did you know she was going back so soon? What did you do to ruin this?" Cat's sharp words cut me.

I groan. "Aye. And I didna do anything. She was always going back. This was never gonna be permanent, as much as it pains me to say it." I rub my eyes with two fingers.

"Well, that was daft, wasn't it?"

"What, her going back to her life in America? She's got a daughter in high school and—"

"Nae, you arse, you letting her go. *That* was the daft part."

"She's a good ma, Cat, like you. She would never leave Chelsea. And I'm here. Remember? I got a job. I'm gonna be around for Lucas, finally. Trust me, there's no solution."

Cat sighs loudly, letting me know just what she thinks of my reasoning.

"This is just like you, Oliver Vass. How can you give up and walk away from the best thing to happen to you in, well, I dunno, ever?" Her voice is not unkind.

"Cat. Come on."

"Nae. It's true. She was perfect for you. She was real, Oliver."

Cat's words stab through to my soul. I dinna wanna hear them.

Oh. Ah ken how to make her stop.

"It wasna even real. It was fake." I raise my eyebrows and turn up a cold smile. Now she'll hate me again.

"What do you mean by that?" Cat's voice goes still.

"I was helping her avoid her twat of an ex-husband, and she was helping me to not look like a loser in front of you and my parents. I wanted you to think I had my life together."

There's complete silence on the other line. *Aye, this will do it.* This will make Cat stop preaching in my ear. The last thing I need is the opinion of my son's mum on my love life. Then again, this could completely backfire.

"Cat? In case that wasn't clear . . . we were faking it. The entire relationship was a sham. A business arrangement." A vision of Reese's lips flashes through my mind. Her stony gray eyes. Her laugh. Her smile.

Some fucking business arrangement.

Cat chuckles, then laughs. At what I said? Words that should've angered her. Words that could risk her letting me spend time with my son.

Instead, I entertained her.

"The fuck?"

"Och, Oliver." She breathes in and I can hear the smile in her voice. "You poor, clueless, beautiful man. You know nothing about women. Did you know that?"

"I can honestly say I have no idea what you're talking about, but aye. Ah ken that I'm clueless." I spread my hands flat on the counter and hang my head, trying to figure out what is so amusing to her.

"Exactly." Cat pauses for effect.

"I give up. Tell me."

"That woman was faking nothing with you on Saturday night. She looked at you like you were a purple flying unicorn. A god.

Like how everyone used to look at you when you were at the top of your game. But this time, it wasna about football. Do you know what she did?"

I make a questioning grunt, unable to form words.

"She told off your parents. Aye. She followed them out the front door as they were leaving and fucking chastised them for being unsupportive, both now and when you were growing up."

"What?" My head snaps up.

"Can you picture it? It was quite brilliant, actually. And brave. Your parents can be scary as shite. I saw Reese slip out the front and went to make sure she was okay. When I peeked my head out, I witnessed it all."

"For fuck's sake." I cover my mouth with my hand. I'm not sure if I'm going to laugh or cry or swear. Maybe all three. She told off Ma and Da? She stood up to my parents? No one's ever done anything like that for me. No one would dare. No one has cared enough—ever.

"I would say this woman loves you, Oliver. You. Not your fame or your game. You."

I run my hand down my neck and leave my mouth gaping open.

"And you, Oliver, you. You were looking at her like she was a bespoke gift from the heavens. Like you'd never seen a woman before. I dinna give a shite what kind of agreement you stupidly made. That's the realest I've ever seen you."

Rewind. Cat thinks Reese *loves* me?

"She doesna." My throat is bone dry, and my voice comes out raspy and weak. "She doesna love me." There's no way. Cat has no clue what she's talking about.

"Maybe. Maybe not. What the hell do I know? But *you* sure looked like you were quite fond of *her*. So dinna tell me it's fake. Tell yourself whatever bull you want, but dinna spew those lies to me, of all people."

I shake my head and back up to collapse on one of the hard kitchen chairs.

"I've got to go. Go fix this, Oliver. Figure it out. Dinna tell me it's impossible. You need to get yourself together. Not just a job, although that's a start, isn't it? Figure this out with Reese. It'll make you an even better da to Lucas, yeh ken?"

She hangs up, and I drop my head in my hands.

What is she talking about? There's nothing to figure out. There's nothing to fix. I said goodbye to Reese. She's gone now, and everything is on the right track for me.

But I think about that first whisper in Reese's ear, the way her hand felt in mine on the field when we met. The kiss at Melrose Abbey. The night with wine and cheese at her flat that was supposed to be another get-to-know-you date but ended up in mind-blowing sex. The way she touched my tattoos, examined my drawings, appreciating the one of Lucas on the River Tweed. The way she was there for me on Saturday night, giving me the confidence to be a da to Lucas.

The way she sees me.

My knee bounces and I bury my hands in my hair. I growl into the empty house.

Cat's fucking with my head. I know what I have to do: pack my stuff, move to Crenshaw-on-the-Sea, and build my new life here in Scotland.

All my decisions have been made, and there's no going back now.

31

REESE

Departure Day
Edinburgh Airport

The worst decision I've ever made was to fake date Oliver Vass. What made me think I could handle such a thing? Fake dating is a professional-level tactic. I'm not even playing rec.

The flight attendant walks by, scooting around passengers, helping to stuff bags in the overhead bins.

I sigh and glance down at my phone, where the group text with my sisters glows on the screen.

STELLA

I'll miss having you on the same continent, even if we only saw each other once.

MADDIE

Stella, you should just move back to the US.

STELLA

Sorry, no can do. I have a big career and a very important life in London.

MADDIE

Whatever, Miss Independent.

STELLA

Reese, I can't believe he showed up yesterday when you were with Adrian and Britt.

MADDIE

Super swoony move.

STELLA

Let's not go overboard, okay? But it was pretty sweet.

MADDIE

Reese, are you sure it's over? Like really over? He didn't run after you in the airport and beg you to take him back? Remember that scene in Love Actually when that little boy did that? He pushed through the security line and sprinted to the gate to find the love of his life.

I squeeze my eyes shut. Why do they keep asking me if it's really over? Or maybe it's me asking myself the same question that feels repetitive.

ME

It's over. Like we planned.

MADDIE

Boo.

ME

But that was a great scene.

STELLA

I still can't believe you pulled off fake dating.

Did I, though?

ME

> Have to go. Doors are closing. Love you both
> so much.

I click out of the text chain and glance at Chelsea in the window seat, her noise-canceling headphones on, eyes closed, head bopping. Adrian and Britt are a few rows back. I didn't think this through when I changed my return flight . . . This was the cheapest option, and naturally it was the one with all of them on it. I literally can't get away. Luckily for me, Chelsea's still pissed at them for telling her about Oliver, so she swapped her seat to an empty one next to me.

My hand vibrates with an incoming text and a breath catches in my throat.

Stella was joking about Oliver running through the airport after me, but while we waited in the security line an hour ago, I'd kept looking behind us, hoping against hope that he'd show up at the airport in some kind of romantic grand gesture. There are certain parts about *Love Actually* that have not aged well—like seriously problematic—but that scene isn't one of them.

Only the text is not from Oliver.

MARISA

> This little dude can't wait for you to get home.

There's a picture of Peanut Butter sitting in the middle of Marisa's kitchen table, staring accusingly at the camera.

MARISA

> Actually, I'm not sure he noticed you were
> gone. He's hardly noticed me—especially when
> I try to get him off my table—and he's been
> living here for a month.

I snort and download the picture, forwarding it to Chelsea, even though she's sitting next to me.

I can't get Oliver's blue eyes out of my mind. The look in them when he finally told me about Lucas, with a mixture of shame and resignation. How he thought I'd just walk out. The way he always showed up when I needed him, even in the end for our fake breakup. But now I'll never see him again. I'll go back to my home in New Jersey and live my boring, pained life where I attempt to avoid my ex-husband, just like I did before.

I've accomplished nothing in Scotland.

The flight attendants stand in the aisle and mime the actions in the plane's safety video. I pull my hair over my shoulder and tug until it hurts just a little.

"Aw, Peanut Butter misses us."

"You think?" I turn my head to my daughter—her headphones are now around her neck—and smile. "Marisa's house is bigger, so maybe he's happier there."

"Ugh, Mom, what is that look on your face?" She crinkles her smooth forehead. "You look like you're going to bite me or something."

"It's a smile. I'm smiling." I try, but it feels like a grimace, not a grin.

"Please stop."

I sigh and lean my head back against the airplane seat. "Sorry. I'm excited about going home. Are you?"

"You're acting so weird." Chelsea turns her whole body to face me. "It's about Oliver. How'd you leave things with him?"

I groan. "Fine. I left it fine. And I shouldn't be talking to you about this."

"Come on, Mom. I think we're past that now. We can talk about boy stuff together. Did you talk to him again after you came to see me yesterday? Did you guys make up?"

Pressing my lips together, I shake my head. "No, sweetheart, I told you yesterday. We ended things. I didn't talk to him again."

Chelsea gasps. "Oh no. Mom."

"What did you expect?" I frown, curious about her reaction. Did Chelsea think Oliver and I would try doing the long-distance thing? "My life is with you in New Jersey, and his is in Scotland with his son."

She rolls her eyes. "You guys are all so this or that."

"You guys?" I bite back a grin.

"Old people," Chelsea says with a savagely straight face. "When will you learn that *everything* is negotiable in life? I'm not saying you should go run off and get married or do something ridiculous, but it doesn't have to be all or nothing, Mom."

"Doesn't it?" I say to myself. "Besides. It wasn't even real. It was mostly pretending."

I can't believe I said that out loud to Chelsea, that truth I'd tried so hard to keep secret. But was it a truth, that we were faking things? Or am I telling her a lie, because we weren't faking things at all?

She looks confused, but then again, so am I.

"What does that even mean?"

"Chelsea." I attempt a chastising stare to stop her from questioning me further. I fail.

She flutters her eyelashes at me. "It's so funny. I *knew* something was up with you this month. Every time we met up, you had this silly grin on your face, and you just seemed . . . different. Happy. Even with Dad and Britt showing up. I couldn't figure it out."

"It was the fresh Scottish air." But there's a lump in my throat.

"Mom." She shakes her head and continues. "And then I saw you two walking together at Edinburgh Castle and I was like . . . what's going on there? He touched your back, but then you guys disappeared around a corner." She twitches her lips into a smile. "It all makes sense now. You were so into each other."

She saw us at Edinburgh Castle? That could've been a disaster. Or maybe not.

"Honey, sometimes things really are black and white." My heart feels like it's breaking into a million pieces. Like it did on Saturday night, when Oliver and I had our fight over the picture. And yesterday at the coffee shop, when we staged that not-fake breakup scene. And even now, today, when I wonder if I tried hard enough.

"Mom? Want to act out a desperate love scene and go running back through the airport?"

"No. Listen to your music."

"Fine." Chelsea pouts and puts her headphones back over her ears.

I'm definitely not going to tell her I was thinking that exact same thing. At least she's not pushing me any further, because the thing is, I want to wallow in the impossibility of it all. Kids—even sixteen-year-olds . . . *especially* sixteen-year-olds—don't know what it's like to be an adult with children and real responsibilities. They think they understand so much about life, but they really don't.

This summer was nothing like I expected. It was incredible. I think that's what makes it hurt so much more right now. If I'd had a quiet, uneventful month in Peebles, I imagine I'd feel rested and relaxed right now, not full of turmoil. Not contemplating— grieving—something I'll never have.

Because I was right all along: love is fake.

I'm a complete failure for myself, Oliver, Chelsea. Instead of being an independent, strong woman and mother, I'm a heartbroken, almost-middle-aged version of that person. On a plane to New Jersey.

No more beautiful, green Scottish Borders or trips to Edinburgh. I never even explored the Highlands, or pet a sheep, or picked thistle in a field. What kind of summer in Scotland is that, anyway?

Am I at rock bottom?

The flight attendant slams shut the last overhead bin. I check my phone once more. No new messages. I consider one last text. Goodbye? Or maybe ask him his favorite movie, or when he had his first kiss. How did we not cover those two?

There's so much left unsaid, but at the same time, no reason to get to know each other any further.

I tap my phone into airplane mode and close my eyes. It's over.

32

OLIVER

Wednesday, 24 August
2 Days After Reese Left
Crenshaw-on-the-Sea, Scotland

The drive from Peebles to Crenshaw-on-the-Sea, a touristy village northeast of Edinburgh and almost up the coast to Aberdeen, is less than three hours.

Minutes after checking into a hotel in the town center, a stone's throw from the water, I'm itching to leave again. I canna sit around feeling claustrophobic in this nondescript, sad room. Not when the ocean is so close. I also dinna have the strength to search for flats like I'd planned to do, either online or by calling the estate agent I'd connected with yesterday.

Instead, I cram my phone and pencil into my pocket and clutch my notepad in one hand. I run through the village to the water's edge and along the path that turns from moored boats to moss-covered rocky cliffs bordering the sea, climbing the path until I'm high above the water. The wind is strong, and the salty taste of the ocean is prominent in the air. Seabirds circle and dive above me.

There are worse places to live. Worse runs to take every day. I picture it. I'll find a good flat, get to know the local pubs, run daily, see Lucas whenever I can get to Stirling. It's a few hours' drive, but I could easily do a day trip. What else do I have going on?

I wish I'd taken Reese to a place like this. Instead, we chose to lie in bed and stare at each other. Actually, no regrets there.

Maybe she can come visit.

But the jarring idea crushes me with its impossibility. She's gone, and she's not coming halfway across the world to the middle-of-nowhere Scotland to see me.

Inspiration washes over me, like the harsh waves crashing at the bottom of the cliffs, and I halt and squat on a rock. I thumb to the middle of the notebook, ignoring the previous sketches of footballs, empty fields, a Highland cow, and even more drawings of Lucas. Once I'm on an empty page, I sketch a woman in front of the sea, her back to me, dark hair blowing around her head like a shadowed halo, long dress skimming her feet and flying to one side, her fingers splayed next to her thighs, as if she's opening herself up to the sea. It's rough and wild and I love it.

On the next page, I sketch a woman—the same woman—with wide eyes and a subtle grin on her face, holding her finger in front of her lips as if she's shushing someone.

I wish I could show it to Reese. She'd laugh with me at our terribly kept secret. I'm not the best at drawing faces, but there's more than a passing resemblance to her.

If only we could be together one more time and talk about everything. Tell each other all of our truths. Revise the scenes of our relationship that left so many words unsaid. But I canna do that to her. And what are those unsaid words, anyway? I know nothing. I'm just as clueless as Cat said.

I flip back to the first pages in the notebook and stop at the rough sketch of entwined hands. I'd made a note to examine Reese's hands after being dissatisfied with how the woman's hand turned out. Now, crouched in front of the sea, I add more details to her arm. Fingers are delicate but long, nails cut short. I add the heart-shaped smattering of freckles on the top of her hand.

I snap a picture and send it to Patrick.

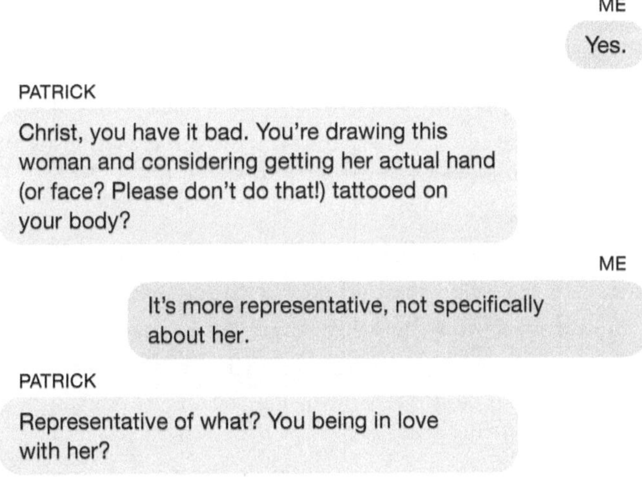

I send him pictures of the other two drawings: the woman from behind and the woman with her finger in front of her face, knowing I'm starting something with him. Sending these to Patrick is a cry for attention, like a footballer rolling around on the field after barely getting touched.

I freeze. The wild ocean roars against the rocks. There it is. The thing I wasn't going to let myself even consider, and Patrick just comes right out and says it.

Me? In love? Nope. Not possible. I've never been in love with anyone. Never. And honestly, never plan to be.

But a voice objects with a whisper-scream in the far corner of my mind. I also never thought I'd be a good da, and that's something I'm trying to do. Reese spent weeks convincing me I'm not just a footballer.

So is it *that* unbelievable I could be in love with her?

The hairs on my arms raise right up.

PATRICK

Listen, mate. You've been texting about her for the past month. You've sent me So Very Many Pictures of you and her together. I have literally never received a picture of you and any other woman you've dated. Yet you claim this was all fake.

ME

I claimed it because it's true.

PATRICK

That's absolute bollocks.

"Fuck," I scream, my voice swallowed by the crashes of waves.

I've fought so hard to keep the words from entering my brain, and now they're written right there in front of me, a blinking neon sign I canna unsee.

Even when Cat called me Monday, I wouldna let myself consider it. Even when she told me she thought Reese was in love with me. How would she know that? And what makes Patrick think *he* knows anything about this, all the way from Ireland? They haven't been here. They dinna ken.

ME

Have you been talking to Cat?

PATRICK

What? Does she agree?

ME

She might have said something similar.

PATRICK

Well, Cat despises you, so I guarantee she's
holding nothing back.

ME

Why did I text you again?

PATRICK

Because you need the truth.

I grip the phone in my hand and squeeze my eyes shut. Is it possible I let the woman I'm in love with just leave, like she was a casual summer fling? I would know if I was in love with someone. It's something that obviously happens, right? Not something that sneaks up on you in between stolen kisses in an abbey or sharing secrets above a fish and chips shop. Or when you're mesmerized by how the corners of her eyes crinkle when she laughs.

Or when she links our hands together and her mere presence gives me the strength to face my ex, my son, my parents, and my entire life.

She made me realize that I can do more, *be more*, and I deserve all the things I want.

I'm here, on what feels like the edge of the world, about to begin a new life, and it all feels so wrong.

Because I should be with Reese.

Because I'm in love with her.

But it's too late. She's gone, and it's my fault. I should've tried harder. I should've fought to keep her, any way possible, at any expense.

ME

Shite.

PATRICK

Realizing I'm right and you fucked up?

ME

Aye.

PATRICK

What are you going to do?

ME

Know anyone in New Jersey?

There's a pause, and I dinna expect a real answer.

PATRICK

As a matter of fact, I might.

I slip my phone into my pocket and stand, eyes now open wide, barely seeing the epic scenery in front of me. And yet, suddenly, everything is clear.

I yell again, letting out heavy layers of repressed feelings, giving them to the ocean to suck down to her depths. A suffocating weighted blanket lifts off my heart. I can breathe. I can see. I understand.

It might be too late to win back Reese. Surely it is. And right now, I canna imagine how it would work. How can I have her and also be a father to Lucas? No matter what Cat said, no matter how much she loved Reese, I suspect she'd be less than impressed at me prioritizing a girlfriend over our son.

There's no way it could work. Is there?

But I have to try. I have to do something.

I know I willna ever have a chance at being happy if I dinna get my arse to New Jersey and beg her forgiveness for not knowing what I had when I had it. For not realizing that she's the realest thing that's ever happened to me.

That I'm madly in love with her.

What will I say to her? What will I tell my new job? Sorry, gotta run a quick errand in America, be back in a week?

I turn and pick up a jog back toward the town center, clutching the notepad in one of my hands like it's a treasure map to a life well-lived. And maybe it is.

The words run through my head, insistent like an announcer at a World Cup final, relentless like a little boy who willna ever stop trying to perfect the Maradona footwork.

I love Reese Hart.

33

REESE

Wednesday, August 31
9 Days After Leaving Scotland
Sharontown High School, New Jersey

I've dropped into some kind of alternate reality.

How is it that ten days ago, I was in gorgeous Peebles, gazing out at the beautiful rolling green hills of the Scottish Borders, dotted with endless white sheep and a purple haze of heather under a moody gray sky?

Contrasted to now.

It's a hundred degrees outside, and the sun and humidity are relentless. I'm in Chelsea's AP English classroom, attempting to listen to her teacher review the syllabus. What I'm really doing is planning my escape route—loop around to the front and dash down the aisle next to the window and out the classroom door—so I don't have to walk to the next class with Adrian and Britt. I've avoided contact with them over the past nine days. There's been only a handful of logistical text messages back-and-forth with Adrian about Chelsea.

There's not even been an invitation from Britt to meet up for coffee.

After that intense goodbye ten days ago at The Peebles Beans, Oliver and I haven't spoken or texted a word to each other. Now it feels too late to even say hello. What would be the point? So we can be pen pals? We don't have anything in common—not really—absolutely nothing to talk about. Yet somehow, the silences between us were never uncomfortable.

It's hard to believe I was kissing him in a park by the River Tweed a heartbeat ago.

"Reese?"

I come back to reality. I'm still sitting in Chelsea's classroom, but most of the parents are heading out the door. Shit! I missed my opportunity for a sneaky exit.

I turn my head toward the voice. Marisa is in the doorway, peeking into the room. Adrian and Britt are chatting with the teacher at the front.

"Hey!" I grab my purse and shoot up, darting out into the hallway to my friend.

"Have you recovered from your summer yet?" Marisa had swung by the night we got home and dropped off Peanut Butter, who, as predicted, was less than impressed by my presence.

Mom and Maddie came over a few days later, and I got to visit with Great-Aunt Evelyn, so I intend to tell Marisa that I'm glad to be back, that it's nice to go away, but coming home is even nicer.

That's what I mean to say.

"I miss it," I say instead, a slight hitch in my voice. "I mean, it's so beautiful there. So romantic." I sigh. "But I came back, so I guess I might as well get over it. Yay Jersey?"

But saying Jersey reminds me of Oliver's nickname for me. My stomach tightens, thinking of his lilting accent.

Marisa blinks at me. "Well. My summer just involved the pool, camps, the beach, kids fighting all the time, the usual suburban mom bullshit. You know how it goes."

I let out a squeaky grunt. "Thanks for taking care of my

grumpy cat. I'm not sure I said it properly when you dropped him off."

Marisa waves her hand in the air. "Anytime. But can we get back to the part where you called your summer romantic? Did you have some wild fling with a hot man in a kilt?"

My eyes widen as—not for the first time—I picture Oliver in a kilt.

"Uh . . ." I'm so distracted by the thought that I don't notice her piqued curiosity.

"Holy shit. You did, didn't you? Spill, woman!"

Marisa and I have spent extraordinary amounts of time with each other over the years at youth sporting events. There's been many inappropriate thoughts shared between us casually at rainy soccer tournaments, huddled under large umbrellas in wet captain's chairs. Even so, I haven't told her the details of the divorce.

"I mean, I don't even know—"

Britt appears out of the classroom, pausing in the hallway, holding my ex-husband's hand, then dropping it when she sees me, as if I've caught her doing something she shouldn't.

I groan.

Adrian nods at me and looks away, as if I'm a greeter at Walmart he's trying to avoid.

"Hi, Ree! Can we talk after the next class? I feel like we haven't connected since we got back from Scotland."

"Sure." I do some kind of face contortion that might resemble a smile.

"Great." Britt waggles her fingers at me and the pair walks away.

When they're gone, Marisa turns to me, her jaw hanging open. "What did she mean, *since we got back from Scotland*? I thought you were going to be there alone?" Marisa's eyes narrow.

"They came to Scotland, too. It was just a ridiculous coincidence that we all changed our flights, and no one told anyone else."

"What?" Marisa grabs my arm and leans forward. She drags me further against the lockers to dodge the parents milling about the classroom entrance.

"Literally. That's what happened."

"I cannot . . ." She shakes her head aggressively.

I understand her horror. I lived it.

"But you weren't far off on the hot Scottish man thing . . ." I quirk my mouth.

Her gasp makes it all worth it.

"No! Are you serious? I want all the details. I need them!" She glances at her phone and groans. "Ugh. I have to run to AP Chemistry. But, Reese?" She smiles at me and tilts her head. "You falling in love with a hot Scottish dude is the best thing I've heard all year. Maybe ever. I'm texting you, like, immediately!"

Marisa skips away—actually skips!—and I crack a grin at the joy I just brought her.

I'm already late to Chelsea's next class, so I take my time walking around the corner, enjoying the quiet hallway. Then it hits me what Marisa said.

You falling in love with a hot Scottish dude.

I grind to a halt in front of Chelsea's next classroom.

Marisa vocalizing the words gave voice to the quiet thoughts that have been floating around in my head since I left Peebles. I know for sure that I miss Oliver. Could I have fallen in love with him?

All at once, I know that's right. The words that I'd fought so hard to suppress are now all I can think.

I love Oliver Vass.

There's a stabbing in my chest. My throat tightens and tears fill my eyes. I lean back against the lockers outside the classroom, placing my hand on my chest and trying to breathe. I close my eyes and Oliver's image springs up in my mind. His wide smile, given freely to me. His piercing eyes, pulling me inside his soul. His strong hands, hard stomach, tattoos littering his body like the most beautiful graffiti.

Oh, no. I squeeze my eyes shut.

We were supposed to be fake dating. Pretending. There was to be no falling in love.

I chuckle, eyes still closed, as if I'm alone in my living room and not leaning against a locker in a high school hallway. *No trying to get me to fall in love with you*, I'd told him that night at The Old Forge, when we talked about terms and conditions. I had been *joking*. Only I did fall in love with him. And he didn't even have to try.

I'm such a loser. There's no way he could love me back. Obviously. If he did, he would have texted, called, emailed, sent a carrier pigeon . . . something. But me, a pathetic little soccer mom from New Jersey, dropped the guard down on my heart long enough to let him in.

"Reese?"

My eyes spring open. Britt is hovering in front of me, brow furrowed, hands clasped in front of her.

"Are you okay? I came out to look for you."

Here she is, once again intruding on my solitude as I try to figure out what the hell is going on in my brain. Before Scotland, I was committed to a friendship with Britt. But while we were over there, things shifted. I can't do it anymore. I can't pretend.

"Britt . . . I don't think I can do this with you." I let my hand drop from my chest, freeing the truths that have been hiding there.

"Do what?" But she knows. Her eyes open wide—Britt's classic hurt look—then her mouth turns down. "Oh."

"I can't be friends with you. I tried. I thought it'd be fine. I thought I could do it."

"Is this about Oliver? I'm sure it was hard to leave him. It's only been a week since we left, so I get it." Her face contorts. "And again, I'm so sorry for telling Chelsea. I'm glad she was okay about everything in the end."

As usual, she looks genuine in her concern for me. I curl my toes. I don't want her input, or her pity, or any kind of commentary on my life. I don't want to share my thoughts and feelings with her.

And I don't want to feel bad about any of that.

"You'll find someone," she continues, biting her lip when she pauses. "Someone here, in New Jersey, which makes a lot more sense. And he was kinda not your type?" As soon as the words are out of her mouth, her eyes grow wide.

"My type?" Angry lava bubbles up inside me.

"I'm sorry, I didn't mean that . . ." Britt slides a hand behind her neck, cringing.

"Like Adrian? Is that who you think my type is?" I stop there. Still biting my tongue, even now.

Chelsea's words from that Sunday before we left Scotland echo in my head. She'd said: *It'd be okay if you told her to fuck off every once in a while, you know.*

I've bit my own tongue enough times to keep the peace. I've given Britt what she wanted, including my blessing on her relationship with my ex-husband. And now . . . I'm done.

"Britt." I lift my chin. "How I'm feeling right now, about Oliver, about anything in my life, is none of your business."

She flinches.

"I can't do this thing between us anymore."

"No," she whispers.

"I can't be your real friend. We can't rebuild our friendship."

"But you said . . ." Her face crumples, as if she's bracing herself for more hurtful words.

"I tried. I really did. I'm sorry. I wanted to be there for you after your father died. I thought I could. But I just can't. Too much has happened."

"Ree—"

I shake my head violently at first, then slow down. "I'm sorry, Britt. The best we can do is be co-parents. Acquaintances. That's it." This hurts. It's like I'm breaking up with a long-term boyfriend or a husband.

Adrian appears outside of the classroom.

"Everything okay?" He takes his place next to Britt, studying her face, then mine.

"Reese is upset," Britt whispers.

Adrian slides his arm over her shoulders and pulls her close before turning his gaze to me with questioning eyes.

"I decided to stay in Scotland for the month so I could get my head on straight. To reset my life, figure out all the things I was feeling. Then you guys showed up. And that was really hard." I keep steady eye contact with Adrian.

"We didn't know you were going to be there," he says, all logical and reasonable.

"I know. It was nobody's fault. No one did anything wrong." That seems to be the theme of my life these past few years. No one was to blame for my divorce either, not really. But still, that doesn't mean I have to be okay with what happened. "I didn't get a reset, but I figured out a lot of stuff. Notably, that I can't be friends with you guys. It's too soon. Maybe I need more time. But maybe there will never be enough time. I suspect that might be the case." I glance back and forth between them, biting my cheek to make sure I don't do anything dreadful like cry.

There's so much more I could say. I could tell Adrian that I'm better off not married to him. That we were strangers at the end, and our marriage wasn't making either of us happy. I could tell Britt that she betrayed me, and I'm not sure I can ever get over that. I could tell them to leave me the fuck alone.

But I don't say any of it. They know, though. The looks in their faces betray their knowledge of the truth.

Regret stabs me in the belly at the loss of my friendship with Britt. She's going to be impossible to replace. She crosses her arms and turns to Adrian, burying her face in the crook of his shoulder.

But I needed to stand up for myself. I need to take care of myself, not just the people around me.

Parents pour out of the classrooms. It turns out I missed all of Chelsea's European History class, and that was the last one I had to attend for today.

I spin around and stride away from my ex-husband and former best friend, my insides squeezing and swirling. Pushing away that interaction as I dodge groups of parents to exit the school, I go back to the realization I'd had right before Britt interrupted my moment of solitude.

I'm in love with Oliver.

I slide into my car and lean my head back, relieved at the truth, imagining what I'd say to him if he were in front of me. I'd tell him I love him for exactly who he is. Not the ex-professional soccer player. Not a soccer coach. Not a dad, or a friend, or a fake boyfriend.

I love him for who he is inside. The one who draws on the banks of the River Tweed. The one who is desperate to be accepted by the people around him. The one who makes me laugh and forces me to try gross orange Scottish drinks before kissing me like I, alone, can pull him from an angry ocean.

But it's too late for all that, and the joy at knowing who I love fades when I remember how far away he is, and how impossible it would be for us to be together.

Yeah, if he were in front of me, I'd tell him those things. I'd give him a proper goodbye, full of truths. But he's not going to magically show up here, in this shitty New Jersey town. I open my eyes and glare down at my phone. I could call him. I could text him. But that wouldn't be fair to him, or me. And who knows what he'd say. I can't do that just to get it off my chest. I need to respect him and let him be who he wants to be without meddling.

It's just like they always say—I didn't know what I had when I had it. And I'm going to have to live with that for the rest of my life.

34

OLIVER

Saturday, 3 September
12 Days After Reese Left
Train to Sharontown, New Jersey

I've been twenty-five miles from Reese's home in New Jersey for the past week, just a bus, underground subway, and train ride away. Like Reese was doing in Peebles, I'm resetting my life with a wee bit of help from Patrick and Ian's tattoo parlor connections in New York City.

Things happened so fast after that run in Crenshaw-on-the-Sea.

Self-doubt, my constant companion, worms its slithering presence up my leg, my torso, and finally tightens around my neck. I scratch at my throat, forcing myself to take deep breaths. Maybe I should've gone to see her right away. Maybe I should've warned her I'm coming. What if she doesna want to see me?

But first, I wanted to make sure this tattoo parlor situation was going to work out.

The distance between us gets shorter by the second. The commuter train barrels through suburban New Jersey towns, the scenery morphing from tall, towering buildings and stopped traffic to rows of single houses, main streets, schools, and sports fields. I shake my hands and roll my neck, hoping to calm my body.

I wanna look at her again and take time to memorize the lines of her face and the curves of her body, like I didna do enough of in Peebles. I wanna slide my hands on the sides of her face and pull her lips to mine, feeling the electricity between us, converting the unspoken words to spoken ones.

I wanna tell her I love her.

It's something I'd have rolled my eyes at before I met Reese. This over-the-top grand gesture, showing up at her house thousands of miles away from where she thinks I am—from where I'm *supposed* to be—to confess my love.

"Fuck," I whisper, then cringe and mouth *sorry* to the mom with her kids and partner seated across the aisle from me, facing each other in pairs.

I've changed the course of my life because of her. I truly have. When I texted David to let him know what I was planning, he called me right away to try to talk me out of it. How could I give up the coaching job at Crenshaw FC, the one I'd claimed was my dream job? What happened to establishing my life in Scotland, near Lucas? I told him everything. How I feel about Reese. My conversation with Cat and Lucas. My plans.

I'm doing the right thing for me. I'm listening to myself. And the people who care about me most understand that.

But bloody hell, what if she rejects me? The self-doubt snake pops back around my throat, making it hard to swallow. Och.

I didna think this through. I'm gonna get off at the next train station and then what? Use my newly downloaded ride app to get dropped off at her house? Just show up? What if she's not there? Do I sit on her front step like the desperate loser I am? What if she sends me away? Do I walk back to the train station? Request another car right away? Ask the person who drops me off to wait, just in case?

Quit my new job and head back to Scotland?

Fuck.

This time I dinna say it out loud.

The small boy giggles as his mom plays peekaboo with him, and the older boy is dealing cards to his dad. The parents canna be much older than I am, the boy around Lucas's age.

I press my lips together and let my imagination run away. What if I'd stayed with Cat? Would my life be like that, maybe? I could've played football, returning to my family in the offseason and when we had breaks. Then, when it was all over, I'd have gone back to a waiting family. A house and a garden, like the one Cat shares with Grant and Lucas. Maybe *we'd* have had another child, given a sibling to our son much closer in age.

Do I want that kind of life? I'm not sure. I think I want my version of it. With Reese. *Our* version.

I touch my new tattoos, still tender. Patrick quickly put me in touch with his old mate, Thor, who owns a tattoo parlor called Dublin Ink in Brooklyn. Ian worked with Thor for a time in Dublin and both Patrick and Ian vouched for the Irish bloke. After talking on the phone, Thor invited me to come check out his facility. Four days later, I stood at the reception desk of Dublin Ink in Brooklyn. A mere twenty-five miles from Reese.

That felt too much like fate to ignore.

Dublin Ink is incredible. I could tell it was clean and organized the second I walked in. It has tablets with screening questions, digital books of custom art to look through, and a front office manager who makes sure everything runs smoothly.

And Thor is an incredibly talented tattoo artist. So on my fourth day shadowing him, I asked him to ink my new tattoos. I knew by then I wanted to work for him in an apprenticeship, if he'd offer me the role. And yesterday, he did. I accepted.

The train pulls to a stop and I sling my backpack over my shoulder and head off, the summer humidity choking me as soon as I step onto the platform. I look around, and thick moisture in the air reminds me I'm not in Scotland.

I tap through to the text message chain from yesterday.

ME

Jersey. Alright?

There'd been a long pause. And lots of dancing dots that would disappear, then reappear. Finally, her response arrived.

REESE

I'm good. It's so nice to hear from you. How's the new job?

ME

I think it's going to be a perfect fit. I wanna send you something you forgot. Can you give me your address?

Another pause.

REESE

What did I forget?

But she sent through her address right after, and I told her I had to run, not answering her question.

Now, I request a car with her address as the destination, and before I can overthink it, I send Reese a new text.

ME

What's your favorite food? Mine's Thai, but I never tried the place in Peebles.

I picture Reese staring down at the text. Confused? Curious? Baffled as to why I'm asking? Hopefully she's not busy, or out, or on a week-long vacation.

REESE

Well, I missed bagels and good pizza while we were in Scotland, so I guess that's my answer.

A short honk gets my attention, and I climb in the back of the car, not lifting my eyes from my phone. There are dots, then none, then dots.

> **REESE**
>
> City or country? I like a bit of both, which I guess is why I live where I do. We're just a few miles from New York City.

Thank fuck she's engaging with me. I don't know what I would've done if she'd blown me off when I'm a minute from her house.

Och, hell, we're here.

The driver pulls to a stop and tells me to have a nice day.

"Thanks, mate." I step out of the car and it departs, leaving me standing at a front walkway leading to a tidy, two-story brick home with a one-car garage and an SUV parked out front.

My chest thumps with nerves, and I can barely hear my own swirling thoughts. What am I doing here? I shift from foot to foot, considering going for a quick run around the block to calm myself. But that would be weird. Imagine she looks out her window and I'm jogging by? And then I'm a sweaty mess, like I was that Sunday at The Peebles Beans? But this time, I'd be even sweatier because of the humidity.

What is my plan?

An approaching car disturbs my thoughts. It slows. I breathe in sharply and wish I wasna frozen to this spot. The car turns into Reese's driveway. *For fuck's sake.*

A teenaged girl in the driver's seat stares at me with wide-eyed curiosity before looking down at her phone.

Then I realize. She's here for Chelsea. I turn to the front door just as it's opening. This is about to get awkward.

Chelsea appears in the doorway, a football bag over her shoulder, curiosity already on her face. The girl in the driveway must've texted her.

Her jaw drops at the sight of me. "Coach Oliver? What are you doing here?" Her face crumples with confusion.

"Hallo, Chelsea, uh . . ."

And then her face clears and her eyes open wide. "Ohhh. You're here for my mom." She gasps, spins around, and pushes the door back open. "Mom! Come here now! Like, immediately!"

In the driveway, the car door opens and Chelsea's friend steps out and leans against the car, as if she's waiting for some kind of performance.

All the breath disappears from my body.

Chelsea turns back to me, a huge smile on her face.

And then . . . Reese appears behind her. Her jaw drops, and she covers her mouth with a hand.

"What . . . Oliver?"

Chelsea looks back and forth between us and chuckles. "OMG. Old people are so funny." She then jogs down the front steps to her waiting friend. "Let's go."

"We're leaving? Now?" her friend says with a whine.

Chelsea laughs. "Get in the car. They'll never be able to do this with us watching."

The girls pull out of the driveway, leaving Reese and I staring at each other.

"Call me, Mom!" Chelsea yells from the passenger seat's open window.

All words have abandoned me. She is a vision, wearing a tight tank top, short shorts, and bare feet, her hair down and over her shoulders.

I clear my throat. "I like a mix of the country and city, too. Peebles is probably perfect. Or Stirling, really. Enough shops and places to eat, a good pub or two. But not too intense with tourists and crowds."

Reese quirks one side of her mouth. "And a coffee shop, obviously."

"Naturally, although I'm fine with a cuppa at home. And I like cities sometimes, too."

She makes a nondescript murmur. "What are you doing here, Oliver?" Her face is soft and open, a smile lingering on her mouth, but her forehead creases in confusion. "Come in, come in, it's so hot out here." She waves me inside and I finally get my feet to move into the foyer of her home.

"I was in New York City, so I thought I'd stop by."

"What? New York? Do you have some kind of coach training in the city?" She crosses her arms, her eyes searching my face for answers.

"Training of sorts." I shake my head, then nod. "So, yes and no. I went to Crenshaw-on-the-Sea as planned, but . . ."

I pause, searching for the words to explain how I've revamped my life yet again.

"But what?"

". . . but it wasna right. It wasna the right thing to do."

Her face scrunches up, the space between her eyebrows creased. "I thought this was all you wanted? To coach? Be close to Lucas?"

I flinch, then nod. How I explain this to her will be important.

The first thing I did after talking to Patrick was drive my arse to Stirling to talk to Cat. I told her everything I was feeling. I told her I felt like all I could ever do was play or coach football, and that was someone I no longer was. That being a father to Lucas was the most important thing to me.

That I am in love with Reese. Cat was right about us.

Cat's response to my confessions made me realize she loves me as a friend and would support me in whatever I have to do. She reminded me she'd already told me to go fix this thing with Reese, however I had to do it.

"Being a father to Lucas is the most important thing in the

world," I say firmly. "And I'm going to do that. I am that already. But I need . . ."

How do I say this without sounding ridiculous?

Reese steps forward, uncrosses her arms, and reaches for my hands.

"What? What do you need?" Her eyes are as wide as the ocean that was between us. Her touch sends tingles up my arm, and I shift, and her eyes flit down to my left forearm, still raw from the design. Her eyes follow mine and she breathes in sharply. "You got a new tattoo."

Reese's hands cradle my arm, and she stares intently at the new ink.

"Aye."

"It's not a soccer tattoo." She states the obvious, her fingers running over the fresh lines.

"It's not done yet." I watch her as she takes in the tattoo. It's a more intricate version of what I sent to Patrick when I was at the cliffs in Crenshaw-on-the-Sea. Two hands entwined, with the background of the cliffs overlooking the ocean, wild in the distance.

She breathes out, her eyes flitting from mine to the tattoo.

"I got another one, too. Of Lucas. On my leg." I tilt my calf so the tattoo is facing up at her. It's Lucas from the front, standing with his hands on his hips on the banks of the River Tweed. He's smiling and hopeful and I imagine he's looking at me while he does it. "It'll be my reminder that I'm his da. Just like you told me I could be."

Reese stares down at my leg, not letting go of my arm.

"It's gorgeous," she says. "And this one . . ." She runs her finger along the hands on my arm. "I love it."

"I'm gonna be in New York City for the next year. Working as an apprentice at a tattoo parlor. It took me about an hour to get here by public transportation."

Reese gasps and looks up from the tattoo. She's so close to me.

All I want to do is kiss her.

"I don't understand." Her cheeks are pink, even with the air-conditioning. "Why?"

"Because I dinna want to coach football. I enjoyed it, and I could make a life doing it, but I need more. You helped me realize that I can have more than that. Or, rather, that I can be different from that. That I deserve to be multiple things in my life, and even though I need to be a real father to Lucas, I also need to be true to myself. And I couldna do that with football, not anymore. I've always dreamed of working at a tattoo parlor, even though I'd not quite admitted it to myself. Now I get to try that dream out."

"I'm so glad you are figuring things out, but . . . couldn't you work at a tattoo parlor in Scotland?" she whispers the last words, holding our eye contact as if it's her thin tether to life.

"Yes. But *you're* not in Scotland." She must know the truth by now. She has to understand why I'm here in the foyer of her house in New Jersey.

Her hands grip my forearm, our eyes locked. The tension between us as fragile as glass and as electric as lightning.

"That's true. I'm not in Scotland." Her words are breathless as she waits for me to continue.

"I'm in love with you, Reese, and I couldna live with myself if I didna tell you in person. I needed to be here and take a chance that you'd want to try things out with us. For real."

A squeak escapes her throat, but she doesna speak.

"And . . . even if you don't feel the same way, even if this thing between us was just a fling, nothing at all, like you said to your sister that day in the park—"

Her eyes widen. "Oliver . . ."

"—I still wanted to tell you how I feel."

There. I've said it. Relief washes over me. I was true to myself. What happens next is out of my control. I want to grab her and kiss her, but something in her face tells me it's not right yet . . . And maybe it never will be.

35

A hundred thoughts are swirling in my head at once. So many questions, so much I don't understand. But I heard the words he said.

He loves me?

Am I dreaming? I've spent the last three nights grappling with the fact that I'm in love with Oliver, and now he's here, in my house, telling me the same thing? It feels impossible.

But there's a new tattoo on his forearm, and sweet baby Jesus, I'm pretty sure it's our hands, or at least, it represents us. His yearning for connection. His commitment to the relationships in his life.

Part of me feels a soaring joy and fragile hope, but another part of me wonders if it could really be true. If it could be right. He's giving up the life he was working so hard to establish in Scotland . . . to be here? I don't want him abandoning his dreams for me. What if he stays, and in a week or a month, realizes this wasn't the right decision? That he should be in Crenshaw-on-the-Sea, coaching? On the same continent as Lucas?

But what if coaching *isn't* his dream? I'd heard him say it in

Peebles. He feels like he *has* to be a soccer coach, like it's his only option.

"What about Lucas?" I blurt, dropping my hands and crossing my arms on my chest. "How is that going to work? It's one thing not being a coach, but your son . . . I know he's the most important thing in the world to you."

Oliver wanting to be true to himself is music to my ears but giving up his chance at being a good father—at least what he thinks of as one—is not acceptable. He'll never forgive me. He'll never forgive himself.

Oliver slips his hands into the pockets of his shorts and nods.

"I talked to Cat before I came here. A lot. As soon as I realized I didna want the coaching job, I drove to see her and Lucas. She was incredible about it, actually. Cat adores you, Reese, and she was the first one to tell me she thought . . . That she thought there might be something real between us."

"She did?" My voice is a whisper.

Again, he nods. "She was a big fan of your little performance with my parents when they were leaving Lucas's party."

"Oh shit, she saw that?" I bite my bottom lip. Damn, that wasn't meant to be witnessed by anyone.

"Aye." Oliver's mouth quirks up.

"You'd be so far from Lucas." I feel sick. He's here, the man I love, and I want to throw my arms around his neck, but how can I trust it? It seems like he's choosing me over his son.

Oliver nods.

"Cat and I worked that out. I'll see Lucas four times over the next year. First, for Christmas, which I'll spend in Stirling. Then, Lucas will come to New York for his half-term break in February. I'll go back to Scotland in April when he's on spring holidays, and then he might come back again next summer for longer with a friend, and we'll travel somewhere together. After that . . . I'm not sure."

"Oh," I breathe out.

"So I'll see Lucas more than I ever have before. It's a start."

He's thought it through. Coming here wasn't some impulsive decision. He planned it, took into consideration other people's feelings, and made a conscious plan to ensure everyone will have what they need.

And that *he'll* have what he needs. He finally figured it out.

And it's me. *I'm* part of what he wants.

Warmth blooms in my chest. I'd kept the seedling in a locked box until now, away from sunlight, where hope for a future with Oliver was impossible. But now? I think I can let myself feel that. I can let myself feel everything. *Including love.*

We stare at each other. It doesn't seem real that he's in my house, waiting patiently for me to say something. I swallow and uncross my arms, letting them fall to my sides.

"What would you do at the tattoo parlor? What does an apprentice even mean?"

He grins. "I've been there for almost a week. First, Thor loves my art, and wants me to design tattoos in bulk for clients to choose from."

"That's perfect for you. You're an amazing artist."

"Thank you."

I bite my bottom lip. "What else?" I want to know, I do, but mostly I'm delaying what I need to say back to him. I had speeches prepared, but they were goodbye speeches—ones I could have used if I'd said a proper farewell to Oliver at the airport instead of a rushed one at the coffee shop in front of Adrian and Britt.

I gaze into the endless icy pools of his light-blue eyes, imagining swimming in there forever. I can see it.

He loves me.

"I'll also train to give tattoos." Oliver's voice is slightly breathless as he holds eye contact. "To be a proper tattoo artist, you need to have a long apprenticeship with an experienced artist. Once that's over, I can work anywhere I want."

He takes my hands in his. They are suspended between us,

linked, our physical connection that I don't want to sever. Ever. My thoughts are swirling. Do I just tell him I love him? Just like that?

"Jersey."

I blink and swallow hard. "Picasso."

"Did I fuck up by coming here?" His face contorts.

"Oh, no. No. You didn't. I'm just . . . overwhelmed." I move my hands to his chest and slide them up, stepping forward to let our bodies touch, the familiar electrical charges between us grounding me. "I haven't stopped thinking about you since I left Scotland."

Why are the words so hard for me? There's one last rocky section of the wall that's still surrounding my heart, a part that refuses to fall. I want to go at it with a wrecking ball.

"I thought I'd imagined it all." I missed the ridges of his chest. The way they feel beneath my hands. "I thought it couldn't possibly be real between us. I think that's one reason I let myself go with you in Scotland, let myself be, well, myself. Because we'd said from the start that it was fake. I thought that if we pretended—and we both knew it—that it'd be okay to be myself. Does that make any sense at all?"

"Aye." Oliver slides his hands around my waist. "That makes perfect sense."

"I don't believe that romantic love is real. I mean, I didn't . . . That's why it's so easy for either person to break it off and move on." I'm rambling. Trying to convince myself of something.

Oliver pulls me tighter against him, and I move my hands from his chest to around his neck so our bodies press against each other. We're close. So close, it would take just a tilt up of my chin to kiss.

"Do you still believe that, Jersey?"

Do I? With Oliver pressed up against me after declaring his love, and knowing that I am also inexplicably in love with him? How can I deny real love even a second longer?

"No," I whisper. "I believe."

"Reese."

"I'm in love with you, Oliver Vass."

A groan comes out of his throat. "Thank fuck. Can I kiss you now?"

Instead of answering, I pull his lips to mine, burying my hands in the back of his hair, my fingers getting lost in his waves. His mouth is impossibly soft as his tongue gently enters my mouth. I can't imagine letting this go. Letting *him* go.

He pulls back, pressing our foreheads together and breathing.

"I don't know how you did it." My heart is racing.

"Did what?" Oliver slides his hands under my tank top and his fingers splay on my bare back.

"Convinced me to love you." I shiver as he presses against me. "I was looking into getting a tattoo."

"What? Like for real, not just that game you used to seduce me in Peebles?" He leans back and quirks his mouth, deep pink from our kisses.

I laugh. "I'm still trying to figure out what it should be. But now that you're here . . . maybe you could do it."

His eyes grow wide. "What if I fuck it up?"

"You won't." I run my hands down to the hem of his shirt and tug it upward. "But I'd like to do some research, just to make sure I'm making the right decision."

He holds up his arms and pulls his shirt over his head in one smooth move, tossing it behind him.

We've got a few hours till Chelsea gets back, and I know how I want to spend them. In this man's arms.

"You're impossibly sexy, you know that?" I slide my fingers over the hard muscles on his chest, tracing the bear tattoo. Leaning forward, I kiss his neck, starting with the claws, and slide my hands over his abdomen.

He groans and pulls my hands away just as I get to the front of his shorts.

"Nae. You first." His lips meet mine again, this time more intensely.

"Want a tour of my house?" I ask with a smile pressed against his mouth.

He laughs. "Aye. Let's start with the bedroom." But when I try to turn around, he pulls me back against him.

"What?"

He pushes back a strand of my hair. "I love you."

"You already told me that." But my heart skips a beat again, and it comes out as a whisper, not snarky banter.

"Ah ken. But I'll keep saying it, if that's alright with you."

"It's okay with me." I pause. "And I love you, too."

He smiles and leans in to kiss me.

And with that, I lead this impossibly hot, sexy, shirtless Scottish man down the hall and into my bedroom.

36

OLIVER

Saturday, 10 September
One Week Later
Reese's House

I finally feel like I'm home.

Ever since leaving Stirling for my football career, I never felt like one town, city, flat, house—no matter how nice—was my home. I traveled all the time. Never really went back to where I grew up. My parents werena home for me and I was too shite of a father to go see my son regularly.

But now, lying next to Reese in her bed in New Jersey, I feel the most at home I ever have in my life.

I know I canna stay forever, because I need to be there for Lucas. Lucas is also my home. Fuck. Nothing's easy, but I canna worry about all of that now. Not when I have this gorgeous woman lying next to me.

I run my hand down her arm, into the curve of her waist, over the swell of her hips, thankful for her current lack of clothing.

"What are you thinking?" she asks.

"About doing dirty things to you."

Reese laughs. "No, really."

"Really, I am. But also, I wish I could spend every single night with you."

"Your crappy apartment in New York not doing it for you?"

My flat in the city is . . . very small. And I share it with two other lads, both Irish. My room is a closet with two drawers and a tiny bed. Literally, it's a closet.

But it's around the corner from Dublin Ink, and for now, it works.

It's also close to the public transport that gets me to Hoboken, where I can jump on a train to Sharontown.

To Reese.

"Only because you're not there." The rule for now is that I'm only welcome to spend the night when Chelsea is with Adrian, which I understand. I'm hoping Reese will relax that restriction eventually. I intend to be a part of Chelsea's life as well, and even signed up to help coach her team.

We're not faking this, and we're not hiding it, either. Just trying not to worry about Chelsea hearing us have sex.

"I need to sleep some nights, you know. And you should, too, given you're working with giant, scary tattoo needles."

"So you're not sick of me being around yet?" I trace a circle on her hip with my finger.

"No," she says. "Definitely not."

"Good." I slide my hand onto her bare butt and scoot her closer to me. "I was wondering if you managed to get the reset you wanted. Even with everything that happened."

She smiles at me and rises to her elbow, leaning her head on her hand. Hair falls on her shoulder and over her bare breast. I brush it away and graze her nipple with my thumb, loving the way it hardens as she squirms. I canna get enough of Reese, both in and out of the bedroom.

"Not quite in the way I thought I needed."

"Tell me more." I lean in and kiss her shoulder, then her collarbone, then let my lips fall around her nipple, sucking.

Her breath speeds up, and she lets me pull one of her legs over my hip.

"I thought I needed to find myself. To understand who I am without other people breathing down my neck."

I slip my hand between her legs and stroke her center, loving the feel of her muscles squeezing my fingers.

"But I really just needed to find you." Her voice is breathless. Wispy. Distracted. "That's why I went. To fall madly in love with you."

She pulls me on top of her and I slip inside, my breath catching in my throat, my heart squeezing at the sight of her face contorting with pleasure from my movements.

I'll do anything to keep this woman happy. Ah dinna ken what will happen in a year, or even in a few months, but I finally found my purpose in life.

It's Reese Hart.

37

———————

REESE

Saturday, September 17
Another Week Later
Reese's House

The wedding invitation sits on my countertop. I lean on my elbows, sipping my steaming afternoon coffee, and stare. I can't quite figure out how it makes me feel. Something stirs in my belly. Anger? I don't think so. Hatred? No, definitely not. Jealousy? Uh-uh.

It's gorgeous. Of course, it is. Britt has impeccable taste. The sun streams in through the window over my kitchen sink, highlighting the thick cardstock like some kind of golden halo.

But that tingle in my gut? I think it's nerves for Chelsea and how this will affect her. The divorce, the engagement, the people her parents become next. It feels like something she'll deal with in therapy.

My phone vibrates with a group video call from my sisters. I'm not even going to bring up the invitation to them. It doesn't matter enough.

"Hello." I grin at their images.

"So? What's the decision about the holidays?" Stella demands. "Ever since we started talking about you all coming to London in December, I've been desperate for your plans."

It'd been amazing seeing Stella in London before Chelsea and I got to Peebles, but it hadn't been for long enough. She's clearly going through some stuff with her boyfriend. We need more time together. With Maddie, too.

"Well," I say. "I'm still working on details, but Adrian has Chelsea for that week, and Oliver will be in Scotland for the holidays to visit with Lucas, so . . . I'm in. I'll be there the day before Christmas Eve."

Stella squeals. "Really? Maddie?"

Maddie nods, but looks less excited. "It's almost impossible for me to get off over the holidays, but I haven't taken even a day in ages. So I'm going to just do it."

Stella yelps. "But have you talked to Mom? And what about Aunt Evelyn? We can't leave her alone for Christmas."

"I saw Mom this morning." I pause for dramatic effect. "She said she's been itching to go to London during the holidays. Mom and George are going to fly over on Christmas Day night *after* seeing Aunt Evelyn." Mom's husband is madly in love with her and would do anything she asked.

"It's perfect!" Stella lets out another scream. "And I'm paying for your plane ticket, Maddie," Stella says when she stops screaming. "Nonnegotiable. I make way more money at the agency than you do at the restaurant. Please, let me do this for you. For me. For all of us."

Maddie bites her lip and her face crumples. "Stella . . ."

A knock echoes on my front door.

"Have to run, sisters. Talk soon." I give a quick wave and abandon my phone on the kitchen counter.

The only thing better than Christmas in London with my sisters and mother would be Christmas in Scotland with Oliver.

But he's going to fly down to meet us after seeing Lucas so we can head home together.

I yank the door open and find Oliver standing on my front step, a wide grin on his face, a backpack on his back. My heart lurches and warmth bursts from my core.

This man? He's mine. He loves me. I know it from the words he says and the way he looks at me and the actions he takes every day. I don't know how I missed it in Scotland. Even before he'd said it, in hindsight, his love was obvious. He looks at me like I'm his entire world.

And now, he's mine.

"Jersey," he says.

I step outside until we are inches apart, then reach out to grab his hand. I think back to the first time I saw him, the first time we talked on the soccer fields in Peebles, when I took his hand and whispered in his ear, like I'm about to do now.

"Picasso," I say, my lips inches from his ear. "I love you. And next time? Just come in."

He chuckles and slides a hand around my waist, nuzzling my neck and pulling me flush against him. "I fucking love you, too."

I lean back to look at his face, memorizing the line of his nose, the curve of his jawline, the light in his eyes.

I don't know what life is going to be like for the next year or even after that. But I'm going to enjoy every second I have with this man.

"Can I come in?"

I nod and he leads me backward to step inside the house, keeping eye contact with me and pulling the front door shut behind him.

"Now I need you to kiss me, even though no one is watching."

"Come here, hen."

And then Oliver presses his lips onto mine.

EPILOGUE
REESE

Friday, December 30
Three Months Later
Stirling, Scotland

This wasn't the plan, but I'm here for every second of it.

I spent Christmas in London with my sisters, and Mom and her husband flew over on Christmas night after spending the day with Aunt Evelyn.

London is delightful at Christmas. Everything is festive and decorated and I felt like I was walking through some kind of holiday romance movie. We even went ice skating at the National History Museum. There was a giant Christmas tree in the middle of the rink—which we might have run into once and ended up in a heap—and delicious cakes and hot chocolate with decadent cream waiting for us when we finished. There were festivals and light displays all over the city, and everything closed on the holiday and Boxing Day, the day after Christmas, so we just sat in the flat and drank red wine and giggled together on the couch.

It was perfect. I even got the scoop on Stella's love life. I'm not sure she and her boyfriend are going to last much longer. He doesn't understand her. Doesn't *get* her. But I don't think she sees it yet. It's coming though, I know it.

Oliver never joined us in London.

When Maddie, Mom, and George flew home this morning, I hopped on a flight to Edinburgh, where Oliver picked me up and drove us to Stirling. Apparently, Cat decided she wanted to get married before the baby was born, and at around eight months pregnant, it was now or much later. So we get to go to a romantic holiday wedding in Scotland.

That's what led me here, around the corner from Cat's house in Stirling, to The Red Lion. They decorated the privately rented pub with endless twinkling fairy lights, red poinsettias in every corner, and evergreen wreaths on the walls to celebrate both Christmas and the wedding. Bright-red tartan tablecloths and plates full of mince pies adorn every surface.

Honestly, I never thought I'd go to a wedding at a pub, but I can't imagine anything sweeter.

Before we got here, Oliver also drove me around the corner and found a sheep for me to pet. I've got that image captured forever on my phone. And tomorrow, we're heading into Edinburgh for Hogmanay, the big Scottish New Year's Eve celebration.

I snuggle up next to Oliver on a cushioned corner bench, wearing a long gray dress with a plunging v-neck and loose sleeves, my hand resting on his thigh, his arm around my shoulders.

Oliver is wearing his kilt, the one that was in storage until a week ago when he retrieved it for the wedding. I'm definitely going to make him bring it back to the US, and I make a mental note to go to every single formal event we get invited to, or anything that would be an excuse to get dressed up.

Except Adrian and Britt's wedding, which was last month. I'd responded with a polite, but nonnegotiable, checkmark next to *Will Not Attend*. I'm staying firm in my boundaries with those two.

I glance over at Oliver, his legs splayed, blue and green tartan kilt laid over his thighs, skin showing just above his knees, a button-down shirt, bowtie, and formal jacket . . . I mean, I'm not even sure if he's wearing underwear.

I can't get enough of him.

Maybe I made the wrong decision about Adrian and Britt's wedding. Maybe I should have gone, just to show him off.

Nah. I've matured too much for that.

Cat and Grant lean against the bar, him drinking champagne and her drinking something sparkling but nonalcoholic, resting her hand on her round belly. Lucas is laughing and playing cards with Grant's nephews at a table, and friends and family mill around.

Even Oliver's parents are here. His mother gave me a tight-lipped grimace when I said hello, perhaps afraid I'd go off on her again. Oliver bit back a laugh at the interaction. After initial pleasantries, we've pretended like they don't exist.

"One day this will be us," the hot man in a kilt next to me says calmly.

I whip my head to look at Oliver, who is watching his son's mother and her new husband. "What?"

He looks at me, eyes flitting to my lips, then leans in to kiss me. "You heard me, Jersey."

I press my lips together and smile. "I hope you don't mean pregnant at our wedding, because that's not happening."

"Our wedding." He grins. "I like the sound of that."

"Holy shit," I whisper. I can't believe we're referencing *our wedding*, even theoretically.

"What?" He slides his arms down and pulls me onto his lap, nuzzling into my neck. "That's better. I like you as close to me as possible."

"Well. It's only been five months, so maybe you should cool it on the marriage talk." I wiggle on his lap and think that maybe he's not wearing underwear after all.

Yeah, it's too soon for that. Even though we're madly in love.

Even though I miss him every night he's at his apartment in the city. Even though he volunteered to help coach Chelsea's soccer team and is attempting to further his relationship with her.

Even though I can't imagine my life without him.

"Ah dinna ken. I guess I can wait." Oliver moves his lips up to nibble on my earlobe, one hand around my waist and the other holding me in place just below my hip. "But I'm a virgin groom, yeh ken, I canna wait forever."

I laugh, appreciating his subtle groan as I shift on him. "You're definitely not a virgin."

"Virgin *groom*. Not an actual virgin. Obviously." He slides a hand around my neck and pulls my mouth to his for a long few seconds.

Thoughts swirl around my brain. My chest is full of him, this man I love, who loves me so much he's talking about marrying me. I never thought I'd be here. Never thought I'd even want to entertain the idea of marrying someone again.

"When can I ask you to marry me?" he murmurs against my lips.

I lean back, speechless, unable to respond with words. My heart is overflowing with warmth. Instead, I kiss him again.

"How about this summer?" His words trace my mouth.

I find my voice again. "This summer." If he asks then, I'll say yes. If he asks tonight, I probably would as well.

"It's happening, Reese Hart. Prepare yourself to say yes to me."

"I'll be ready."

But I'm ready now. And I think he knows it.

MORE FROM CHRISSY

Loved *If We Pretend*? Leave an honest review on Amazon or Goodreads. It helps so much!

Want to read one more chapter with Reese & Oliver? Get the bonus epilogue, where Reese gets her first tattoo and Other Things Happen. Subscribe to Chrissy's newsletter on her website: www.ChrissyHopewell.com. Bonus epilogue will be live 10/10/23! Also available only to Chrissy's newsletter subscribers: *One Hundred Lights*, a free prequel novella with Britt & Adrian's love story.

Stay in touch:
Instagram: @ChrissyHopewell
Facebook: ChrissyHopewellAuthor
TikTok: @ChrissyHopewellBooks
Email: Chrissy@ChrissyHopewell.com

Stella Hart's happily ever after is next! Check out *Unless It's You*, releasing Spring 2024 and available for ebook pre-order in Fall 2023 on Amazon.

Unless It's You

Stella Hart is sure there's nothing wrong with cheating her way through someone else's bucket list. She hates being told how to live her life, even from her beloved late great aunt. But the stuffy lawyer says she has to complete the bucket list her aunt wrote for her within thirty days or the entire estate—meant for her and her sisters—will go to charity. It's absolutely unreasonable, especially the part where she needs to find an advisor to help her through the list, and the other part where she needs to face The One Who Got Away.

Ethan Fraser, a grumpy, bearded, English rugby player and Stella's ex's best friend, is trying to deal with the loss of his estranged mother, who always made him feel like second choice. But Ethan can't even bring himself to enter his mum's flat, let alone empty it, and he's got a month left before the landlord trashes it all. He definitely can't bring himself to ask for help from his golden boy best friend, to whom he owes so much already.

When Stella and Ethan end up forced to collaborate on an advertising project, they both find it hard to keep that one night buried in the past. The night they kissed, days before Stella got together with his best friend. The kiss that made Ethan want to hate her, but never quite succeed. But with matching thirty day deadlines, they realize they can help each other. Even as they get closer, Stella knows she's not girlfriend material, and she's off limits to Ethan, who cannot trust that she won't pick someone over him again. Before their time working together ends and they disappear into different corners of London, they both have to choose between a vulnerable new life or the familiar walled-off existence that protects their hearts.

ACKNOWLEDGMENTS

Writing a novel involves a lot of alone time, just me and my laptop: typing, deleting, typing, laughing, screaming, crying, typing, deleting some more. I'm so thankful for the amazing support network I have, especially my Pitch Wars community: Paris, Lillian, Hannah, Lisa, Roma, Gabriella, Bella, Tiera, and so many more. I feel so lucky to have met you all! Also, my high school besties who cheer me on every day, and my husband and kids who watch me with a curiosity akin to observing a circus performer. *Mommy, when is your book coming out?* (As soon as possible, my dear child.) *Mom, are you going to be famous?* (Nope, definitely not.) *Mommy, can I read your book?* (Lord, no.)

And all my beta readers and CPs who made this book so much better: Lillian, Tiera, Andrea, Paris, Sarah, Alex, Cate, and Victoria, one of my Scottish beta readers who helped me not embarrass myself quite so much.

Finally, I'm so thankful to my editor, Brenda Chin, who helped me make Reese and Oliver's story the most compelling possible, to my cover designer, Stephanie Anderson at Alt 19 Creative, for plucking my cover vision right out of my head and creating a cover I adore, and Lindsey Hinkel, for painstakingly proofreading every last word of *If We Pretend,* including the Scottish slang glossary. I'm lucky to have such a great team! Hope you're all ready for the next one.

And thank YOU, reader, for getting this far in my debut romance novel. Can't wait to share my next story with you soon!

Love, Chrissy

SCOTTISH SLANG DICTIONARY

Ah - I
Ah dinna ken - I don't know
Arse - ass
Aye - yes
basturt - bastard
Bawbag - asshole
Braw - nice, good, pretty
Bevy - drink
Bonnie - pretty
Boke - vomit
Canna - cannot
Coulda - could have
Couldna - couldn't
Complete rager - hot mess
Crabbit - grumpy, upset, annoyed
Cuppa - tea
Cut aboot with 'em - hang out with them
Daft - stupid
Didna - didn't
Dinna - don't
Dinna fash - don't worry
dobber - jerk
Doesna - doesn't
Dunno - I don't know
Eejit - idiot
Fae - from
Fashing - stressing

Feartie/ feart - afraid
Ferra - for a
Football boots - cleats
Gaun yourself - you can do it
Goan - go on
Hadna - hadn't
Hasna - hasn't
Havena - haven't
Isna - isn't
It's nae bother - not a problem
Ken - know
Lad/ bloke - boy/ man
Lassie - girl
Nae - no
Neigh a - not a
Och - light curse word
Outta - out of
Pure barry / dead brilliant - awesome
Rank - disgusting, vile, hideous
Right gent - gentleman
Slainte mhath - cheers in Gaelic
Shite - shit
Shoulda - should have
Shouldna - shouldn't have
Wasna - wasn't
Wee - little
Werena - weren't
willna - won't
Wouldna - wouldn't
Wanjker - jerk
Walloper - jerk
Yer aft yer head - you're crazy
Yeh ken - you know
Yer - you're

BOOK CLUB DISCUSSION GUIDE

1. Why do you think Reese was so confused about her feelings for Britt during much of the story? Would it have been the same for you, or was their situation black and white?
2. What do you think about the emotional sacrifices Reese made for Chelsea? Did she have to do that? What kind of pressure do moms feel today to be the perfect example for their children, especially daughters?
3. If you had to go somewhere for a month to reset your mind, where would it be and why? Have you ever studied abroad, traveled for more than a week, worked in another country, etc?
4. Have you ever thought about the different roles you play in your life as a child, parent, friend, spouse, employee, other? How many roles do you think you can play in your life and still do them all well? 3? 4? 5, maybe?
5. Have you ever thought of what it's like to be a professional athlete? Some of their childhoods might have been more 'normal', but maybe some of them were under intense pressure to perform from a young age. Would you want your child, friend, or loved one to be a professional athlete?
6. Did Oliver do the right thing by moving to the US for a year to be close to Reese? Or should he have stayed close to Lucas and Cat?

7. What do you think about the intersection of life and art? Oliver felt like his drawing was his secret and no one would understand. Chrissy thought there was an interesting parallel to how many writers treat their novels, keeping them a secret from family and friends. Why would someone do that?

8. What do you think about the secret Oliver kept from Reese about his son? Why didn't he just tell her, even though he was intimidated by the kind of mother she is? Can you see why someone might keep their child a secret from someone they're dating, or is it never acceptable?

ABOUT THE AUTHOR

Chrissy Hopewell started her love for romance novels by sneaking her mom's steamy books in middle school. She has spent varying amounts of time overseas, including working at a pub in Dublin, waitressing at a hotel in the Scottish Borders, and studying and living in London. Because of these experiences, international flair and accents often show up in her writing. Chrissy now lives in the suburbs of Cincinnati, Ohio with her family, and she no longer has to sneak what she reads.

instagram.com/chrissyhopewell

tiktok.com/@chrissyhopewellbooks

facebook.com/chrissyhopewellauthor